VENICE
BLACK

Other Titles by Gregory C. Randall

NONFICTION

America's Original GI Town: Park Forest, Illinois

FICTION

The Sharon O'Mara Chronicles

Land Swap For Death
Containers For Death
Toulouse For Death
12th Man For Death
Diamonds For Death

The Tony Alfano Thrillers

Chicago Swing
Chicago Jazz

VENICE BLACK

An Alex Polonia Thriller

GREGORY C. RANDALL

THOMAS & MERCER

Text copyright © 2018 by Gregory C. Randall
All rights reserved.

No part of this book may be reproduced, or stored in a retrieval system, or transmitted in any form or by any means, electronic, mechanical, photocopying, recording, or otherwise, without express written permission of the publisher.

Published by Thomas & Mercer, Seattle

www.apub.com

Amazon, the Amazon logo, and Thomas & Mercer are trademarks of Amazon.com, Inc., or its affiliates.

ISBN-13: 9781542048699
ISBN-10: 1542048699

Cover design by Jae Song

Printed in the United States of America

This book is dedicated to my late father, John Charles Randall.

THE BALKANS

For more than a thousand years, the Balkan people have been the unwilling victims of warlords, kings, sultans, fascist dictators, petty tyrants, and communists. The rugged Adriatic coastline of the Balkans includes countless islands, deep fjords, fishing villages, and smugglers' beaches. The region's inland is mostly mountainous, with an extensive succession of valleys, each with its own assortment of villages and cities. Since around the time of the Crusades, three major religions have established themselves in these mountainous lands: Roman Catholicism among the Croats and Slovenes to the northwest; Orthodox Christianity among the Serbs, Bulgarians, and Romanians to the east; and, starting with the Ottoman conquest of Serbia in the fourteenth century, Islam. However, these are just generalities. In reality, all three religions are mixed together in a stew of resentment and distrust.

Bordered by Italy in the northwest and Greece in the south, today's Balkan countries are but present-day chapters in a bloody book that will perhaps never be finished. At the very end of the eighteenth century, Napoleon ended the centuries-long control of a stretch of the eastern Adriatic coast by the Republic of Venice; the rest of the region belonged to either the Ottomans or the Habsburgs. After the conclusion of World War I—which began with the assassination of the Austrian archduke Franz Ferdinand in Sarajevo—the Kingdom of Serbs, Croats, and Slovenes was formed (renamed Yugoslavia in 1929), only within twenty years to be occupied and partitioned by the Nazis. The Ustaša, the fascist organization in the independent state of Croatia, operated many of the vilest concentration camps of World War II. Their goal was to ethnically cleanse Croatia of Serbs, Jews, dissident Croats, and Gypsies. Around half a million men, women, and children were systematically liquidated.

In the last decade of the twentieth century, Slovenia and Croatia declared independence from Yugoslavia. In many ways, this declaration was the result of the collapse of the Soviet Union and its withdrawal from the regional politics of Eastern Europe. Chaos reigned. Over the following decade, other countries in the region asserted their right to self-determination. The resulting social and political anarchy led to another brutal and repressive wave of government-sanctioned massacres and cultural and institutional retribution, much of it justified by various leaders.

An uneasy solution was eventually negotiated through the offices of the United States government. The Dayton Accords, as it was called, brought stability to the region; some even called it peace. However, in Bosnia and Herzegovina mass graves full of massacred civilians are still being found twenty years later. The politics and beliefs of the dead are now immaterial to the march of time. But to many, those dead are not irrelevant; they are missing parents, sisters, brothers, and children—and in the Balkans, as it has been for a thousand years, revenge is left for the living.

MONDAY

CHAPTER 1

Pula, Croatia, Present Day

Marika Jurić sat uneasily in the back seat of the Pula taxi. The Croatian driver and his vehicle smelled of rancid cabbage and stale tobacco. She was exhausted and wanted nothing more than to sleep for a week. She wiped away the moisture on the inside of the window with her sleeve, and through the wash of rain drumming on the taxi's roof, she waited for the signal from the motor launch that she had arranged to meet her. She had been waiting for almost an hour.

Eleven hours had passed since she'd taken the last seat on the one o'clock afternoon bus from Zagreb and, for the first hours of the trip, sat soaked in her black wool suit. The rain had caught her as she slipped out the rear service entrance of the Palace Hotel overlooking Zrinjevac Park and walked to Zagreb's Glavni Kolodvor bus station. She had waved off taxi after taxi, positive that foreign agents drove them, probably Serbians, or worse, Albanians. Rumors were that the bounty on her now very wet blonde head was a hundred thousand euros—alive only. Dead she was worth nothing. It was too cheap; she'd have paid ten times that to stay alive. Her black canvas bag, almost as wet as she, sat on her lap, its single long strap still over her shoulder. After the numbing trip across Croatia to the Pula bus station, she had chanced the only cab at the stand. Now soaked and shivering, she waited in the back seat of the fetid Pula taxi.

"You need a drink, comrade?" the driver now asked, holding up a bottle. "You look like you could use one." The meter said six hundred and forty-four kunas.

"No, I'm fine. You are being paid to wait, not talk."

"No problem, comrade, just asking." The driver raised the bottle and tipped it to his lips.

The storm had followed Marika from Zagreb to Pula through the afternoon and into the night. It was as ardent now in its embrace of the wharves of Pula as it had been with the cobblestones of Zagreb. Thankfully, she'd finally dried out. If only her damp and clingy underwear didn't feel so uncomfortable.

The Volkswagen Golf taxi sat at the end of the long wharf, the rain veiling any view of the Adriatic Sea. She again wiped away the moisture on the window and continued to stare into the storm. The man on the phone had said the price was ten thousand euros and to have it ready when the boat arrived.

"Pay the man when you board," the voice had said. "His name is Pavelić. The deckhand is his son, Boris. After you board, tell him where you want to go—I don't want to know."

"Anything else?"

"No, just make sure you have the money. I get my cut from him." After the instructions on which wharf and the time, the man had offered something about luck and fortune. For most of her forty-two years, Marika Jurić had made her own luck and her own large and well-hidden fortune. However, a fortune can only buy you things; what Marika wanted was retribution.

She reached into the damp canvas messenger bag and ran her hand across the Beretta pistol to the bundle of euros in a Ziploc bag. Then her fingers passed over the money and touched the small thumb drive sewn between the layers of cloth. With a cursory look, no one would see or notice it. She traveled lightly and wished now she had at least placed some fresh underwear in the bag. Her clothes and suitcase were still in her room at the Zagreb hotel, along with an old passport and other identification. Those in her coat pocket were well-worn fakes. On these well-stamped pages, she was a Bulgarian. When they searched her Zagreb room—as she knew they would—they would think she had just gone out to dinner or a concert or a quiet and indiscreet assignation. The thought of dinner made her stomach rumble.

"You say something, ma'am?"

"No."

A week earlier, she'd finished her last interview in a small café three blocks from her hotel. The woman had given her affidavit and photos of her sons and husband to Marika. The woman, a Bosnian Muslim, was sure they had been dead for twenty years. The faded images of a strong-looking man and two intelligent boys of maybe twelve and fifteen with thick black hair were all that she had left of them.

"I do not expect them to be found, maybe their bones someday. I have left DNA with the United Nations people, but only Allah can help now. I am not sure what I will do if they are found. Rebury them with our ancestors? I don't know. I just don't know."

Marika was never sure what to say. The questions had been asked: the usual who, where, when. No one asked how—to think of it was too painful. It had been her tenth and last interview from the same Bosnian village, all with women. She had found no men to interview, and the few grown boys from that time had been too young then to be a threat to the Croatian executioners.

Now, on the wharf, all the paranoia that had been building for the last six months again began to manifest itself. Her hand shook as she removed it from the bag.

"Maybe a sip," she said.

"Sure, comrade." The driver passed the bottle over the seat.

Marika held it to her nose. The bottle smelled like the taxi, but the vodka was tolerable. She passed the bottle back.

"Not so bad, yes?"

"It's swill," she answered. But it did give her a quick shot of warmth, something she had not had all day.

Through the gloom, a strobe light flashed through the rain, once, twice, then a third time. Each time a different series, the sequence the man had told her over the phone.

"I'm leaving," Marika said, threw a hundred euros over the driver's seat, and reached for the door handle.

"You going out in this shit? Maybe you should wait for it to stop."

"No questions."

"Whatever you say, comrade." The driver began to gather up the euros scattered on the seat.

The door opened into the storm and rain immediately began to fill the interior.

"If you're going, be quick. I don't want my cab soaked—comrade."

Marika glanced at the back of the head of the annoyed driver and pulled her pistol from the bag. Instead of firing a slug into the man's skull, she swung the pistol's muzzle and sharply rapped the side of the man's head. He slumped forward against the steering wheel.

"Sorry—comrade."

She slipped the pistol into her jacket pocket and walked to the edge of the wooden wharf illuminated by an overhead streetlamp. Without its light, she would have stumbled over the low iron railing and fallen into the harbor. The motor launch silently slipped up to the narrow-planked walkway secured to the face of the pier. A young boy holding a thick rope leaped from the launch to the planks.

"Who are you?" Marika asked in Croatian.

"Boris, ma'am. You?"

"The woman with ten thousand euros."

She climbed down an iron ladder secured to the stone bulwark and then stepped onto the stern of the launch.

"Go," she said and looked up through the rain to the boat's bridge.

A man in dark clothes stared down at Marika, then turned away. Seconds later, the sound and vibrations from the engine under Marika's feet began to increase. The launch slowly turned away from the small pier and into the storm. Within minutes it was lost to the receding lights of Pula and Croatia. Marika was soaked, again.

CHAPTER 2

Marika climbed the ladder to the bridge. A broad-shouldered man stood silhouetted by the array of red lights from the electronic gear spread across the cabin's console. His bearded face and heavy brow reflected off the bridge's window. He wore a watchman's cap favored by sailors in the Mediterranean and the Black Sea. He didn't turn to look at his passenger.

"Your name?" she asked.

"Pavelić. Like Pavlov, the scientist who discovered why mangy dogs drool."

She slowly drew out the pistol and held it to her side, out of sight.

"Where are we going?" Pavelić asked in Croatian.

She looked about the bridge. It appeared new and well equipped. A large radar screen was mounted to one side, its probing band circling over and over. On the screen's bottom, a line of dense green light reflecting the coastline pulsed with the radar's rotating signal. The top of the screen reflected nothing but the open Adriatic Sea.

"Okay, let's start somewhere else then," Pavelić said. "What should we call you?"

"Unimportant," she answered in Croatian.

"That's a strange name, but in my line of work, I hear it often. Do you have the money?"

"Yes."

"Good, place it on the console."

With her free hand, she did as directed.

He turned to look at her for the first time. "Good, now where?"

She heard the sound of a footstep behind her. Looking at the reflection in the window, she saw Boris standing behind her. His hands were empty.

"My son," Pavelić said.

"We met."

"Good. Now that the rituals of smuggling have been completed, I still need to know which way to point my *Irena*. South to Ancona, north to Trieste, or west to Ravenna, maybe Venice; just tell me."

"Venice."

The captain smiled. "You are not the first I've taken there, but you're the prettiest."

"Enough fuel?" she asked, ignoring the compliment.

"Plenty."

"Food?"

"Much."

"Good, then Venice."

"Damn, I told the boy's mother that I'd be gone maybe one day—now it's two." He looked at the bundle of euros. "It will be morning when we arrive. This storm will pass in about three hours, and the seas are reasonably flat, so we should make excellent time. Unless, of course, we are delayed."

"Delayed?"

"Yes, the Italians are not big fans of smugglers and sneaking people into their little bit of heaven. All these Syrian and Afghan migrants are making business difficult for me. The Italians, along with their European brothers, are sure the next refugee is some Syrian jihadi terrorist. This rain is a good cover, and maybe we can use some of the larger ships to hide our small radar signal. I can pay the fines, but I can't lose my boat; the *Irena* is all I have. Also, for once I have nothing to hide—except you. So, I hope you are not wanted by Interpol or some government. You look like a Croat. That's at least in your favor. I won't deal with those Serbian pigs—ever."

"Those that want me are probably wanted by their own governments, so the less you know, the better."

"Excellent, just what I wanted to hear." Pavelić lit a cigarette.

For a half hour, the boat droned on into the storm, the slapping of the windshield wipers providing the tempo. Pavelić pointed to a small blip that appeared in the lower left of the radar screen. "Dammit, no miracle today."

"What?"

"Maybe a Croatian patrol boat. They are always interested in who comes and goes."

"Heading toward us?"

"Maybe, we'll watch." He edged up the two throttles, and the cruiser gained speed. "The next few hours will tell. At least this storm keeps away helicopters or aerial surveillance."

Thirty minutes later the coast of Croatia, with its brilliant radar return, had disappeared from the radar screen. The only return came from the single boat to the east—and it was gaining on them.

"How far?" she asked as Boris handed her a large sausage on a plate and a mug of coffee. "Thanks."

"Refill mine, son." He passed his mug to the boy. "Five miles, but closing. I think they want to see who would go out into this weather."

"And?"

"I hope they think we are a fishing boat."

Fifteen minutes later a large return blinked on in the upper-right quadrant of the radar screen.

"What's that?" Marika asked.

"My guess is a cruise ship. They travel at night so their rich passengers can pillage our fair cities during the day. She is about ten miles out. I have an idea." The captain adjusted his course and aimed his boat directly at the ship. "At this speed and theirs, we should pass each other in fifteen minutes. Look, our friend is increasing his speed. He may have figured out my idea."

Marika ate the sausage, and the grumbling in her stomach eased. The coffee was tolerable.

"You okay? Sometimes my guests get seasick."

"I have spent time on the ocean. I'm good."

"Excellent, we don't want you puking all over my nice clean deck. Boris is not fond of cleaning up after our clients." He nudged the throttles; the cruise ship was now closer by half. "I'm going to pass him on our port side." The captain nodded left. "As we get closer I'm sure they will hail us. Too bad my radio doesn't work in this weather." He reached for a package of cigarettes on the console, shook another one out, and lit it. "You want one?" He offered her the pack.

"No, I don't smoke."

"A man—or a woman"—he nodded to her—"needs their vices. I think that smoking is one of the lesser of the evils. Even Boris nags me to quit, but what am I to do?"

The following radar blip was now fewer than two miles to their stern and closing fast, the cruise ship three miles ahead.

"If they are who I think they are, the boat is already at top speed." He tapped the glass. "Damn, too fast. He's still gaining on us."

"Can they catch us?"

"Maybe."

"He can't."

"He won't."

Through the rain, the cruise ship appeared like a great white city lit up for the holidays. Lights extended down the length of the upper decks and superstructure and then disappeared into the overhanging gloom two hundred feet above them.

"Big bastard," Pavelić said.

The radio crackled again. "This is the *Diamond Princess*. To the boat approaching us on our port bow, please turn away. You are on a collision course."

Pavelić left the microphone in its receiver and turned to Marika with a smile.

"How close?" Marika asked.

"Maybe a hundred feet. Hold on—it will be rough."

Their shadow was now three-quarters of a mile behind them but still gaining. The *Diamond Princess* rose ahead of them with its great bow lit with floodlights. It was like an iceberg closing on them at almost fifty miles an hour.

"Can't this boat go faster?"

"Maybe."

In a matter of seconds, the great, blinding-white hull of the ship filled the windshield as they passed over the bow wave and raced the length of the liner. In a flash, they passed the entire length of the thousand-foot-long ship. When they cleared the stern, the launch lurched hard left and right as Pavelić took the wake head-on. Then it was dark and they were lost in the rain. The massive stern of the receding ship was rapidly consumed by the storm.

"Now we can go," Pavelić said and pushed the dual throttles to the top of the control. The boat jumped like it had been kicked in the ass.

"Why not earlier?"

"And make them think we're smugglers? We have a few minutes before he understands my trick. We are now lost in the shadow of the big boat. He will be confused, and when they pass he will look for us, but we will not be where he thinks. My hope is that he will give up the thought of chasing us, and with this weather, he can't ask for helicopters. Maybe my ruse will work. We will see."

Five minutes later. "Shit."

"What?"

"He's still coming and is faster than us. There is nothing in the Croatian navy, sad as it is, that can catch us. Yet these guys are gaining on us." Pavelić turned to her. "Someone chasing you?"

"Possibly."

"What do you mean *possibly*? They are, or they aren't. It looks like they are." Pavelić pushed the throttles, trying to squeeze another knot out of the *Irena*. Boris returned to the bridge with more coffee.

Steadily, the return radar blip on the screen inched closer. Every fifteen minutes it closed by another two hundred yards. At this rate, the chase boat would catch them in an hour.

"Boris, get my pistols and the rifles. I don't want to be surprised."

Boris disappeared down into the boat and returned minutes later. Boris set two AK-47s and three magazines on the large plotting table behind the console and handed his father a gun belt with two pistols secured in their respective holsters.

She noticed Boris's belt and holster. "I see you have run into trouble before," she said.

"One must always be prepared—I was told this is the Boy Scouts' motto."

"I wouldn't know," Marika answered.

"If there's trouble, I want you to stay out of the way."

Marika reached for one of the AK-47s, expertly removed the magazine, placed it on the table, and then pulled the ejection slide on the weapon. She deftly caught the ejected bullet. She then reloaded the bullet into the magazine, reinserted the magazine, clicked off the safety, and charged the weapon.

"And pistols?"

"More experience than I may have wanted during the last couple of decades."

"Then at least stay behind me. Boris, in the locker in my cabin there is a steel box under the trap door. Please bring it."

"Steel boxes, trap doors? What other surprises do you have?"

"Some I'd hoped not to have to use."

Boris returned and set the box between the rifles.

"Ten minutes, then we will see what we have. This rain gives us some cover, but the radar doesn't let us hide. Boris, lights out."

In seconds, it was as if the Adriatic Sea had swallowed them. Pavelić turned all the instruments off or put their screens on the lowest display settings. Only a few red dots the size of fingertips glowed in the darkness. Outside of that, they were invisible from the outside.

"Son, take the helm and put your headset on. I'm on channel three." The captain eyed her. "Stay here in the bridge. I don't want a dead woman's money."

"But you'd keep it anyway."

"Yes. But I wouldn't be happy about it. I've never lost a client."

"Maybe they are coast guard?"

"They would have hailed us. No, these are friends of *yours*. I assume you don't wish to go with them?"

"Not willingly."

"Good."

"I'm going with you; I have a stake in this."

He looked at Marika. "It *is* your ass, after all." He took a quick look at the screen. "Two hundred meters. Grab one of those rifles and put on this headset."

She secured the band of the headset over her damp head and inserted the earpiece. Then she picked up one of the rifles.

"Son, when I tell you, throttle down and put us in reverse as fast as she can handle it. Watch for the backwash. With any luck, they won't expect this and will roar by us. We will see."

Pavelić took the steel box with them up on deck. Marika and Pavelić, with the steel box between them, waited in the dark behind the gunnel. The rain had eased but not by much. Again she was wet. The deep hum of the *Irena*'s twin engines and exhaust masked all other sounds, especially that of the onrushing vessel. Marika didn't know what to expect.

"Can you hear that?" Pavelić said. "Fifty meters off the starboard quarter. They are not coming straight on."

Marika heard nothing outside of their boat. She looked where she thought Pavelić said he heard them. It was then that something massive materialized and replaced the rain: the sharp, high bow of a black speedboat veered toward them, its bridge fully illuminated.

"Now, son, now!" Pavelić yelled into his headset. "Hold on tight."

The *Irena* slammed into the next wave and then instantly slowed. The black speedboat roared by, and multiple pistols fired on Marika and Pavelić. Bullets broke out the windows, and she heard wood splinter.

"My poor *Irena*!" Marika heard Pavelić yell at the same time he opened up with his AK-47. Unlike their boat, the speedboat was lit up like a Christmas party. Three targets stood at the stern, continuing to fire. One fell as Pavelić found the range and allowed for the motion of his boat. Marika aimed for the center and the engine and sprayed bullets into the hull just above the waterline.

The boats veered apart; she could just make out the other boat in the rain.

"Boris, you okay?"

"Yes, the windows were shot out, but I'm good. Radar says they are returning."

"Try to get us out of here, see if we can gain some separation and distance."

The engines roared, and Boris turned the launch to port in a large curving arc. The shooters had turned the opposite direction and lost valuable time and distance. Marika could just barely hear the other boat over the sound of their engines.

"They are catching up, Father. To the starboard stern quarter."

Pavelić pointed, and Marika could just barely make out the direction from his arm. Again the boat, still lit up, approached fast and hard.

"We're losing speed?" Pavelić said.

"Losing oil pressure in the port engine; we may have been hit," Boris answered.

"Dammit. Son, kill the port engine. We'll make do with one. As the boat pulls up, I will tell you when to pull hard to starboard. Let's shake them up a bit." He turned to Marika. "What's your real name, Ms. Unimportant? When I'm yelling, it's easier to use a real name."

"Marika."

"Pretty. I knew a girl named Marika when I was a boy. Died in the war."

The speedboat's bow pulled closer when Boris killed the damaged engine.

"All the shooters must be in the stern," Pavelić said. "Open that box, will you?"

She clicked open the metal hasp . . . *Holy hell.* "Grenades?"

"Gifts from our troubled past here in Croatia. They are everywhere for a few kunas. Hand me two."

The speedboat rapidly gained on them. It tried to slow down to match their speed, but it was too late, and within seconds the rear deck area again was exposed. More gunfire erupted from the speedboat. More bullets struck the *Irena.*

The captain held both grenades out to Marika. "The rings, pull them."

If Pavelić could have seen her eyes in the almost total darkness, he would have been surprised by how large they were. Marika reached out and put both her hands on his. She felt the tops of the Russian-made grenades, and her fingers easily hooked into the rings.

"Now!" he yelled.

She pulled the rings free and fell to the deck as the boat pitched from the impact of the speedboat's wake. Rolling over, she watched him throw the two grenades, one after the other, toward the passing boat. One hit the railing, bounced off into the sea, and exploded twenty feet behind the boat. The second landed in the middle of the stern deck, unseen by the shooters. Their gunfire continued. In the blackness, she felt Pavelić flatten himself next to her on the *Irena*'s deck as the second grenade ripped apart everything in the stern, and the lights in the speedboat's cabin went out. The speedboat immediately stopped, the explosion having obviously destroyed some part of its propulsion system. As the *Irena* turned west, back on its original course toward Italy, the shattered black speedboat drifted powerless in the Adriatic Sea.

Chapter 3

Marco Polo Airport, Venice, Present Day

Alexandra Polonia, dressed in black boots, black jeans, and a short black leather jacket, stood braced against the cold early-morning wind that blew off the lagoon, a leather backpack hung on her left shoulder. Her single black ballistic-fabric carry-on bag sat at her feet. The narrow walkway of the quay was filled with groggy tourists newly arrived on early local and international flights. All, like her, waited for either the next *vaporetto* or available water taxi. Most were silent.

For at least thirty of her forty-two years, Alex Polonia had wanted to see Venice, Italy. She had dreamed of its exotic canals, romantic gondolas, and pigeon-filled Piazza San Marco. Hers would be a stylish trip, not one of those youth-hostel adventures that required sleeping in bunk beds with a dozen other people snoring well into the night. No, not *her* dream trip. She would have four bags: one for her cosmetics, one for her shoes, and two for her clothes so she would be dressed properly. It would be the romantic adventure of a lifetime—Venice, Florence, and Rome, and of course all with her husband, the once great love of her life.

Right now and for the next twelve years, however, Detective Ralph Cierzinski—her piece-of-shit ex-husband—was lounging in the Ohio State Penitentiary in Youngstown for criminal conspiracy and operating a meth lab in a garage on Cleveland's south side. Cierzinski, a veteran Cleveland police detective, received only twelve years because he turned on the other two cops involved in his operations. Cierzinski, to his credit, testified that his wife, Alexandra, a detective with fifteen years on the same Cleveland police force, knew nothing about his illegal business interests. Testimony that, except for Alexandra's partner, her captain, and commander, no one believed. In article after article, Cleveland's rag of a newspaper painted her with the same brush as her husband. She was told to sue the newspaper; she didn't. At least the man had the balls to sign the divorce decree the day he climbed into the bus for the trip to Youngstown.

Standing on the water taxi quay at the Venice airport, her one black bag at her feet, Alex Cierzinski—now with her maiden name Polonia—was completely and entirely exhausted. The past year had been one insane day after another. Initially, before Ralph's arrest, she had been placed on a joint task force with the DEA to find the source of the meth. When they discovered, during one of the sting operations at a south-side high school, that Ralph, using some of the students, was the dealer, she was immediately suspected of being involved. After her house was raided by her own people, her only way out and to save her own butt was to help the prosecution. She became part of an elaborate sting to collect evidence, nail her husband, and get the drugs off the street. Every day was an entanglement of deceit and lies.

Within weeks of Ralph Cierzinski and some of his crew having been arrested, one of the codefendants, another cop, retired by putting a bullet in his brain, believing that his family would get his pension. They got jack shit. The other defendant, a policeman with Parks and Recreation, swore that he would have every member of Cierzinski's family killed within a month, but the criminal justice system is often unjustly fair. Someone, while the defendant was in county lockup awaiting trial, shoved a broom handle up his ass. He died two weeks later from the ensuing infection. As far as Alex Cierzinski knew, the dead cop never gave the kill order. Besides, the moron was as broke as the Cleveland budget. It was a contract no one would take.

During Ralph's trial, she began the process of taking back her maiden name, Polonia. She'd never particularly liked the name Cierzinski. Her father was pleased. He'd told the story many times: "When my grandfather arrived at Ellis Island on a steamer from Gdansk, Poland, the immigration official was Italian and couldn't understand what your noble, yet sadly illiterate, great-grandfather said his name was. Our family is from a small village south of Krakow—Polanka is its name. The official said the name sounded like Polonia, the Italian word for Poland. It stuck. Since then, we have always had a connection with Italy."

Alexandra Luisa Polonia . . . She'd loved her given name and now felt whole again, even though her life had been torn to shreds by the man she'd married. At least—one of many "at leasts"—he'd kept the accounts, dollars, and profits separate and hidden from their personal accounts. She paid a forensic accountant twenty grand to make sure that all their—her—remaining assets weren't seized by the state. It took more money to prove to the Feds that her taxes were correct and that they didn't need a piece of her soul for unpaid taxes on *his* illicit gains. The one piece of information that the state and the Feds never dragged out of Ralph Cierzinski was where he had hidden his money. When asked, he smiled. When threatened, he smiled. When told that they would ruin his wife, he smiled. The number thrown about in court was twenty million dollars, twenty million that the government wanted. When Cierzinski heard the number, he smiled. The government was no different than he was. They were just thieves with lawyers. The only time he didn't smile was when he was asked who his backers or partners were and adamantly answered, "I have no partners."

The damp wind from the lagoon blew her shoulder-length blonde hair away from her face. She held the strands in place with her fingers and gazed across the water to a surreal landscape of towers and red-tile roofs that floated an inch above the lagoon. Around her, in the crowded harbor at Marco Polo Airport, hundreds of motor launches and water taxis jockeyed for positions against the pier. One massive municipal vaporetto, "Actv" stenciled on its side, slowly pushed its way through the chaos, almost upsetting the smaller boats that surrounded it.

"American?" a voice from one of the launches asked.

She looked at the young man and nodded.

"Excellent. Signora, you need a ride, maybe?"

Alex looked down at the gleaming mahogany motor launch; its bright work and chrome furnishings were immaculate. A length of hemp rope was wrapped about one of the colorful mooring sticks driven into the mud of the harbor. A young man in a striped shirt stood at the boat's gunnel, fending off the stick, the wharf, and the other boats. "You need a ride? What hotel, I take you. Best price. These others"—he waved at the boats—"are pirates. I give the pretty signora a good price."

The twelve hours from Cleveland's Hopkins International Airport to Philadelphia to Venice had drained every thought and dream from her head. She stared at the man.

"Signora, you waiting for someone. No problem, I wait. Signora?"

Alex slowly focused on the boat and the question, and affirmatively nodded her head, again tucking a windblown length of hair behind her ear. She picked up the bag and handed it to the driver, then climbed into the rocking launch.

"Sit anywhere you like. My boat and me, Giuseppe Anatole, are at your command. Please, signora, sit."

Almost falling as the boat pitched in the turbulent water, she dropped her bottom on the brightly colored striped, upholstered bench on the port side.

"Someone else coming?"

"No, just me."

"Where are you staying, signora?" Giuseppe asked as another boat pulled in between theirs and the pier. Horns blared from all sides.

"What?"

"Hotel, which hotel."

She unzipped her backpack, hunted through the pockets, and extracted an envelope. She opened it and removed a piece of paper. Squinting, she read the small print: "The Aqua Palace Hotel."

After crossing the lagoon through a watery road fixed by marker piers, the motor launch turned into a narrow gap in the broad and colorful façade of buildings that fronted the lagoon and slowly made its way through the intricate maze of canals.

"A shortcut, signora," Giuseppe said. "Is this your first time to Venice?"

She looked up at the man, who couldn't have been any older than twenty-five. "Yes," she said, loud enough to be heard over the rumble of the engine.

"It is a magical place, even if a bit cold today. But she will still warm your heart," he said as he slowly moved his way past three gondoliers and their boats.

Alex stared in wonder as they motored through the canals that were the streets of Venice. The ancient buildings, their foundations built deep into the mud, rose up on either side. She watched the boatman wave at the tourists as he maneuvered the launch under a series of low stone bridges. Many of the tourists were wearing masks and colorful costumes.

"Are they always dressed like that?" she asked.

"No, signora, it is Carnevale. We are a few days from the start of Lent, when we have to atone for our sins." A big grin crossed his face.

When they entered the Grand Canal, a million images, indelibly imprinted from her youth, flooded Alex's head. It was all a whirl in her mind. After passing under the Rialto Bridge, Giuseppe turned into a side canal and wove between four- and five-story brick and plaster buildings that crowded the waterway. Even in her transatlantic stupor, she was mesmerized by the architecture and the total disconnect from

Cleveland. The boat idled along the canal at less than walking speed as more gondolas sculled their way past.

"Giuseppe, do you ever get lost?" she asked.

"I never get lost; this is my home. I grew up here. Just a few hundred meters more."

The boat eased around a corner and then hugged the canal wall as a barge motored past them. It was full to the gunnels with crates of fresh fruits and vegetables. Giuseppe waved at the young man helming the barge.

"I know that kid since I was a bambino. Some of us never leave the islands and the canals."

Giuseppe allowed the boat to gently drift to a stone stoop that led up to the entry of a hotel. A small sign on the wall said "Aqua Palace." He tossed a rope to the doorman, who secured the line to a mooring pole and took Alex's bag from Giuseppe. The boatman then swiped her credit card and returned it. She counted out a few extra euros and handed them to him.

Giuseppe smiled at the tip and gave her a business card. "Please, signora, call anytime. I am at your service."

With his arm to steady her, Alex stepped onto the stone stoop and, like a princess being delivered to a dream palace, felt for the first time the solid ground of Venice under her feet.

CHAPTER 4

Marika stood in the bridge with Pavelić and watched as the morning turned the black sky gray. Ahead, lights twinkled like brilliant Morse code dots and dashes from the windows of the buildings on the low strand of land stretched across the dark horizon. This barrier island, called the Lido, protected Venice and its enclosed lagoon from the direct and eternal ravages of the Adriatic Sea. She had once spent a week there with her family. Two stark and squat lighthouses flanked the narrow entry into the lagoon from the Adriatic. Beyond them, the lights of Venice still lit the low clouds that hung like a veil over the ancient city. Boris sat on a chair in the back of the bridge, his wounded arm bandaged and in a sling.

"We were lucky," Pavelić said as he blew smoke into the dark cabin. "Risky, very risky. Your friends were stupid. They have now learned not to screw with me." He throttled back the one still-functioning engine. "One engine always makes me uneasy." An hour earlier, Pavelić had aimed his boat at the lighthouse from the first moment it flashed on the horizon. "I can breathe more easily now. I have a friend in the north end of the lagoon where I can get my *Irena* repaired. Luckily, there will be dozens of boats at the entry—they come and go all the time. After we enter the harbor, I'll drop you at a small pier near the ferry stop. The ferries start their rounds early. One should soon come along."

"Thank you," Marika said. "Can't say it wasn't interesting."

"Yes, it was that. Your money might be enough to get my *Irena* fixed. Not a very profitable trip."

"Sorry."

"No problem, maybe I should just kidnap you and sell you to whoever was chasing us. You must be worth a lot of money."

She tightened her grip on the pistol in her pocket.

"Don't worry, if I were to do something like that, the word would be out in hours—and my livelihood and my life would be worth nothing. I hope that those you are running from do not find you. They appear to be dangerous as well as stupid."

"Yes, they are."

As the cruiser slowed, Boris leaped to the dock and with his one good hand fended off the *Irena*'s bow from the tarred wood of the pier. He waved to Marika, who followed. As Pavelić backed away from the pier, Boris nimbly vaulted back into the craft.

Before Marika even reached the end of the dock, the *Irena* had disappeared into the morning mist.

It was good to feel the solid land of the Lido after the last several hours on the *Irena*. Her body still felt the rocking of the boat; her stride was like a tipsy sailor's. At the San Nicolo vaporetto pier, a dozen people waited for the ferry to make its stop. Like Marika, they would transfer at the Sant' Elena water-bus stop and then proceed to their destinations on one of the three main islands that make up Venice.

As Marika waited, she avoided the eyes of the commuters. She knew she was a mess. On the *Irena* she had tried, with limited success, to untangle the rat's nest of her blonde hair with a small brush from her bag. She had succeeded only in shaking out some of the dried salt water. Three men, dressed in suits and ties, stood off to the side, watching her and smoking. The vaporetto was ten minutes out across the lagoon. She craved a cigarette. She'd lied to Pavelić: she did smoke. She reached into her bag and retrieved a sodden pack of Ronhills, and after squeezing out what seemed like a cup of water, she threw the pack into a litter bin.

One of the men held up his cigarette and motioned to her.

After offering her a cigarette and then lighting it, the man said in halting English, "Are you okay, signora?"

The fellow thinks I'm a tourist.

She responded in fluent Italian with a touch of Milanese. "Yes. And thank you for the cigarette—I needed this."

"You look like you have had a tough night. Can I be of assistance?"

Italian men—even at seven in the morning. "No, I'm fine. My so-called business associates took me to a party on the Lido, then left me on the beach, in the rain. Some friends. All I need is a bath and a gun— I'll show them." She smiled. The frown on his face when she said *gun* pleased her. "Are you going to San Marco?"

"No, signora, we will transfer at Sant' Elena. We work near the cruise ships."

"*Sì, sì.* I've seen those cruise ships. They can be very intimidating, especially close-up," she said, remembering her recent encounter.

"Ah, they're just big hotels full of tourists with nothing to do. They are wrecking our city. Maybe they will have to go elsewhere, but then I'd lose my job and have to move to the mainland. I'll worry about it later. Say—you want to have a drink tonight?"

She smiled. He seemed like a nice guy, for an Italian. "Sorry, but I'm leaving this afternoon for Milan. But I appreciate the thought, thank you."

He pulled out a business card and slipped it inside the cellophane of his Marlboros. "You take these. I have some at work. However, if you change your mind and decide to stay in Venice, give me a call. I've lived here my whole life. There are many secret spots I can take you to."

She continued to smile at the man, who was easily ten years her junior—*and so early in the morning.*

While waiting at the Sant' Elena stop, Marika bought a ticket from the machine for the No. 1. She took a seat in the rear of the vaporetto and for the first time relaxed.

"Tourist?" a dapper gentleman asked in Italian. "Staying on the Lido for your holiday?"

"No, Bulgarian," she answered, also in Italian.

"Can I be of assistance?"

What is it with these men? This one is ten years older.

"Thank you for asking, but my husband is waiting for me at San Marco. He's the jealous sort. You know those Bulgarians."

The ferry cruised along the waterfront, making three more stops. As they approached the San Marco stop, she watched the great campanile's tip disappear in and out of the low clouds. The dapper gentleman sat just a little too close to her the whole time. The vaporetto slowed as it approached San Marco, and she stood and waved to no one in particular. Surprisingly, one man waved back. Startled, she said, "See, there he is."

The ferry bumped into the dock, and without waiting for the boat to tie up, passengers walked on and off. She turned to the dapper man still on the boat and, with a flamboyant flick of her wrist, saluted him and walked into Venice.

Marika crossed the open Piazza San Marco. A cold wind had followed the rain; it swirled about among the surrounding colonnades of the square. This early in the morning, only a few people wandered the piazza; their Nikons and iPhones, pointing in every direction, gave them away as tourists. The pigeons, all scrunched up and immobile, waited for the sun to crest the basilica. Heads down with heavy coats and thick scarves, the locals came and went through the narrow alleys cleaved between the buildings with their peeling walls and empty flower boxes. Marika's coat had finally dried, but her skin itched under the heavy sweater that Pavelić had given her. The smell of the man pushed its way up through the coat's buttons. She lit another cigarette and silently thanked the Marlboro man.

How did they know she was leaving from Pula? How did they know she was heading to Venice? *Why did they risk chasing me across the Adriatic? Why didn't they take me in Pula? That damn taxi driver must have been in with them. I should have taken care of the drunk. Luck was with me—Pavelić and his luck. I will need a lot more of it before Thursday.*

She walked hastily through the city to the Campo della Fava and the Ai Reali, her hotel. When she entered, a man dressed in a tailored dark suit and tie instantly became excited and started to wave his hands about.

"What has happened to you? My dear Ms. Jurić, for the love of God, what has happened?"

CHAPTER 5

Too tired to care or even unpack, Alex had washed her face and fallen into bed. Three hours later and after a luxurious shower and a touch of makeup, she dressed in black jeans, a boldly striped gray-and-white cotton sweater, and the black leather jacket. Over-the-calf boots matched her shoulder bag, which replaced the backpack. It was a comfortable look she'd perfected as a detective—it just felt right.

She pushed open the room's thick leaded-glass window. After having melted the morning clouds away, the sun had returned and now found its way into the canal just below her window. Inching between midday gondolas, another barge motored along, filled with stacks of plastic-wrapped bottled water and boxes of vegetables. She assumed it was destined for some restaurant or hotel. The gentleman holding the tiller in the stern looked up and smiled. *"Buon pomeriggio signora, non è una giornata meravigliosa?"*

She understood the first half but not the second. When he waved upward at the crisp blue sky, she got the gist of his remark.

"Sì, it is a very nice day," she answered.

The man went back to his business, like thousands of others had over the millennia. While the islands of Venice were magical, they also needed lettuce, radishes, and bottled water. To some, it might have taken a touch of gilt off the dream, but it only made her happier. Even after the past year, she knew that life would go on, and there was no earthly reason to be upset—not now.

She crossed the hotel's elegant lobby to the concierge desk, where a cute girl with the name tag "Sonia" stood writing something in a large ledger.

The girl closed the book as Alex approached. "What can I do to be of help, Mrs. Polonia? By the way, a pretty name."

"Thank you," she said, "and it is Ms. Polonia. I am divorced." She thought how easy it was to say now.

"I am sorry."

"Please, there is no need to be sorry. I'm not. It is not something I want to think about. But today, I would like to have a wonderful lunch for my first meal in Venice. What do you suggest?"

"Oh, there are so many. Do you want seafood, traditional pasta, beef?"

"Seafood with a view and a bottle of Soavé—does Venice have anything like that?"

Sonia smiled, then put her hand to her chin and looked at the ceiling, as if pretending for a moment to earnestly ponder Alex's joke of a question. Then she laughed, opened the massive leather-bound binder, and leafed through the pages until she stopped, ran her finger down the column, and then turned the book toward Alex. "This should do nicely. Not too expensive but not, how you say, too cheap either. A wonderful view of the Grand Canal and one could lazily spend the whole afternoon just watching Venice drift by."

"Sounds perfect," Alex answered, then turned at some commotion. A few people in the lobby were holding decorated masks and wearing plumed hats. She remembered what Giuseppe said about Carnevale.

"It's Carnevale di Venezia," Sonia said once Alex turned to face her again. "Lent starts on Wednesday, so tomorrow is our Mardi Gras—Fat Tuesday in English, Martedì Grasso in Italian. There are parties and events late into the night, then thankfully the peace of Ash Wednesday. It is really quite fun."

"I never knew. Will the restaurant be too crowded?"

"Never in Venice. We will take care of you. Let me show you where the restaurant is."

Sonia extracted a map from under the counter and with a bold red pen marked Alex's route through the city's jigsaw-puzzle-like streets.

"Should not take ten minutes. If you get lost, just ask a shopkeeper where the Rialto Bridge is. The restaurant is just on the other side of the canal; you can see it from the bridge. I have other choices for later in the week, but this is a good place to start. The wind is cold, but this restaurant will have some protection, or you can sit inside. And Ms. Polonia, try to avoid Gypsies and men too eager to help—they are trouble. I don't need to warn you about pickpockets. Keep your handbag closed at all times. They are very good at what they do."

"Sonia, *grazie*. I think I'll be just fine. I'm a police officer back home."

The girl stiffened and smiled as a large man strolled through an office door directly behind the reception desk. "Ms. Polonia, I would like to introduce you to Signor Portero, our hotel's manager."

"Signor Portero, a pleasure. What a wonderful hotel."

"The pleasure is ours; if you need anything, just let us know. Where is your home?"

"Cleveland, Ohio. Have you been there?"

"No, I have been to New York and Los Angeles. Is it nice?"

"I think so, but then again I grew up there. Venice has been a dream of mine since I was a child."

"I hope you enjoy your stay with us, Ms. Polonia. Sonia will be most helpful if you need additional assistance."

"Thank you." Alex folded the map and slipped it into her back pocket, left out the door, crossed a small bridge over the canal she'd seen from her window, and dived into the alleys and passageways of Venice.

Alex prided herself on her sense of direction, but Venice's layout was confusing, far different than Cleveland's tidy grid. Somehow, five minutes after leaving the hotel, even with a map and cell phone in hand, she was lost. It wasn't as if she were stranded alone in the wild: frumpy, picture-snapping tourists and well-dressed Venetians surrounded her. But the narrow streets and the lack of any familiar landmarks didn't make things easy, the alleys provided limited views, and the narrow canals and steep bridges all began to look the same. After fifteen minutes, she was sure she had crossed the same bridge twice. She'd seen the same two men on the steep steps of the next bridge, staring down at her as she approached. Their black leather jackets and their glares reminded her of a Russian gangster she'd arrested a year earlier. Something about the men clicked: she'd first seen them in the alley when she left the hotel. They were casually smoking, trying their best to not notice her. But she'd spent fifteen years doing stakeouts and surveillance, and all this meant only one thing: they were following her. *Now, why the hell are they doing that?*

The two men blocked the bridge ahead. She turned and quickly wove through the crowds. She turned to the right and, through the windows of a shop selling trinkets, saw that the men had gained on her. She walked faster. The crowds and the well-lit shops thinned the farther she went from the plaza. She spun around, and her pursuers were gone.

Somewhat relieved, she turned into another alley, this one narrow and dark. At the end were the bright reflections of boats passing by and sunlight on the far side of a wide canal. She made for the light but soon found herself at a dead end. Just below her was a small dock with two mooring poles stuck in the mud. The surge from a passing vaporetto rolled up against the low stone wall that was the end of the alley. She turned to go back. The two men stood directly behind her. They both stood six inches taller than Alex and looked as hard as steel.

Her eyes never left the men. They wore black T-shirts under black leather jackets, no hats. Their haircuts were close, similar to those of the skinheads she'd busted. The men were white and looked Slavic—the same type of Eastern European that had flooded certain Cleveland neighborhoods during the past fifteen years. They were often trouble and most had criminal pasts.

One of the men pulled out a cell phone, hit a speed-dial number, listened, and said something she did not understand. He turned to the other man, said something else, then clicked it off. Continuing to stare at Alex, he slipped it back in his pocket. In one quick motion, the second man seized her arm and held it in a viselike grip.

She heard the man with the phone say something that sounded like a command.

"Let go of me, or you *will* regret it," she said. Her English seemed to confuse them for a second. "Now," she demanded, grabbing the hand of the man holding her other arm. His grip tightened. "Let go!" she said loudly and swung a fist quick and hard toward the man's right cheek. She was shocked when all she found was his left hand now completely enclosing her right fist. His reaction was like a snake's.

"Marika Jurić, you come," the man said in broken English. "Come now, no trouble."

"Like hell." She stomped on his toe. Nothing. His shoes had steel toes.

Professionals.

The first man grabbed both her arms. She lifted her knee to employ a woman's strongest defense. He turned to the side, and all she got was the side of his thigh; it felt as hard as the toe of his companion's boot.

"I said you must go with us." The two men began to pull her up the alley.

Seeing an opening, she grabbed the first man's middle finger and pulled it back and away from her forearm. Her move was as quick as the second man's when he had grabbed her fist. She pulled it back farther, hoping to hear it snap, the pressure forcing him to release his grip. Then she drove her elbow into his face, which dropped him to the stone paving. She released the finger, now broken she was sure, and turned her attention to the other man. As he reached inside his jacket, she slammed her fist into his throat, then spun past him and jammed her knee into his lower back as he tried to catch his breath.

She kicked the first man in the knee, surely damaging his cartilage. "Asshole."

The gagging man withdrew a Glock. Using her boot toe she caught him in the wrist and sent the pistol clattering across the stone. Her back was now to the canal.

The first man was slowly standing, regaining his wits. He smiled at her as if excited that she wasn't a defenseless woman, after all.

Shit.

He lunged, his arms wide. She waited a split second, then ducked, turned as the man rushed by, and shoved him toward the edge of the canal. With nothing to stop his momentum, he tumbled head over heels into the frigid waters.

She grabbed the Glock and spun back to the other man. Still trying to catch his breath, he straightened and raised his hands when she pointed the pistol at his face.

"No, please. Do not shoot."

"What the hell's going on?" she said, listening with some pleasure to the sloshing sounds of the first man struggling to climb out of the canal. "Who is this Marika? Talk, you asshole."

"You—you are Marika, bitch."

Not waiting for the floundering man to reach the paving, Alex turned and started running toward the end of the alley. She jammed the Glock into her jeans' waistband under the back of her leather jacket. After three turns, and more confused than ever, she stumbled into an odd-shaped courtyard. A hundred tourists wandered in and out of the four openings at the corners. A small café with bright-yellow awnings filled the far corner. In its windows were displayed hundreds of cookies, bread, and pastries. She saw a table to the far side and, still breathing hard, walked toward it.

"Marika, wait. Marika Jurić, wait a moment."

Alex turned and saw an incredibly good-looking man with Latin features, a head of black hair, and dark eyes. He was walking toward her.

"Who the hell are you and what was that all about?" she said to the approaching stranger.

A confused look on his face, the man said, "Ms. Jurić, I did not know that you spoke English so fluently. In fact, it's quite good."

"That's twice in the last ten minutes someone's called me Jurić or Marika—you and those jerks." She pointed toward the courtyard opening she'd just used. "I'm not Marika, whoever she is."

The man studied her face for a moment. "What jerks, where? Did something happen? Are you all right?"

"Get away from me," she said once she'd reached the café table.

The waiter walked up to her. "Signora, is this Gypsy bothering you? Should I call the *polizia?*"

"The police will not be necessary," said the man who'd called her Marika. "You sure look like her, in fact too much like her. What's your name?"

"Wait just a goddamn minute. Why should I tell you my name? You know those guys that tried to grab me? What is this all about? And who the hell are you? I'm taking a leisurely stroll on the vacation of my life when two of you fools try to jump me. Now you, whoever you are, say I look like someone else. So, answer my questions—now!"

"I'm sorry, ma'am, I don't have the time. I have—"

"Ma'am?" She pulled her cell phone from her coat pocket and snapped a picture of the man's face. "You speak English like an American, so I'm sure you're in some felony database. I can start there." She spun around and started to walk away.

"Wait a sec, okay. Sure, a cup of coffee, that'll be fine. Please sit."

She turned back and, without taking her eyes off the man, sat down at the table.

"Due espressi," the dark-haired man said. The waiter, still with a serious and concerned look on his face, nodded and walked away.

Alex waited as he sat. She flashed a look at the gun inside his open jacket, also a Glock.

"Name," she asked.

"You first."

"No, you tell me yours. You seem to think I'm somebody else, and I assume that person knows you. So, since I am the one at a loss, you first." She crossed her arms. "Or should I wave over the gendarmes there?" She pointed to two policemen who had just arrived and were standing in a strip of warm sunlight beneath the campanile. "Hell, maybe I will, there's something else I'd like to tell them." She started to rise.

"They are called carabinieri, and they are good at their jobs. We do not need them. My name is Special Agent Javier Castillo. I am assigned to the Milan branch of the Central Intelligence Agency. And you look a lot like someone I am to meet with later this afternoon."

"CIA? Here in Venice? Really?" Alex said with a snort, and then examined the man. "I look like someone else? I pity them. Show me your creds, Mr. CIA."

Agent Castillo retrieved a small wallet from the inside of his coat and opened it. Alex inspected the picture, the gold badge, and the information. She nodded and glanced up, then slouched in her chair. Across the piazza the two men who tried to grab her had arrived. They stared at every face and, like stalking cats, worked their way across the square. Using the CIA man as a shield, she hid from their line of sight.

"You know those two?" Agent Castillo asked. "Were they the earlier trouble? One appears to be wet."

"Yes, they were the trouble. One accidentally lost his footing, and I helped him fall into the canal."

He smiled. "You were lucky. They are paramilitaries from Croatia or Serbia, hard to tell them apart. Not very nice, only the Albanians may be worse. So, now your turn."

"You said I remind you of someone?"

"First, your name."

"Not nearly as exciting. Alexandra Polonia, police detective from Cleveland, Ohio. I assume you know where that is. By the way, you sound like a Texan."

"Yes, and I've even been to Cleveland. Born and raised in Waco, Texas, though."

"Thought so. Aren't we a long way from home?"

CHAPTER 6

Alex sipped her espresso. She watched the mysterious CIA agent drink his like she'd seen the Italians in the café drink them: in one swallow.

"I was on my way to lunch from my hotel when those thugs attacked me," she explained to him. "Why, I have no idea. Now I'm on an adrenaline rush and famished. My stomach sounds like Friday night at a Parma bowling alley. So, Mr. CIA Man, do you have any restaurant ideas? Even with my map and cell phone, I'm totally and utterly lost. When those thugs found me, I was heading toward the Grand Canal to a restaurant the hotel suggested and got all turned around." She pointed in one direction; he pointed in the other. "That way? I *am* all turned around."

"You are not the first," the agent said. "This island will do that. Yes, I know a great place for lunch, ten minutes away, tops."

"That's what the concierge said just before I left." She finished her espresso, stood, and peered into the dark eyes of the good-looking guy that had literally dropped in on her. "Care to join me, Mr. Tour Guide?"

Special Agent Castillo looked at his watch, then Alex.

"Places to go, things to see, nations to spy on?" she said.

"Something like that, but after those two Croatians, I'm intrigued. So, yes, I'll join you."

"Lead on."

Mr. Tour Guide strolled next to Alex the whole way, pointing out various churches, museums, shops, and places to eat. He said *fabulous* more than three times; her stomach said a split with the seven and ten pins still standing. They turned a corner. He stopped and waved out his hand like a conductor. The whole of the Piazza San Marco spread before them. She stopped. The crowds and the noise faded away, and soon all she saw was the campanile and the white façade of the basilica beyond, lit by the early-afternoon sun.

"I take it you've never been here?" he asked as Alex wiped a tear from her cheek.

"I have never been anywhere. Venice? Only in my dreams and in movies. It's more than I imagined—larger, grander, more wondrous."

"Lunch is a little farther on, just off the colonnade. I know the owner. Good guy. He can whip up an excellent omelet. The seafood is also wonderful."

Openmouthed, Alex rubbernecked the surrounding colonnade and arcades, and followed the agent as they wove through the tangle of tourists. Some wore masks and outlandish, brightly colored costumes. The pigeons, harassed by children, flew in all directions. Even the cold wind off the canal failed to dampen her excitement.

After her tour guide had exchanged niceties with the restaurant owner, they took a small table in the front window where she could watch the theater of the piazza. The owner pulled a "Reserved" sign off the table.

"He knew you were coming?"

"No, but he does hold this for special guests."

"Nice to meet a special guest on my first day—and a spook as well."

"Dominic, the owner, likes to tell the story of when Hemingway would stop here for breakfast. His grandfather owned the place then. It is one of the few restaurants that serve a full American-style breakfast. Seems the Venetians like to eat a quick *colazione*. Dominic lived in Brooklyn for some years before returning home to Venice, so he knows all about Americans and their big breakfasts. The Venetians save themselves for a grand lunch and a late dinner. So, I suggest a grand lunch.

And I am not a spook, just a middling special agent on assignment. Now, Ms. Alexandra Polonia, did you leave your husband at the hotel, are you trying to ditch your travel friends, or are you traveling alone?"

Before she could answer, the owner walked back to the table and said something in Italian. Castillo answered, pointing to her. The owner left.

"What was that?"

"I ordered for you. He makes an incredible omelet, and you look like you could use one right now. Also, a bottle of Soavé, is that okay?"

"First of all, Special Agent—"

"Javier to my friends."

She paused and studied the man. "Javier, first of all, I'm a Cleveland cop. I'm here alone because my ex-husband was also a cop—and is now in prison. He ruined my reputation. Now I'm on my first vacation in so long, I don't remember when, or how many years. And this morning, after arriving in this fabulous city—a place I've dreamed about my whole life—I am accosted by what you call Croatian paramilitaries, I throw one of them in the canal and nearly crush the throat of the other, all because, according to you, I may look like a woman named Marika wanted by those same Croatians."

"Actually, they may be members of a Croatian paramilitary group that some say murdered thousands of Bosniaks during the Bosnian War. Nasty killers. Did you see a wolf's head tat on their necks?"

Alex thought for a moment and recalled that when she'd thrown her elbow into one man's face, she'd seen a tattoo of something on the side of his neck. "Yes, there may have been," she said.

She was already on her second glass of wine when lunch arrived. It was as good as Javier said it would be.

"So, you think I was mistaken for this Marika Jurić woman?" she asked.

"Probably," Javier answered. "I've never met her, but you look a lot like her picture—in fact, amazingly so. We have talked by phone a few times."

"And why are you here?" she asked.

"That is confidential. Needless to say, if these guys are after her, it has become much more serious."

"Were you also following me?"

"No, that was coincidental. I was walking through the piazza, and your blonde hair caught my attention in the sunlight. And we were a block from where Marika is staying, so naturally, I thought you were her. The Croatians did the same and followed you until you were someplace less crowded."

"Can't say I'd have liked my chances with those guys. I only had a second to surprise them. I'm resourceful, but they outweighed me by three hundred pounds. And that one fella was stupid fast with his hands. My hand still hurts."

"They're well trained through years of practice—it was an awful civil war. And a war that is just the latest chapter in a long story of religions and people hating each other."

"Is that why you're here? Does this woman have information the United States wants?"

"Good guess, Detective. But as I said, it's all confidential."

"Not really a guess. I could tell from the passion in your voice. I've been a detective for a long time. My job is to put two and two together and get five."

"So, your ex-husband is a scumbag, in jail, and you're free. Now this—life just isn't fair, is it? These guys still think you are Marika Jurić, and that's not going to change until she comes forward. Until then, keep your head down."

"Do you think I'm going to hide in my room?" Alex said. "I survived interrogations about Ralph—he's the ex-husband—interrogations by my friends, no less, and two days on the stand during his trial. I've dealt with gangbangers, white supremacists, Albanians, Bulgarians, and a few Russians during my days in Cleveland. I'm on so many hurt or kill lists, Guinness might call to see if I hold the record. The crap with my husband brought out a lot of old shit and new opportunities for payback. I have wanted to see Venice my whole life, and this is my first chance. Do you think a couple of thugs are going to interfere with my fun?"

Javier smiled and shook his head. "These guys are nasty—very nasty. Just keep your wits about you, okay?"

Alex leaned back and felt the Glock muzzle's sharp edge. "So, when are you meeting my twin?"

"In about an hour."

She laughed. "Need backup?"

"No, you go and enjoy Venice. Where are you staying?"

"The Aqua Palace, seems nice."

"It is, and it is just a block from Marika's hotel. I can see why the Croats were confused."

Alex signaled to the owner and waved like she had a pen in her hand.

"My treat," Javier said.

"No way, I pay my debts."

The owner walked to the table and said the bill was already paid. Alex looked at Javier, who said, "Done and done. Remember, I'm the one working and on a government expense account. You are on vacation."

"So, how do I get back to my hotel?"

"Let me have your map."

She handed it to him.

"From here walk past the campanile, then turn toward the canal. A few hundred yards beyond is the San Marco vaporetto stop. Buy your ticket, get on, and ride up the canal until you come to the Rialto stop. You can't miss the bridge. Then go this way." He marked a trail even she could follow.

◆ ◆ ◆

After Javier had left, Alex spent an hour strolling through the grand arcade of shops that surrounded the most famous piazza in the world, then went into the Basilica di San Marco. Her Catholic upbringing gnawed at her, and her current lapse in the world of Catholicism had drifted into a longing that seemed hard to come to terms with after the past year. She'd been raised a good Catholic: Saint Ann's Catholic School, communion, confirmation, and the usual sacraments. But being a cop made being devout difficult. The basilica brought her to her knees, and she lit a votive candle for her grandmother. Looking up at the glorious ceiling, she was taken in by the rich, ornate art created in religion's name. Then she remembered the cynical remark Javier had made about Bosnia and the war and realized it could also be said about countless dead from other senseless wars where religion was the excuse.

She took an open seat in the vaporetto and reached back into her childhood and her dreams of navigating the Grand Canal toward the Rialto Bridge. Granted, the dream didn't include the forward compartment of a crowded vaporetto, but the dream was strong enough that even the whining of a tired child sitting next to her couldn't steal away the magic. She stepped off the boat and walked onto the Riva del Ferro, pulled out the map, and rotated it. She noted the Rialto Bridge to her left and the street sign reading "Calle Mazzini." She dived back into the passageways, or *calli*. She passed a hotel named Ai Reali and wondered if that was where her doppelgänger was staying. Ten minutes later, she walked into her hotel. Sonia was at the desk.

"Did you find the restaurant?" Sonia asked.

"No, but I found something even more interesting."

"And what was that?"

"An enigmatic Texan."

CHAPTER 7

Marika wiped the condensation away from the bathroom mirror. She desperately needed a hairdresser. While she was able to wash out the salt and other debris that had nested in the tangle of blonde hair, its texture had devolved to that of a golden Brillo pad. But the hair would have to wait—her appointment with the CIA agent was later today.

She toweled herself off, dressed, and sorted some of her luggage, which she'd shipped to the hotel a week earlier, into the room's drawers. Stylish gray slacks, a Florentine leather over-the-shoulder satchel, a designer handbag—things she couldn't have dreamed of owning growing up on the streets of Communist Zagreb. But she had invested wisely after selling her software company five years ago and was now comfortable. Every kuna she had made was deserved, every euro used to pay for her son's education was earned, and every English pound and American dollar sitting in Geneva banks was hers. She owed nothing to anyone. And her early retirement from software had allowed her to return to her roots as an independent investigative journalist.

She reflected on her life's twists and turns—doors opened and doors closed. Some opportunities seized, others forgone. But most of her life had hinged on one twist, one turn: a single day almost a quarter century earlier. The day she had left Zagreb and taken a bus up into the hills of Bosnia. She had been so full of hope and aspirations. Croatia was now a free and independent country, centuries of oppression by despotic governments, one after another, gone. Yugoslavia, always a political imposter, was gone. Croatia and the rest of the puzzle pieces of the Balkans were beginning to take their place in the modern world of Europe.

Her room's phone interrupted her reverie. She picked it up. "Yes?"

"The afternoon wake-up call you requested, signora."

"Thank you," she said and hung up. Not as if she needed the call anyway—her circumstances had left her restless.

She rechecked her small pistol's magazine, cleared the chamber, and grabbed her satchel. The pistol fit comfortably into its custom holster just under the flap.

"Ms. Jurić, good afternoon," the manager said a few minutes later, once she'd reached the lobby. "I hope you had a chance to rest. Was your luggage as you sent it? I was concerned."

"Signor Baradino, everything, as usual, is very satisfactory. However, I could use a few more towels, and there is a plastic bag in the bathroom that needs to be removed. I cannot stand to look at those clothes again. So, if you would, please."

"Certainly, as good as done. Anything else?"

"Messages?"

"One moment. I believe so." Signor Baradino disappeared into an office behind the reception counter. "Yes, here it is. It came as an e-mail." He held a small gilt tray; an envelope lay on it.

"If you would excuse me," Marika said and turned toward a small sitting area off the lobby. She sat on a velveteen couch with a carved dark-wood base and arms, placed her satchel next to her, and opened the letter. She smiled.

Mother,

I will see you in Venice on Monday afternoon. I'm arriving on the five o'clock train from Milan and will meet you on the platform. I have sent this to Mr. Baradino, whom I know you trust. I hope that your trip was a success. I look forward to seeing you.

Con affetto,

Ehsan

She refolded the letter and held it next to her heart. *How could the time have passed so quickly?*

"Is everything acceptable, signora?"

"Yes, thank you, Signor Baradino."

"It will be good to see Ehsan again. If I were to have a son, he is the man I would want."

"He is my treasure. Moreover, as a man, far more than that. Is the small wine library available this evening? I may have some guests and, of course, Ehsan. Could you be kind enough to see?"

"I know for a fact it is available. Would eight o'clock be acceptable?"

"*Perfetto.* I have errands to run, and then I'll be back. Thank you for taking care of the room."

The CIA agent had suggested they meet at three o'clock in the Campo Santi Giovanni e Paolo, and she'd agreed. He was a curious man, his accent unlike those she'd heard from Washington, DC. His was softer, with a twang, yet formal at the same time: he had called her *ma'am* many times during their phone conversation. She was interested in meeting this Javier Castillo—very interested. But first she needed to complete a couple of errands: get a card for her son (his birthday was this Friday), and retrieve cash from the ATM. The timing of his birthday was unfortunate, but at least they'd celebrate it together.

She soon completed her errands. The birthday card was simple and direct—Ehsan would enjoy the thought, even though it was in Italian—and the five hundred euros now in her bag would be helpful.

She had fallen for Venice as a young woman. Her parents had brought her here when she was eighteen, around the time the Soviet Union collapsed and Yugoslavia began to change. Old hatreds arose; boundaries were carved in blood; politicians conspired. Her parents discussed leaving Zagreb for Italy. She remembered her father saying something about a job he might be able to find near Milan. What it was she couldn't recall. He was a mechanic, his hands always dirty, his clothes always smelling of gasoline.

In Venice they toured the countryside in open cars and bright sunshine, drove on snowy roads in the mountains, and spent the week on the canals. A week that just the three of them enjoyed, not knowing it would be the last vacation they would ever spend together.

Then the war came. Her father was conscripted by the army. She never saw him again. Her mother died soon after he did, from a broken heart. A couple of years later, all Marika had was her son, Ehsan, a small apartment in Zagreb, and an idea. Ten years after that, her software company was a success; she even opened an office in Milan. In time, she and her heart returned to Venice.

She had an hour before her meeting with the CIA agent. She stopped for a glass of Campari at a small bar that overlooked the Rialto Bridge and lit a cigarette.

As the waiter set the glass before Marika, two men pulled out chairs from the table next to hers, spun them around, and sat directly across from her. Shocked, she started to stand.

"Sit, Cierzinski," the thinner of the two men said. "We need to talk. There is much to discuss."

"Who the hell are you?" she demanded, her English—unlike theirs—thick with an Eastern European accent.

"You know why we are here," the other man said. "Is this why you skipped out of Cleveland, to come to Italy and get your husband's money?"

"Money? What are you talking about? What is this *Cleveland*? I don't know you, and I have no husband. Go away, or I'll call the polizia."

"The money, I know you know where it is. Since he doesn't need it, it's ours. Just tell us and no one will be the wiser. So, blondie, where the hell is it?"

She studied the men: cheap suits and white shirts under short trench coats. The man on the left had a narrow face, pasty skin, red hair, and green eyes. The other had a fuller face, dark skin, three-day stubble, and brown eyes. Both had receding hairlines and attempted to style what was left into something that they probably hoped made them look ten years younger. They reminded her of the EU bureaucrats she had dealt with in Brussels, but they sounded American.

"Who the hell are you?" she demanded.

"Really, is this how you are going to play this?" the narrow-faced man said. "You don't remember me? How could you forget your old friends, Agents Duane Turner and Bill Damico? We have a history. I am hurt, aren't you, Bill?"

"Very hurt," Damico said. "I wonder if she treats all her friends this way."

"Probably, women can be so bitchy, forgetful, and mean."

Marika started to stand.

"Sit," Turner said.

Marika sat back in her chair and placed her bag on the table. "I have no idea what you are talking about. I am a tourist from Croatia; I am not this Cierzinski person, whoever she is." She opened the flap of her bag, brushed her hand over the pistol, and removed her passport. She opened it and held it up to Turner's face. "Now, based on your gangster appearance and your English, I assume you are some type of an American thug. Who the hell are you?"

The men looked at each other, then back at her.

"You are not Alexandra Cierzinski?" Turner asked.

"No, obviously not."

"Did Cierzinski have a tattoo on her arm?" Turner asked Damico.

"Not that I know of."

Turner grabbed Marika's hand and twisted her arm to show Damico her tattoo, a dagger with flames erupting from its edge. Marika pointed her pistol at Turner, and he promptly let her go.

"Yes, the tattoo is a cherished memory from my past," Marika said, pulling her left arm back. "I suggest that you two gentlemen move along. It seems your embarrassment is a case of mistaken identity. I don't know an Alexandra Cierzinski or even care. Shall we just say your mistake was an honest one before it becomes a regrettable one?" She smiled at the men as they stood.

"Jesus, I could have sworn it was her," Turner said.

"Sorry, lady, we didn't mean anything by it," Damico added.

The men walked away and didn't look back.

"Americans," Marika said as she slipped the pistol back into its holster and closed the flap on her bag.

Chapter 8

An hour later, Marika entered the Campo Santi Giovanni and carefully inspected the dozens of plastic tables set up at restaurants around its perimeter, until she caught the eye of one man, a Spaniard by his looks. As she approached, the man stood. Something about the CIA agent reminded her of her son. He also looked confused.

"Special Agent Castillo, it is a pleasure to finally meet you."

"And you too, Ms. Jurić. Please sit," Javier said, still staring at her.

"The afternoon is chilly despite the sun," Marika began as she sat. "But then again what I am doing does not abide pleasant days and warm sunshine. Has everything been prepared?"

"Yes," Special Agent Castillo said. "You requested the transfer to be low key. That is not a problem. But we will need some time to review the information before we can go public."

"Yes, I understand, but Kozak will arrive here any day, and the conference is on Thursday. Your State Department has assured me there will be enough time."

"After the transfer of the information, it is out of my hands, but I will do my best."

"Thank you, Special Agent Castillo. I have waited more than twenty years to have this man erased from the history books. He is not the future of Croatia. If we Croats wish to play on the same field with the other European countries, we must show them our resolve."

"I understand, Ms. Jurić, but I am just the messenger. My government needs to be sure."

"Like your President Clinton waited to be sure as thousands were massacred? As he and your State Department did nothing while my people died and thousands of murdered Bosniaks were thrown into ditches and the women and children raped? Like those same plutocrats and politicians of the European community who also waited to be sure, safe in their glass-walled bureaucracies in Brussels?"

"If this is your opinion of us, why am I here? There's the French, the English."

"They are not to be trusted. Hundreds of years of mischief and meddling is behind their words and promises. No, all I have now is the United States—I have faith in your current president."

"More than many of his fellow citizens," Javier added.

"No matter, my goal is simple: to eliminate this man as a candidate for the presidency of Croatia. The man is a monster, and it cannot be permitted."

"The information?"

"My son is bringing me the rest of the material, and the film, later today. I will give it to you tonight at my hotel." She stopped and studied Javier. "Is something bothering you, Agent Castillo? You keep looking strangely at me."

"I apologize for staring," Javier offered. "I am sure you remember an old adage that says we have a double somewhere—a person that looks so like yourself that even your mother might not know the difference. It seems that earlier today I met yours. It is perplexing, specifically right now."

"I have a twin, fascinating."

"Sorry if I offended you. I apologize."

"On the contrary, I thought I had lost an earring, or my makeup was a mess."

"No, you are just fine. It is just that the two of you are so alike, you might be easily mistaken for the other."

"That explains what happened an hour ago," Marika said. "I was interrupted by two Americans as I was having a Campari at a bar near my hotel. They mistook me for a woman they called Cierzinski, Alexandra Cierzinski. After I had shown them some identification, they seemed confused. I told them to go away. They did, but it was very strange." *No need to tell him about the gun.*

Javier's smile at the coincidence turned to a stern look. "That explains the other men too."

"What other men?"

"Earlier today I was walking through the neighborhood near your hotel. You are staying at the Ai Reali, correct?"

Marika nodded.

"I noticed a woman in one of the piazzas that I thought was you, so I introduced myself. When she protested, and I realized that she wasn't you, she told me a story of being attacked by two men—Croats by her description. She managed to escape them and she is staying nearby."

"Interesting. And this is the woman who is my double?"

"Yes, and other than the clothes and your accent, to most anyone you would be twins."

"A fascinating story. Is this something your CIA has concocted?"

"Ms. Jurić, Attila Kozak is trying to either kidnap you or in some way compromise you. I would not put it past him to find a way to eliminate you."

"Others have tried and failed. Kozak's a thug and a gangster. He only knows violence and brute force. Those sorts of men are easier to deal with than a politician or bureaucrat, who wrap themselves in laws and regulations. The thugs are easier to spot. Unfortunately, sometimes their violence must be met with violence. The war in Bosnia did not end entirely through the actions of politicians. A few appropriately placed bombs dropped by your American planes did a lot more to bring Kozak and his militia to the peace table than fancy words."

"Did these Americans give you their names?"

"Yes. Duane Turner and Bill something . . . Bill Damico. They said they were agents, I assume of some American agency. What is this all about? Are they with your CIA? I assumed they have something to do with this woman. They wanted money. Money she supposedly knew about. Now, Agent Castillo, can you tell me why these men are following Ms. Cierzinski?"

"Her name is Polonia, Alexandra Polonia. She changed it before coming to Venice. She is also a policewoman."

"How suspiciously convenient. These men had a reason for accosting me as well as following this Polonia woman. I wonder what it is?"

"I don't have a clue."

CHAPTER 9

Javier and Marika left the campo and walked back to her hotel.

How can there be some other woman who looks so much like me—and here, now?

"Agent Castillo, I do not believe in coincidences. They are only in movies and books."

"Ms. Jurić, I think even your son would have difficulty telling the two of you apart. She has the same eyes, height, complexion, and hair color, and you are both the same age. It is too strange."

"One must never discuss a woman's age," Marika said. "So, this woman is a police officer?"

"Things are different in American police departments," Javier said. "In fact, in some cities, the chief of police is a woman. They are respected and, more importantly, obeyed."

"That would be difficult to find anywhere in the Balkans. We are, as you might believe, a male-dominated society." At an overlook of the Grand Canal, Marika stopped and lit a cigarette. "That is where many of our problems begin: the men and their testosterone and foolish bravado. Eventually, it changes to the lust for power, with old hatreds an excuse for violence. I have studied this man Attila Kozak for a long time. He started as a small-time hoodlum working for a small-time tribal chieftain, smuggling in goods, drugs, and girls from Turkey, Romania, and Ukraine. All to satisfy a man's wants. It was not hard to move on to murder on an industrial scale."

"Your information and data—are they truthful and undeniable?"

"Of course, I would not be talking with you and risking my life if they weren't."

"Vendettas can change a person. I've seen it."

"Special Agent Castillo, this has changed me. I cannot deny it. This vendetta, as you call it, changed my family, my beliefs, and my life. Yet if it were not for this man, I would not have my son, who would not have lost his family, and likely would have been killed too. I am here to stop this Kozak monster."

"I understand."

"I hope you do. You Americans are so naïve. You haven't had as much time as we've had to build up hatred and religious righteousness—or the need for revenge. We Croats have long memories when it serves our purposes."

"You said that your son is coming today?" Javier asked. By this time they had reached the Campo San Lio, a short walk to her hotel.

"Yes, on the late-afternoon train from Milan. I am having a small dinner party at the hotel to welcome him at eight o'clock. Please join us—I want you to meet him, and he has the papers I could not carry. I will give you the thumb drive and the original film with the rest of the data. You can do with them as you wish; I have copies. Also, please invite this intriguing double of mine—I would like to see what I look like. Good afternoon, Special Agent Castillo."

Marika turned and disappeared down a passageway.

Special Agent Castillo considered the day's events. No, *events* was the wrong word; it was more like one strange coincidence piled on after another. And the day wasn't even done yet. In his operational orders from the CIA's Milan field office, the mission was described as simple data collection. He was a go-between, nothing more. Pick up what Marika Jurić has on this known Croatian mobster, and military officer turned politician, Attila Kozak. Get the papers, thumb drive, and film back to Milan to be scanned and sent on to Washington. If the US State Department confirmed the information and blessed it, the US would publicly denounce Kozak.

All well and good. He had been briefed about Attila Kozak. However, because the European Union conference was scheduled for the day after Ash Wednesday, Javier had arrived during Carnevale. Everywhere he turned, masked and costumed revelers danced and paraded through the campos and piazzas, some tipsy even at noon. He was sure the EU commissioners had chosen that Thursday so that they could attend the parties and banquets that revolved around Carnevale.

Attila Kozak, the leader of the Croatian Party of God and Rights, was one of six candidates running for the presidency of Croatia. The Party of God had evolved from a succession of Croatian nationalist, conservative, right-wing paramilitary gangs that had now matured into the present political organization—PGR in English. Kozak had some-how managed to hold out an olive branch to both Serbia and Bosnia and Herzegovina. While neither country trusted the man, they had conceded to the United Nations that this might be the first step to some form of reconciliation between the warring states.

During the Bosnian War, Kozak was a young and aggressive colonel in the most feared and beastly of Croatian paramilitary units, the Wolf's Head Battalion, and was suspected of being one of the leaders behind the systematic ethnic cleansing and massacre of hundreds of Bosniaks. The men, and some women, of this unit acted like the heinous Nazi SS that had terrorized the Croatian countryside during World War II. Known for a stylized wolf's head tattoo on the right side of the neck, they definitely were not the peace-loving Party of God and Rights and the future of Croatia. Kozak was also rumored to have established brothels in the cities they controlled, which were nothing more than rape centers populated with detained Muslim women and young girls. But in the aftermath of the peace accords and the eventual arrests and convictions of dozens of Serbian commanders, politicians, and soldiers for crimes against humanity, those Croats that participated in their own ethnic cleansings of the Bosniaks were often ignored. While a few Croats were caught and placed on trial at The Hague, most escaped or were never charged. Kozak was one of those never arrested or indicted.

The dossier that CIA headquarters in Langley had given Javier noted that Kozak grew up in the suburbs of Zagreb, in one of the worst postwar industrial areas built by the Communists. With a drunken father and a mother who had disappeared when Attila was ten, he was raised by his grandparents. His eighty-year-old grandfather filled the boy's head with stories of the war, hatred for the Germans, the Serbians, the Turks—as the Bosniaks were called—and anything European. It was a short step for the ten-year-old to be taken under the strong and embracing arm of one of the local Zagreb criminal gangs that moved opium and other drugs from the east through Croatia into Europe. When the Bosnian War exploded, they shifted their resources into stealing property, killing those in the way, and expanding their control of prostitution.

Kozak was smart and understood the advantages of using the chaotic political turmoil as a way to provide cover for many of his own operations. He enlisted in the army and was selected by a friend to become part of the Wolf's Head Battalion—a government-sanctioned gang that used its cover of legitimacy to pillage and plunder the villages of Bosnia and Herzegovina. A practicing Roman Catholic, Kozak was not shy about using the church as well. On his office wall in Zagreb, in a place of honor, hung a photograph of him kneeling before the pope's ring.

Javier wasn't sure what Marika had. She had been vague as to the scope of the story and the information, but he was now certain that it was her intention to bring the man down. He also knew the dossier listed other witnesses to Kozak's crimes, but they had disappeared. None had been found, alive or dead. When in a rare interview a reporter had asked Kozak about the coincidence of the missing witnesses, he answered, "I don't believe in coincidences. Those people are probably on vacation."

Javier had two days. On Thursday, at the conference center Teatrino di Palazzo Grassi, the European Union would convene the next meeting in the series of post accession economic summits with Croatia and the surrounding Balkan countries. Also included in the EU conference were those European countries that stood to gain or lose something by Croatia becoming a member of the European Economic Area. Being a member of the European Union was one thing; becoming a member of the European Economic Area, with permission to adopt the euro, was something else entirely. The lowly Croatian kuna might not have much international power, but the conversion scared the devil out of Germany and France, and the citizens of Croatia as well.

The rumor was that Kozak would make a political play at this conference. CIA contacts in Croatia suggested he would verbally attack the Germans and again lay at their feet the war crimes of World War II. Millions died in Yugoslavia and Croatia at the hands of both the Nazis and the Communists, but it was the Germans that Kozak still blamed for most of the current troubles in Croatia.

"We Croatians will never again bow to the Germans, no matter how much they wave their precious euro in our noses," Kozak had said at an earlier conference—a conference he'd not been invited to. "They want us for cheap summer cottages, cheap labor, and cheap food. Seventy years ago, it was the Germans that puffed up the dreams of the Bosnian Muslims who owed fidelity to Turkey. While the world may forgive this historic allegiance, we Croatians will never forgive or forget. Remember, it was those Turks, those Bosniaks, that filled the ranks of the treacherous SS Handschar army units for the Nazis. The Germans and the rest of Europe will pay dearly for our labor and access to our country."

Javier understood some of what was going on, but the US State Department had its own reasons for meddling in things. As for Javier himself, he just believed Attila Kozak had to be stopped.

The CIA's motto was "And ye shall know the truth and the truth shall make you free." Javier's experience and eighteen years' tenure in the agency had reinforced every one of those words. He and his fellow agents lived them, but since 9/11 he had grown wary of many of the other expanding bureaucracies of the American government. Their goals often drifted into the world of politics and politicians. Theirs was a gray world of innuendo and marginalization. His own world was simple: collect data, find the bad actors, and then put them away. But now two agents from some American organization had walked into the mix, men who knew this Alexandra Polonia. First he'd have his people in Langley check them out, and then make a few calls of his own.

Even after finding two identical women on the same day in Venice, he did not believe in coincidences. Though, unwillingly, he was beginning to.

CHAPTER 10

The late-afternoon sun was low over the rooftops, and the canal outside Alex's window was darkening. Her thoughts drifted like clouds on a windy day: the Croatian thugs, the delicious lunch, the cowboy from Texas, and the pistol in the room's safe. For the first time in months, she thought, even with all the chaos, there were positive things.

The phone rang. "We need to talk," Javier said.

"Why?" Alex answered. "What could I possibly have that you want?"

Javier hesitated. "Things have gotten a little out of control."

"Out of control? Where?"

"There's a small café just across the bridge from your hotel. Only four tables in front. I'm sitting in one. I have been invited to a small dinner party this evening, and I'm asking if you would like to join me. A little touch of Carnevale might do us both some good. I believe you will find it interesting."

"Are you asking me on a date?"

"Right now, just to talk. Can you meet me?"

She paused. "Sure, fifteen minutes. I just got out of the shower," she lied.

"Nice image. See you soon." He hung up.

Alex tapped the top of the phone. She still had no idea who this Castillo character was, even after an enjoyable lunch. She'd been assaulted, almost kidnapped, had escaped, been picked up by a Texan, bought a nice lunch, and now had been invited to a party. Not bad for her first twelve hours. Yes—why not?

Soon afterward she slipped into the chair opposite Javier as he clicked off his phone and removed his earpiece.

"Why is it that these plastic chairs are not made for our American butts? Some of the Venetian women I've seen—how can I say this nicely?—are not exactly svelte."

"I haven't a clue," Javier answered. "They're comfortable to me."

"You have a tiny ass, whereas we full-figure gals—well, just saying. So, what's so important?"

"Two men, Americans, accosted Ms. Jurić earlier today. They claim to know you. They demanded money of some kind. Their attitude toward you left little to the imagination."

"Two men?" Alex said, an edge to her voice. "What did they look like?"

"Marika said they were white, called themselves agents. They gave the names Turner and Damico."

"Damn, those idiots? They are DEA and have been hounding me over the profits that Ralph supposedly has hidden."

"Is that why they are here?"

"Probably to get the money, money I don't know anything about. I assume they mistook your Croatian spy, or whatever she is, for me?"

"Yes, that's what she said. Maybe for the same reason why those Croats tried to grab you this morning—mistaken identity. It seems that I have two identical women on my hands, wanted by two extremely different groups with different agendas. Marika Jurić is my assignment, and the other, you, has become a pain in the butt—no chair joke intended."

"Cute. What did they say?"

Javier described Marika's encounter with Turner and Damico.

"Damn, I just don't get it. Why come four thousand miles to try and shake me down? If there is something that you would like to investigate, you should check out those two."

"They are not my concern."

"Really?" Alex said. "They should be."

"I have enough to do—I don't need more. Money, what money?"

"Don't care but curious, not good. Somebody came up with a number during the trial; the number was twenty million. Ralph refused to say anything. So, these DEA guys are here looking for the money, how stupid."

"Like hunting a trophy head or something?" Javier said. "I've seen it before."

"Yes, maybe. I think they are in it for themselves. They are a smarmy pair, and I would not put it past them. Besides, that ex of mine knows that if I found it, I'd turn it over to the Justice Department. I'm sure that's why he never even hinted at where it might be. He believes it's so well hidden that it will still be there when he gets out. Damn, I came here to get away from all that, and the jerk still follows me. I'm beginning to have an overwhelming desire to shoot someone."

"That never solves anything."

"Wanna bet?"

Before he called Alex, Javier had been on the phone with his friend, Special Agent Luis Rodrigues of the Cleveland FBI field office. Rodrigues, a Texan like Castillo, was shocked.

"Alexandra Cierzinski is in Venice?" he asked.

"She says her name is Polonia," Javier answered.

"It is. I was informed she recently changed it. However, we still know her as Cierzinski. Nice woman, well respected and a good police officer and detective. This office was directly involved in the follow-up to her husband's arrest. His being a cop put the whole Cleveland police force under a microscope. In fact, my partner, Special Agent Latimer, interviewed her. We found nothing that connected her to the charges; it was hard to believe. Honestly, I was skeptical, but as the weeks went on, even I came over to her side. She was extremely upset about what her husband did and its impact on her—wait, that's not the word. She was furious. I believe her husband, Ralph Cierzinski, kept her totally out of his criminal activities. Maybe he loved her. Who the hell knows?"

"She mentioned a divorce."

"Yes, signed the day he went to Ohio's Youngstown facility. He got twelve years. Might get out earlier for the usual good behavior. Personally, I'd lock him away forever. Meth is really bad, particularly for kids."

"The woman I'm assigned to assist here was mistaken for Polonia and was hit up by two DEA agents, Turner and Damico."

"Interesting, I know them. Average DEA, clueless and opportunistic," Rodrigues said. "You think they are there for the money?"

"What money?"

"The number kicked around is ten to twenty million, but no one knows, except Ralph Cierzinski."

Javier whistled. "Really? Shit, no wonder they are here."

"Seen people go brain dead over a lot less. What's Polonia's connection to your assignment?"

Javier explained the coincidence of the two look-alikes, the Croatian thugs' attempt on Polonia earlier in the day, and the DEA agents' shakedown attempt on Marika in the afternoon.

"I assume your assignment is as good-looking as Polonia? I've seen her," Rodrigues asked.

"Don't go there. I'm working."

"Too bad, nice to have choices. We tried to find the money—nothing. For all I know it could be buried in a box. Our guess is it's in accounts in the Caymans or Switzerland. The fact that he was a cop gave him knowledge your typical meth-lab operator doesn't have. You think this Polonia woman might be in Europe to get it?"

"Not sure. If she is, I think she would have blown me off. Didn't seem like it. Then again, she is a cop."

"Wow, two blondes, party-central Carnevale, millions of dollars out there, government expense account—you dog."

Javier let it slide. "If you hear anything, let me know. This will all be done in three days, then I'm back to Milan."

"As I said, you lucky dog."

Alex sipped her espresso. "This is good, not as good as my hotel's, but good. We could have met there—less windy and a lot warmer. So, did you find those Croatian thugs?"

"No, and probably little chance of it. Since lunch, a lot has happened. These DEA guys, what about them?"

"Quite a pair," Alex said. "I was on a task force with them."

"How did they know you're here? In fact, how did they get here so quickly? You only arrived this morning."

"Since you told me, it's been nagging the hell out of me. Someone told them I was here. No one from Cleveland knows I'm here except my old partner, Bob Simmons, and my parents. Even my captain doesn't know. Can you find out when they arrived?"

"Possibly," Javier said. "I suggest you ask your partner who else knows."

"I will."

Javier studied Alex's face, then continued, "You and Marika look exactly alike, even down to the eyes and smile."

Alex stared at him in disbelief. "So, I have a double. I don't know whether to be thrilled or give her my condolences."

"To be seriously honest, it threw me. You two could be twins. Her hair is just a bit different, she wears more makeup, nice jewelry. Better dressed."

"Really? You employed by *Vogue* or something on the side?"

"Sorry, just wondering what you would look like all dressed up."

"Good enough to knock your socks off, mister. I've dealt with federal agents like you for many years, Castillo. Most look like whiny momma's boys—all straitlaced and such. Until now, I've never run into a Texas stud, with a deep tan, dark eyes, speaks a few languages, and, my guess, is seriously buffed under that shirt. Do you wear big shoes?" She smiled, then tilted her head to one side.

Embarrassed, he returned her smile. "I deserved that. Sorry—I think."

"You will never know," she answered. "So, tell me about this dinner party. Am I going to like my twin?"

"She's tough, been through a lot. She has important information that she wants to pass to the United States. I'm here to get it. There's an international conference this Thursday on Croatian monetary issues, critical to some people. One of those attending is a war criminal disguised as a politician."

"That's not news. Lots of them floating around the world today."

"Yes, but Ms. Jurić has information about this one particular man. I can't do anything about the others. My job is to make sure it gets to the right people. Then I'm done. She has asked me to meet with them this evening."

"Them?"

"She has a son. He's an attorney in Milan with an international NGO; they track down and bring war criminals to justice. I've never met him."

"I assume that I should, at least, wear something not so touristy?"

"It is a nice hotel."

"I would not expect anything different from my twin—she gets to live my nonexistent, yet imaginative, elegant parallel life."

"I will pick you up at seven forty-five. Her hotel is just a block away."

CHAPTER 11

Attila Kozak paced the length of the private car attached to the train traveling from Zagreb to Trieste. The train, a local, seemed to stop every twenty minutes; it waited at a platform, then started again. His private coach was the last car. Curled up in the corner of a velveteen settee was a woman sipping champagne. Kozak looked into her dark-green eyes as he marched up and down the aisle.

Kozak stopped and pointed at the man in a military uniform who was seated at the far end of the car.

"Why the hell wasn't she stopped, Colonel Vuković? How could your men let her get out of Croatia? You had your orders. And me, the future president of Croatia has to take this train, all because of some international no-fly list. Have they found her in Venice?"

"Yes, but before they could grab her, she escaped."

"They could have shot her," Kozak said.

"That would have been worse. You know that, General. However, they are watching her. We need all the information she has. She has probably left copies with someone; we need to know what she has. Then we will take the appropriate action."

"The best action is a bullet in her head." Kozak leaned over and gently stroked the woman's cheek. "What would you do, Maja, my dear?" he asked.

She smiled. "Take our time. Marika has by now contacted the European or American authorities. Even now, those cowards at the EU still do not believe all that happened in that wretched country, Bosnia. We must be prepared; *you* must be prepared. There will be many accusations and charges, but the evidence is long gone. This Marika Jurić has nothing—nothing, my general."

"I wish I could be so certain. Everything we did was necessary. Good God, it was twenty-five years ago. Can't they let it go?"

"Most have moved on with their lives. Now even the stupid Serbs want tourist dollars. The Bosnians are renting out their houses to the British; Dubrovnik welcomes cruise ships. My general, it is all about money. No one cares about the Croats, or the Bosnians, or the Serbs. These Europeans just want clean beaches, wine, and good food. The past is that—the past."

"Fools, don't they see what lies in front of us?" Kozak said. "The Bosniaks still believe the Turks will return and raise them up. And those criminals, the Serbs, are just waiting for their chance to take back everything they claim they lost."

"It's a war no one wants. Least of all the Croats."

"They need to be reminded. These European offspring, these perverts playing naked on our beaches, these children who only want to party and play with their Facebook and Instagram. I have a great fear for my country and its future."

"I do too, my general. I do too. Nevertheless, we will find a way to awaken them, to make them see what is happening. All these migrants and riffraff fleeing Africa, Syria, and Afghanistan are just making it worse. How many are really ISIS? How many are al-Qaeda? How many are the treacherous Saudis and their Wahhabis? You need to direct your people against these Muslims, all Muslims. You must make your people understand the threat they pose. It only takes one fanatic Muslim to change the world. Even if the number of terrorists is a small percentage by NATO's count, there could be hundreds of trained killers."

"And the Venice conference will be my stage to make it happen." Kozak stopped and puffed up a bit. "It is there, with the world watching, that I can make them see how dangerous this all is."

Maja sipped her champagne. "Yes, my general. Venice will be the place where you will take the world's stage."

The train was weaving its way from Zagreb through Slovenia to Ljubljana, then on to Villach, Austria, and into Italy. He would leave his railcar on a siding at the Venezia Mestre station and take the local into Venice's Santa Lucia station. In many ways, he was much more comfortable traveling this way than by plane. All the security and nosiness bothered him. It was an insult to someone like himself. And his luggage would be out of his hands for hours. Good God, what foreign agents could do during that time. Trains had, in the past two centuries, helped form empires. There was something regal about them, unlike airplanes and flying with the "riffraff," as Maja called them. What General Attila Kozak did not want anyone to learn was that he was deathly afraid of flying.

Why did this woman, this Marika Jurić, want to stop him, to embarrass him? She had unexpectedly appeared a year earlier in an article in the *Times*, branding him a war criminal. The interview went on and on about his record during the Croatian army's advance into Bosnia in the spring of 1993. She claimed he had been responsible for massacring Bosniaks, burning villages, and operating Croatian execution squads. How simplistic—she never offered proof, and besides, what does a woman know of war? The criminals were those Serbs under Milošević and his brutal executioners. It was the Serbs who had killed both Croats and Bosniaks. Who was she to challenge the next leader of Croatia?

CHAPTER 12

After her meeting with Special Agent Castillo, Marika, full of the spirit of the holiday, wandered through her beloved Venice. Her destination: a small shop near San Marco, where she bought a simple half mask and a large black hat. The thought of the CIA agent and the other woman annoyed her. She often stopped and looked back to see if someone was following her, including any of Kozak's men who might be watching for the real Marika Jurić. Her simple disguise worked, or at least she hoped that it was working.

Ehsan would be arriving in about an hour; she smiled at the thought. Her son, the love of her life, the reason behind everything she'd done during the past twenty years. When people said she was too young to have a boy his age, she beamed. Yes, when she saved him he had been eight years old, she just twenty. He had been her responsibility, he had been her child, and he had become her son.

It would be good to be with him again; they spent too little time together. Her time in Zagreb the last few years had been spent writing and interviewing the survivors of the last European war of the twentieth century. The demands of the victims—Muslim, Christian, and Orthodox alike—left little time for the two of them. Ehsan's work in Milan meant he spent a great deal of time traveling. She had played a small part, unknown to him, in helping him secure the position. His trips to Slovenia and Bosnia didn't worry her, but his increasingly frequent trips to Turkey and Saudi Arabia did.

"My job is to coordinate various Muslim and Christian organizations," he had explained when she'd asked. "These religions and their political organizations are wary of each other. They all profess great sympathy, but I find they often reflect the politics of their countries. There is among some of these religious and political leaders a zealotry, a dangerous fanaticism. They respect me. I have access where others don't. Maybe it's my past, for those that know it. Maybe it's because I have one foot in both worlds."

That had been three years ago. Ehsan, having lived on his own then for already almost eight years, had come to Zurich to meet Marika, who was interviewing a Bosnian refugee. The woman had, like so many others, lost her entire family during the war. Ehsan was also there to meet his friends Cvijetin Radić and Asmir Fazlić. Radić was living in Zurich, Fazlić in Trieste, the three friends getting together when they could. Cvijetin and Asmir were two of the lucky ones, both having been swept up in an organization that rescued orphans and lost children after the war. They had grown up in a small Muslim orphanage near Budapest, and they had met Ehsan at university. After graduation, when Ehsan went on to Oxford, Asmir and Cvijetin had found jobs in Trieste. In time, Asmir had gone to work for a logistics company, and Cvijetin had moved to Zurich to work in hospitality. The three men's histories, religion, and friendship bound them together.

Marika strolled through the city and across the Rialto Bridge and the Ponte degli Scalzi, the high-arching stone bridge that led to the piazza in front of the Santa Lucia train station. Across the canal from the piazza was the colonnaded façade of the church San Simeone Piccolo. She crossed the piazza and climbed the broad, shallow steps to the station.

The electronic train schedule, posted high in the grand lobby of the station, noted that Ehsan's train was on time; she had twenty minutes until it arrived. As one of the only true gateways to the city from the rest of Italy, the station was packed with tourists, citizens, and business-people. Many carried masks, and a few were even dressed in Carnevale fashions. The women wore imaginative gowns in silk, the men richly decorated costumes of some lost or fantasized era, and all wore hats that defied description. For Marika, it was entertaining, a release from the long, dreary winter days in Zagreb. She held her mask to her face and bowed to one colorful couple. They returned her bow.

The signs above the crowded platform indicated Milan on the right and Trieste on the left. As if cued, the headlamps on both of the bullet-nosed locomotives appeared at the far end of the station. They each slowed and approached the platform, the train from Milan slightly in the lead, then stopped. The porters dismounted first, and the passengers followed, climbing down the steps to the platform.

Marika, her mask now in her hand, stood to one side as the flood of arriving passengers pushed their way toward Venice. She beamed a mother's proud smile when she saw Ehsan step down from the train, a leather satchel in his hand. He saw her at the same moment and waved. Returning the wave, she walked swiftly toward her son, then looked to the opposite end of the platform.

A group of men was aggressively pushing its way through the dis-embarking passengers. None in the group carried baggage. Behind, a woman in a long black coat followed, a man in a gray-green military uniform immediately behind her. And directly behind them, flanked by two large men, walked Attila Kozak. They shoved their way through the crowd like tanks driving through a forest of small trees.

Marika turned to see Ehsan, wide eyed, jogging toward her. Apparently, he'd noticed her staring at Kozak.

"Not now, Mother," Ehsan said once he reached her. "Not now."

The woman in the long black coat touched Kozak's sleeve and pointed at Marika. He jerked his head in Marika's direction. For a moment he didn't recognize her, but the woman said something and a sneer appeared on Kozak's face. Immediately, he headed toward Marika.

Ehsan moved to place himself in front of his mother.

"Marika Jurić, my little viper," Kozak said, looking past Ehsan. "It is a pleasure to meet you again. And I assume this is one of your bodyguards?"

Ehsan started to say something, but Marika grabbed his arm and pulled him back toward her.

Not acknowledging Kozak by name, Marika said, "He is my son, you murderer. We have nothing to say to you—nothing. I suggest you leave before—"

"Before what? Do you think I'm afraid of a woman like you, or this boy? When I am president, I can assure you troublemakers like you will not be welcome in our country."

"The people hate you," Marika said. "You and the criminals you call your comrades."

"Come, Mother," Ehsan said, now pulling her away. "Leave this for another day. This is not the place. There will be a time when this criminal will be properly disposed of—it is just not here and now."

"Shut up, you Turk. I know about you. Yes, this is not the place, but someday—"

Like with after an accident on a busy highway, the passengers on the platform had jammed up against them. People raised their voices to tell them to move on, get out of the way.

Ehsan directed his mother down the platform and away from the exiting Kozak.

"Leave them, Mother. He has betrayed his country, and you will tell the world of this betrayal and his murderous past. Just leave them."

Mother and son watched Kozak disappear into the station. Ehsan leaned down and kissed his mother on the cheek. "I missed you."

"And I missed you," she answered, placing her hand on his cheek.

CHAPTER 13

"After your first day in Venice, you look rested, and quite lovely," Javier said as he met Alex in the Aqua Palace lobby, his hand hidden behind his back.

The intimate hotel foyer was crowded with guests, many wearing masks and costumes. Unlike the revelers, Alex wore a simple black dress and the short black leather jacket. Her blonde hair rested on her shoulders in soft waves.

"How's the jet lag?" he asked.

"You are a little rusty on your compliments," Alex said as Javier took her arm. "But thank you—the nap helped. There's still a touch of fogginess around the edges, but better." She looked at the guests. "I spent a bizarre week in New Orleans during Mardi Gras with some girlfriends, before I was married. But this"—she waved her hand—"is way over the top, very dressy. I see that you are not wearing a mask, Mr. Castillo. And what are you hiding there?"

He offered her a white porcelain mask decorated with black pearls and sequins. "For you."

"Really?"

"Call it a disguise."

"The bad guys are long gone."

"We can wish."

They walked through dense crowds of merrymakers, some costumes inexplicable, others fascinating. Inhibitions seemed to drop, or at least so Alex thought. Some of the costumes were just on the edge of bawdy.

She leaned into Javier. "It seems that the Casanova theme goes a long way here."

"Way too much for my taste. Us Texas boys are not keen on public displays of affection, and some of this is embarrassing, even for a guy like me."

"And what is a guy like you?" she asked.

He turned and whispered in her ear, "A federal agent on the job."

"Spoilsport."

The Ai Reali, its windows glowing from within, fronted the Campo de Fava. As they entered, a small group of laughing, costumed guests pushed their way out. Alex turned to avoid one man that seemed a bit too close and followed Javier into the hotel. *Very nice. In fact, exceptionally nice. Whoever this Marika Jurić is, she at least has some money.* The hotel lobby, bright in whites and new marble, fit right into the faux reality of modern Venice.

"We are guests of Ms. Jurić," Javier said to the man at the desk.

The clerk smiled. "They are waiting for you in the wine cellar. Please, through these doors."

"They have cellars in these buildings?" Alex whispered.

"I believe it is a figure of speech."

The clerk led them through a series of twists and turns down carpeted hallways until they came to a dark-oak door. The clerk knocked and waited.

A handsome man opened the door. "Please come in. It's good to see you again, Special Agent Castillo."

"And you too, Ehsan, it has been months since our meetings in Milan. This is my friend Alexandra Polonia."

If Alex could have been shocked after the past two days of hard travel, jet lag, and Croatian thugs, seeing herself walk across the elegant room would have stunned her. Marika Jurić, in an attractive dark-blue dress, stopped in front of Alex. The expression on Jurić's face was no different than the one Alex wore; each squinted at the other. Then, before any pleasantries, they circled each other, staring like two strong felines warily appraising the other. Jurić, the more forward, reached out with her fingers and touched Alex's face.

"When Agent Castillo said we look alike, I thought he generally meant hair, height, all the usual physical things. You know how observant men can be," Marika said.

"Yes, but it's more than that. I feel like I'm looking at myself. I'm Alexandra Polonia, Cleveland, Ohio."

"Marika Jurić, Zagreb, Croatia. Agent Castillo." She walked to Javier and kissed him on each cheek. She then turned to Ehsan and took his hand. He looked to be around thirty. His face was long and sharp, with a closely trimmed, fashionable dark beard, and he had blue eyes and full black eyebrows. His black hair was neatly combed back and reached the top of his collar. His smile was welcoming, broad, and warm.

"This is all too strange," Marika added.

"Ms. Polonia, the resemblance is amazing," Ehsan said, surprise filling his face as he studied Alex. He looked at his mother. "Mother said that the two of you are supposed to look alike, but it is more than that: you look like twins. You are from Cleveland? Where is this Cleveland?"

"On the shore of Lake Erie in the state of Ohio, halfway between New York City and Chicago. Does that help?"

"I have been to New York and Chicago, so yes. The Midwest, right?"

"Yes, close enough." Alex turned back to Marika. "They say we have a double somewhere in the world; I just didn't think I would find mine in Venice. It is a pleasure."

"Mine as well," Marika said. "Champagne? Or something stronger?"

"A gin martini would be nice," Alex replied. "Very dry, one olive."

"Excellent," Marika said. "I think we will be very good friends. Agent Castillo?"

"A Peroni, if you don't mind."

"Ehsan?"

"Yes, Mother, I will be right back." He headed to the corner where a young girl stood behind the bar. She smiled as Ehsan walked toward her.

"He is a handsome young man," Alex said.

"The love of my life, I will do anything for my son. But more of that later."

With their drinks in hand, they took seats in the corner of the room, wine bottles in elegant walnut racks nearly surrounding them. The couch and chairs were deep-red leather. All in all, a comfortable room.

"I have asked that a dinner of seafood and risotto be prepared," Marika said. "And some delicious wine from the vineyards north of Verona, and a surprise treat for dessert."

"I love surprises," Alex said.

"Not like the one from earlier today, I'm sure," Marika said. "Those Croatian thugs are more than what most tourists want to find in Venice."

"Yes, but it seems that I found a Texas cowboy instead."

Marika looked suspiciously at Javier. "Yes, he is a cowboy. But I believe he is an impatient cowboy. I see it on his face."

"I assume you have all that I need?" Javier asked.

"Yes, it is all there in that envelope." She pointed to a thick manila envelope on a side table. "I have included the film—the original rolls— in the envelope as well. Ehsan brought the rest of the documents from Milan. Now you have all the proof you need."

Alex knew she was not a part of this conversation, but her detective brain wouldn't rest. A hundred thoughts bounced around inside her head.

"Agent Castillo, have you told my twin anything?" Marika asked.

"A few bits, not much."

"I see no harm. After all, there are men about Venice that want to talk with Ms. Polonia about something other than Croatian politics."

"I have no idea why they are here," Alex said. "They are federal agents who may have had something to do with my husband. He's in prison, and they think he's hidden money here."

"Your husband is in prison?" Ehsan asked. "Why?"

"Ehsan, it is not our affair," Marika said.

"That's quite all right. It is the reason I'm here in Venice." Alex told them the story.

"And you think they are here for this money?" Marika asked.

"There can be no other reason. They are opportunists."

A soft knock came from the door, and the maître d' looked in and asked Marika something in Italian. She answered, and the man left.

"Dinner will be in one hour." Marika placed her hand on Alex's knee. "After your troubled year, I am glad that you are here. This is a magical place to lose and then heal yourself. However, ours is a sad story that now has, I hope, a satisfactory ending. If you are interested, I will tell you."

"Not sure it is my place."

"Alex, the world, and most particularly the part of Europe to the east of us, is very different than your Cleveland. I think you will understand us better if I do. Is that acceptable to you, Special Agent Castillo?"

"Ms. Jurić, I am here at your request. Yes, I would like to know more than what I've been told by my office in Washington. Please."

Marika smiled at the girl at the bar. "You can leave us for an hour, then return. I'm sure we can take care of ourselves until then."

"Yes, signora."

They waited until the woman left. Marika looked at Ehsan, then began: "Ehsan is not my biological child, but he has been my son for the last twenty-two years and will be for the rest of our lives. We are entwined like two vines that have become one. He is the love of my life." She turned to Ehsan and touched his cheek. *"Amore."*

"Mother," Ehsan replied.

"It was in the spring of 1993 when we met under circumstances I would never wish on my worst enemy," Marika began.

The Lašva Valley, Bosnia and Herzegovina, April 1993

The Lašva Valley was filled with a dense early-morning fog, the higher ridgelines barely visible through the mist. Our bus—filled with journalists and members of an EU relief agency, some my friends—had driven down from Zagreb that previous night. I was a twenty-year-old student journalist and had managed to secure a seat. After passing through Zenica, we were stopped by Croatian paramilitaries a kilometer east of Dubravica. They'd chosen the spot well: steep slopes rose from each side of the narrow two-lane road. The barricade allowed no room to pass. Flanking the road, sandbags were stacked almost two meters high, and behind each bunker was a pickup truck with a manned fifty-caliber machine gun mounted in the bed. The men at the weapons looked unfocused—I assumed they were drunk. These were, as I soon found out, dangerous men.

I had spent the previous week trying to find a ride into this region of Bosnia. The reports of police actions in the region by Serbian troops were confusing. A school friend had offered the ride, and I'd jumped at the chance. The driver, an Englishman who was writing a book on the war, had rented the bus. There were about twenty of us. We all wanted to see for ourselves the depredations by the Serbs, to write articles for the Zagreb papers, and to tell the world what evil was happening to the Croats and Bosniaks living in this part of old Yugoslavia. Yet, these men at the barricade were Croats—rough men, hardened men, with ready AK-47s. The driver talked with the officer, who stood with one hand on his hip; the other hand held a pistol. The officer met the Englishman's every statement with a shake of his head and, using the pistol, kept pointing back to the road we had just taken. The Englishman pulled a bundle of money from his coat pocket and waved it at the officer, but the man looked at the notes, pocketed them, and again shook his head and pointed with his pistol. Two other soldiers walked to the officer's side and lifted their weapons. The Englishman raised his hands, backed away, and climbed into the bus.

"Not a chance to get through. They say there are Bosniak insurgents ahead who will shoot anything that tries to go down the road. He will not let us pass. It is for our own protection and safety. We will have to find another way."

The Englishman slowly backed the bus up the road until he found a spot wide enough to turn the vehicle around. Just before he started back up the road, I stood and told him to stop. I walked to the front of the bus and turned to look back up the road out the rear window. The curve hid the barricade we had just left.

"Let me out here. I'll walk. I know these hills."

"Not a chance, Marika, no way," the Englishman said. "Too dangerous."

"Not your problem. I came for a story. I'm going to get it."

I secured my backpack, slung my leather camera bag over my shoulder, and pushed myself past the Englishman. Before he could stop me, I was down the steps and had jumped to the pavement. Ten seconds later I was climbing the hill above the bus. I turned to see the people staring out the bus's small windows as I disappeared into the woods.

I climbed and climbed, and five minutes later I reached a clearing high above the road and watched as the bus slowly accelerated and headed east back to Zenica. From across the valley, I heard a succession of concussive thumps. The first mortar shell exploded just in front of the bus, throwing pavement and debris in every direction. The second mortar exploded behind the bus, and the third and fourth shells hit the bus directly on its yellow roof. Before I could take another breath, the bus exploded into a ball of fire. I dropped to my knees. The fire consumed the bus and everyone on board. Two people, each ablaze, tumbled out and ran up the road. Another mortar explosion, this one at the front of the bus, mercifully put an end to their agony.

All I could do was cross myself and say a prayer. There was nothing else. I slipped back into the trees and cried.

For the next five hours, I snuck along a narrow cattle trail that skirted the woods high above the main road. Later I had to crawl through open pastures from one thick copse to another. I was certain there were snipers. The main road lay down a steep slope below me. I saw soldiers and military vehicles heading south. I scanned the vehicles with the long lens of my camera. None had any markings, but surprisingly, they all had Croatian license plates.

At the next crossroad, there were direction signs for Ahmići and Busovača. The fog was lifting, and the spring warmth began filling the air. Through the telephoto lens, I noticed small smoke columns rising from the hillsides. There was no pattern—a column here, another there. I thought it odd that the villagers were starting their fireplaces. The day was warming: Why start a fire? A few minutes later, the columns of smoke grew larger and more furious.

I looked up and down the road, which was clear. My map showed the farming village of Ahmići to the southeast and partway up the hillside. More smoke columns rose from the village. I bounded down the hill, stopped near the roadside, and hid among a thick tangle of thorny berry bushes just leafing out. I checked the road and bolted across. A minute later, as I climbed the hill, I saw three open military vehicles drive where I'd crossed. The men were loud as they passed a bottle among them. A woman in a truck bed tried to stand, but a soldier knocked her to the floor with the butt of his rifle. I took a half dozen photos of the vehicles before they disappeared.

I pushed on toward the columns of smoke, a dozen of them now filling the sky. By this time, I knew these were burning buildings, not merely chimneys.

I crested the hill above Ahmići and paralleled a fence line that enclosed a small sheep pasture. The vegetation along the fence line provided some cover. Once, I thought I heard screams, even gunshots; breathing hard from the climb, I found it hard to hear. I stopped near a slight fold in the hillside. Four houses stood clustered together with small outbuildings nearby. Five farmhouses were on fire. Soldiers stood in the road, watching them burn. They did nothing.

From the first house, a man rushed out holding a child. A soldier calmly aimed and shot the farmer. The other soldiers continued to fire until neither body moved. Someone screamed from inside the building and ran out. The woman, wearing a hijab, fell as the soldiers fired again. The soldiers continued climbing up the narrow lane, firing indiscriminately at farm animals and buildings. Behind and below them more farmhouses began to burn. No one was watching the hills above the cluster of farmhouses. I took photographs as fast as I could, changing my film twice.

The men, interrupted in their business, stopped and waited for an open military vehicle that pulled up behind them. They saluted. A large man emerged from the truck with the letters "HVO" painted on its door. He pointed back down the lane, then up the road to the remaining houses. I took a dozen more photos, then continued along the fence line toward the upper end of the village. I was minutes ahead of this Croatian execution squad.

The road abruptly ended at the last two farmhouses. Beyond, the hill sloped up through open pastures and disappeared into a thick woodland beginning to turn green. I knew it would be suicide to try and stop these murders. They'd thought nothing of killing women and children. I'd heard rumors of rape camps and even worse run by the Serbs, but these were Croats, my people.

Above and behind the last stone farmhouse, I found a small corral and took photos as the two men reached the last house.

"Out, all you Turks, out!" one of the soldiers yelled. "We won't harm you. Out!"

I wanted to yell, to scream, to tell them to run, to escape. The men just stood in the road, waiting. Three soldiers joined them, one carrying a rocket-propelled grenade.

"Shoot the house," one of the soldiers ordered.

The soldier raised the RPG to his shoulder, but before he could fire, the door swung open. A man and a boy, maybe thirteen, stepped out. The soldier with the RPG lowered the weapon. The soldier giving orders waved the two to walk toward him. The boy tried to pull his father back into the house, but the man said something and continued to walk down the road. The boy stood at the door, watching. When the man reached the soldiers, one of them struck him in the head with a rifle butt. As the man tried to rise, the leader pulled his revolver and shot him in the back of the head.

"Now you can shoot," he ordered.

The man with the RPG raised the weapon and fired. The grenade flew wildly high and over the building and hit the corral. When it exploded, a dozen sheep were killed; others screamed in agony.

I flattened myself behind a pile of stones. The explosion was deafening. I looked up. The boy, still at the door, turned to run back inside. One of the soldiers shot him dead with a burst of four automatic rounds.

"You idiot, can't you fire that goddamn thing?" the squad leader yelled. "Again."

This time, after reloading the RPG, the soldier's aim was better. He hit the upper floor of the structure; the stones fell on the doorway and the boy's body, blocking any escape. One of the other soldiers retrieved two bottles from his knapsack.

My ears still rang from the first rocket grenade. The man lit the cloth fuses on the Molotov cocktails and calmly walked to the farmhouse. He pitched the bottles through the shattered windows, and the rooms beyond exploded into flames. Smoke began to rise. As the fire raged, the rear door of the house swung open. A young woman stood in the opening, a child at her side. She leaned down and said something, and the boy shook his head. She said something again. He looked across the farmyard to the sheep pen, where dead animals lay everywhere. She pushed him, and the boy began to run. The woman looked up at the corral. I was positive she knew I was there. The child ran up the gentle hill as the woman looked at me again and began to follow her child. From the lane below, five automatic weapons began to fire indiscriminately at the blazing building. Bullets struck stone and wood; dozens pierced the house. A single bullet hit the woman in the head, and she fell. The child, not looking back, kept running.

The men could not see the child; he was hidden by the building and now by the smoke that blanketed the farmyard. The child stopped when he saw the sheep and tried to get one to move. He didn't understand.

I stood. "Here, come here, child," I said. "You will be safe."

The boy, surprised, again stopped and looked at me.

"Now, boy. Now. We need to leave. Your mother will be here soon. Come." I held my hand out.

The boy turned and looked at his house, now completely engulfed, then back at me.

"Please, child, please come."

He ran the last six meters. I reached through the barbed wire of the enclosure and pulled him to me. The barbed wire tore a ragged slash down my left forearm. We hid behind a pile of rubble; the boy looked at my arm and started to cry. I asked him to remain still. He did, and I was able to cut a piece of my undershirt and wrap it around the wound. It helped to slow the bleeding.

I watched the soldiers work their way back down the hill until they were gone. We carefully navigated our way along fence lines until we reached the woods. Once there, we climbed toward the hillcrest. Through the trees and well into the night, I could still see houses burning.

CHAPTER 14

"How incredibly sad," Alex said, a tear on her cheek. "What is the HVO?"

"The Hrvatsko vijeće obrane, the Croatian Defense Council," Marika answered. "It was a paramilitary organization of Croatians in Bosnia during the Bosnian War, fundamentally a disorganized army of thugs, murderers, and rapists. In the Lašva Valley, some took their retribution out on the defenseless Bosnian farmers." Marika's voice was shaking.

"That's all right," Ehsan said. "Mother, it's okay."

"These men and other Croats living in Bosnia had decided to cleanse Bosnia and Herzegovina of all Muslims. While this was also the policy of the Serbs, this ethnic cleansing was a regression to the worst of man's behaviors—cultural and social genocide. They acted no differently than the SS during World War II."

"I assume that this Attila Kozak was a member of the HVO," Alex continued.

"Yes, initially. He was a colonel but in time took over an internal battalion of thugs, the Wolf's Head Battalion," Marika said. "He is one of the men responsible for massacring the people in Ahmići and the surrounding valley. Over a hundred were killed. Some believe even more, but their remains could not be found in their burned-out homes."

"He was arrested?"

"No. He, like hundreds of others, escaped or was never charged. The EU wanted the big fish, the leaders. The true assassins, those pulling the triggers and throwing the grenades, went back to their families and jobs after the truce. For them, it was like nothing ever happened. They even have reunions. I cannot think of what they talk about."

"This is the information that Marika and Ehsan have pieced together," Agent Castillo said to Alex. "Her photos, affidavits from witnesses, even interviews expressing remorse from a few of the soldiers who participated. She is handing this information over to me and I am to get it to the State Department. They will decide what to do with it."

"What's the urgency?" Alex asked. "Seems that even after all this time a few days won't make that much of a difference."

"For a conviction, yes," Marika said. "But Attila Kozak is a candidate for president of Croatia. He has a sizable right-wing following, with significant support from religious and cultural organizations both inside and outside the country. He is attending the EU conference on Thursday and intends to use it as a platform to show how he can lead his country and expand Croatia's role in the European Union."

"Isn't that a good thing for Croatia?" Alex asked.

"Maybe, but the thought of this man, a man with the blood of defenseless men, women, and children on his hands, leading our country is more than many of us can stand. I do not trust him; many of us believe he is in this for himself. He needs to be shamed and shunned by the European community. He needs to be stopped. This is a forum where it can happen."

"This is an opportunity to set things right, to honor those who were murdered, and to hopefully find some peace for the survivors," Ehsan said. "Like Simon Wiesenthal's work hunting down Nazi war criminals."

"I assume you are that little boy?" Alex asked, looking at Ehsan.

Before either Ehsan or Marika could answer, there was a soft knock on the door, and the manager said that dinner was ready. They all took their seats. There was little gaiety even as the conversation turned to the changes in Venice, the current Carnevale, and the general state of Europe's finances.

"A pox on all their heads," Marika said. "Ehsan, our guests care little for our economic issues here in Europe. I'm sure the problems in the United States are just as daunting."

"Yes, they are, but I am on vacation," Alex said. "I do not want to think about the world, Cleveland, or even my ex-husband. For the next two weeks, and for the first time in years, it's me time."

"Me time?" Ehsan asked as he sipped his sparkling water.

"Yes, me. As in not having to take care of anyone else but me for the next few days. See things, do things, and enjoy things I want to do."

"I envy you," Marika said. "It has been many years since I had that opportunity. I needed money to raise my son and give him the education he deserved. I could not do that on a journalist's salary. I had an idea for a software system—I developed one of the first programs to help coordinate money exchanges throughout Eastern Europe. I made it work, and it was successful. A German company stepped in and bought my business. The sale gave me the freedom to go back into journalism full time. It has also allowed me the time to investigate Kozak."

"And to answer your question," Ehsan said, turning to Alex, "yes, I am that same eight-year-old boy. We escaped over the mountains to Zenica. I remember a bus ride, clean clothes, wonderful food, and a warm bed with sheets whiter than the snow. Twenty-two years later I am an attorney in Milan with an international NGO that tracks down and brings war criminals to justice. My work extends across the Balkans, Middle East, and North Africa, from Turkey to Afghanistan to Saudi Arabia."

"Are you a Muslim?" Alex asked.

"Yes, Mother taught me about my religion and my history. But it was my decision to return to my religious heritage. I am at peace with that decision."

"And I am proud," Marika said.

"You should be," Alex said. She looked at Marika's arm. "Can I assume that the tattoo on your arm covers the wound from the barbed wire?"

Marika rolled her left arm over and looked at the long, thin dagger tattoo. "Yes, the wound became infected and took months to heal. The scar was dark and quite hideous. The tattoo is there to cover the scar and to be a reminder. It is my sword of retribution."

"A bit dramatic, don't you think?" Alex said.

"Most of our lives are dramas. I chose to have this reminder dyed into my skin. A day does not go by that I do not think of that afternoon."

"I don't wish to put an end to this evening," Javier said. "But there are people waiting for the information in Milan. I need to catch the last train. The information will be transferred to a particular State Department official in Washington who will review the materials and, if there is enough evidence, make it public. But none of that will happen if I miss that train."

"Can't it be faxed or emailed or something?" Alex said.

"That will also be done. However, they are old school: they want to see the pictures, inspect the original film, and see and listen to the affidavits. That's what's in the package, and it will need at least twenty-four hours to reach Washington."

"So, this is goodbye?" Alex said, a touch of disappointment in her voice.

"Until tomorrow night," Javier answered. "I will be back. I've been assigned to stay through the conference, more as a liaison for our consular agencies both here in Venice and in Milan. They have limited resources and my language skills will be helpful."

"What else do you speak besides Italian?" Alex asked, happier now she knew Javier would return.

"Pashto, French, and some German. Growing up Latino in Central Texas also pushed a hard Tex-Mex dialect into my Spanish."

Alex stared at the man she hadn't even known existed twenty-four hours earlier. *Can this guy get any more intriguing?*

"And what are you doing tomorrow?" Marika asked her. "With Special Agent Castillo in Milan, you'll have the day to yourself. May I suggest a stroll through the city? There is much about Venice itself that is beguiling, but there is nothing like a walking tour of the city, and hiring a boat to see the city from the water. It can be a pleasant and fascinating day. Then there is Murano with its glass factories and shops, yet another nice diversion."

Alex looked at Marika. "Since Javier will be away, why don't you join me? I would enjoy the company."

Marika seemed to ponder the possibility for a moment. "I cannot in the morning, but I will be free after one o'clock. You can visit Murano in the morning, and then we can wander the canals and alleys of Venice in the afternoon."

"An excellent idea, Mother," Ehsan said. "I don't want you cooped up in this hotel until Thursday. You should get out."

"Marika, I agree with Ehsan," Javier said. "Take your mind off all this, at least for one day, while your information is under review by Washington. I can make a call. There is an excellent tour company that I've used. Their boats are beautiful."

"It would be nice to put this out of my head for a day, or at least an afternoon," Marika said. "Yes, I accept the invitation."

"Good," Alex said. "Can you meet me in the lobby of my hotel? It's just around the corner. Then you can play travel guide."

Marika turned to Javier. "Is she always this bossy?"

"I'm beginning to find that out."

Marika laughed. "Well, before you go, you have to try some zabaglione with berries."

After they left the hotel, Alex suggested that she walk Javier to the train station.

"It's not that late, and I can use the exercise," she said.

"You'll get lost going back to your hotel."

"Probably, but it will be fun anyway."

They strolled across the Rialto Bridge, dodging tourists and masked carnival goers. From either side of the Grand Canal, fireworks erupted, shooting colorful streamers back and forth over what seemed a thousand gondolas. Their sensuous shapes reflected in the mirrored glass of the canal. The noise was deafening, making a conversation next to impossible.

"Magic," Alex said.

"It is that. Hard for a kid from Waco to imagine that someday he would be standing here. I'm sure I didn't even know what Venice was."

They plunged into one of the countless passageways that led to the train station.

"I've dreamed of Venice since I was twelve," Alex confessed. "I had picture books and guidebooks. When my best friend went off to college and spent a summer traveling in Italy, she sent postcards. I still have them."

"Where else have you traveled?"

"I have never been out of the United States—unless you count the extradition trips I made to Toronto and Montreal." She smiled. "Javier, if all my future vacations start like this one, maybe I will travel more."

They crossed the Ponte degli Scalzi and the piazza in front of the train station. Alex waited while Javier bought a ticket, then joined him on the platform.

"How long have you been in Italy?" Alex asked.

"I've been assigned to Milan now for more than a year. I was in Rome before that. It's a nice gig. I won't get much sleep tonight. All this has to get to Washington."

"Try to get some on the train."

"I will," he said, his expression strange. "I shouldn't be doing this. Lord knows I'm breaking a hundred international laws, but take this." He retrieved a thick envelope from his briefcase and handed it to her. "I know you know how to use it."

From its heft, she knew what it was. "I can't." She thought of the Glock in her safe.

"You need it. These people do not play fair. It's a loaner; I want it back tomorrow. I have a ticket on the midafternoon train. Would you care to have dinner tomorrow?"

The announcement of trains and platforms interrupted her answer. Javier, briefcase in hand, looked at Alex and kissed her on the lips.

"Yes," she said.

He smiled and boarded the train. Stunned, she stood there and watched the train slowly pull out of the station.

CHAPTER 15

Alex walked toward her hotel in a soft daze. The smallish Glock 26 was comfortably lodged in her handbag. Along with the pistol and spare magazine, she was surprised to find a cell phone. "If you need me, speed-dial 007," said the Post-it note. *Cute.*

She put on the porcelain mask Javier had given her earlier. It allowed her anonymity: a white face among dozens of other white and gilded faces that pushed their way toward the Rialto Bridge and onto Piazza San Marco. She strolled with the flow as music blared from cafés and *osterie* and people danced and celebrated. The wonderful dessert still lingered, but the wine had worn off.

Venice . . . That's why I came four thousand miles: to eat and drink.

In the Campo San Polo, a restaurant, still open, was snuggled in one corner. She spied an open table under a large bare tree festooned with Italian lights. She sat and looked across the campo; even at this late hour, a small carousel filled with laughing children turned. Around and around it went, to the sound of an accordion. She slipped off her mask.

Within seconds a waiter appeared and slapped down a menu. "Something to eat?" he said in English, his accent New Jersey–ish.

"Just a bottle of Chianti, your best," she said without looking at the menu. "Understand?"

"Sì, sì. I lived a few years in Trenton, New Jersey. I got it. We have four Chiantis. Which one?"

"You pick."

The waiter smiled. "You da boss."

Hundreds strolled through the campo, some in costume, some in heavy coats, and others in the seemingly ubiquitous leather jacket favored by Eastern Europeans. The Americans were easy to spot, all bright and shiny, iPhones and cameras firing away. The others, their international languages preceding them, pointed and waved in joyful chaos. The glowing windows of the two-, three-, and four-story buildings wrapping the campo gave the scene substance.

Magic.

A basket of bread landed on the table while she eyed the campo. Then the waiter appeared with a bottle and two glasses.

"Only me," Alex said.

"Seriously, a woman like you alone in Venice?" the waiter said as he extracted the cork. "I thought your husband was just late. Maybe you are to meet him here?"

If he only knew. "No, just me, but thank you." She tasted the wine. "Wonderful."

He filled the glass, then mumbled something she thought sounded like "bummer" as he walked away.

The theater in the campo continued. Music spilled across the plaza from deep in one of the passageways. Four drummers and three accordion players marched out ahead of an entourage of costumed revelers. She had never seen such silk gowns; they looked to be ten feet wide, with long trains, in bright yellows and pinks, some ecclesiastical purple. The men wore richly embroidered black capes, and their tricorn hats sat on great wigs that fell to their shoulders. Other men, with silk finery matching their partners' colors, danced and preened. Some carried canes; others waved fans about even in the damp, chilly air.

The wine and the music worked their enchantment. For the first time in more than a year, Alex could feel the weight of the past winter sliding away, even though the day, her first day in her dream country, had been so strange.

Is this why I came to Venice? Magic? Texas magic?

After two glasses, the restaurant had emptied to half, and even the campo had quieted. She asked the waiter for a bag. The rest of the wine would be her nightcap. She rose to leave.

"Will you be all right?" the waiter asked as he handed her the credit card receipt.

"Yes. In fact, this is the best I've been in a year."

His eyes went wide as she air-kissed him on both cheeks.

Then she slung her handbag over her shoulder, picked up her mask and the wine bag, and headed toward a passageway exiting the campo. A sign with an arrow said "Ponte di Rialto." She reset the mask on her face as fireworks exploded high over the terra-cotta roofs.

She drifted along with the crowd through the maze of streets. After a turn, she came face-to-face with the Grand Canal. Everyone else turned left onto the Riva del Vin and headed toward the illuminated Rialto Bridge. Alex turned hard right to get out of the flow and moved over to some steps that descended into the canal. She stood with her boots one step above the water's surface. More fireworks exploded over the spot where the canal curved and disappeared. A thousand lights reflected off the canal from lampposts, vaporetti, and restaurants that seemed to float atop a long sinuous mirror.

She took in a breath and slowly released it. She felt a push from behind, forcing her to adjust her footing. She turned to look behind her and bumped into a large man. He said something under his breath, something she didn't understand—in Croatian or some other Balkan language. His breath stank of garlic and booze. She felt a hand trying to grab her arm.

"Get away from me." She elbowed him hard in the gut. It did nothing. "Get the hell off me!" she yelled. A hundred people could have heard her if it weren't for the background Carnevale noise masking everything.

"*Sada, doci!*" he yelled.

She saw the pistol held to his side. His black eyes stared at her; he smiled through yellowed and broken teeth, teeth she had seen that morning. She then noticed another man three paces behind him.

Shit, not good.

If there was one thing she remembered from her police-academy days, something she'd told a dozen rookie partners, it was "Never give the advantage away. If you don't have it, get it." She smiled at the man; his quizzical look was all she needed. She swung the bottle of Chianti at the thug's forehead. The heavy paper bag kept the broken glass from flying everywhere but did not stop the bottle from knocking the man to the pavement.

As he dropped to one knee, the other Croat pushed in to grab her. She deftly seized the attacker's hand and, using his momentum, pulled the man to her, then stepped out of the way. He somersaulted into the canal again, its current soon snagging him and pulling him away as he screamed.

Her eyes had never left the man kneeling on the cobblestones; blood ran down his temple and cheek. As he started to rise, she casually passed him and dropped an elbow onto his shoulder. She thought she heard the bone break. The pistol dropped from the hand of his traumatized arm. She picked it up off the paving, slipped it into her already-crowded handbag, and jogged down the walkway, dodging through partygoers as she made her way to the bridge.

They had to have been following me, but why did they wait? For an hour I sat in the campo, nothing. Then here. What the hell?

Just before she reached the Rialto Bridge, she turned into the Calle de la Madonna, away from the canal and back into the San Polo district. She was sure they would be watching the bridge. She made a left and sprinted another few blocks, toward a small café.

The proprietor, gray haired with a long, drooping mustache, stood behind the antique cash register and told her something in Italian.

"I need just one minute, then I'll go. May I use your bathroom?" Then in Spanish: *"Baño?"*

"Bagno, sì, sì." He pointed.

"Grazie."

She looked down the short hallway to a door she assumed opened to a back alley. A dead bolt locked it from the inside. She pushed her way into the tiny bathroom, looked in the mirror, and took a deep breath. She still had her mask on, and the shock scared the hell out of her. She slipped it into the handbag and put the Glock into the pocket of her leather jacket. The thug's pistol was a Russian Makarov 9mm, its walnut handle well worn, the identifying five-pointed star carved into its checkered grip. She pushed it deep into her handbag. She'd managed to accumulate three weapons in a single day. She retrieved Javier's phone, and as she started to punch in the James Bond number, a loud bang came from the door. Her heart skipped a beat.

"You okay, lady?" Just the man from the counter.

Alex pushed open the door. "Yes, I'm okay."

The man stood in the hallway, his arms across his chest. "No drugs here. Okay? No drugs."

"No drugs, okay." She rummaged through her bag and came up with a twenty-euro note. "Espresso?"

The man looked at the note and raised two fingers. She rummaged again and came up with another note.

"No, no. Espresso, due euro."

She almost laughed as she passed one of the twenties to the man. "It's okay, take it." She slid into a discreet corner seat where she could see the front door but no one outside could see her. She called Javier.

"Are you okay?" he answered after a few rings. "What happened?"

She blurted out everything and became embarrassed as she went on. *For Christ's sake, I'm a goddamn cop.*

"Are you in Milan?" she asked.

"An hour out, still on the train. They are waiting. I have to do this."

"Like you're going to turn around and come to my rescue? Please . . . I'm fine. But if they have my hotel staked out, I'm toast for the night. The chance of finding a room with thousands of drunk partygoers on two small islands is nuts." A few moments passed. "Javier?"

"Here's what I want you to do. In Venice, I'm staying at an apartment kept by a lesser-known government agency. I'm going to call them and set you up for the night. I'll text you the address. Where are you now?"

She leaned over and asked the man where the café was located.

"My apartment is a block from Piazza San Marco," Javier said. "Don't go over the Rialto. Take a water taxi to the piazza—it's safer. Have the driver mark your map with the apartment address. Call me when you get there. Are you sure you're okay?"

"You have to ask the other guys," she answered.

He laughed. "I'll talk to you in an hour. The man at the front desk is Albert Nox; he will have all the info. Be safe."

"You too," she said, not knowing why, and ended the call.

He's the one who's safe. Hell, I've got a bunch of Croats chasing me who think I'm some avenging Croatian bitch. She looked at the clock on the wall over the door. *Just past one o'clock.*

A half hour later she stepped off onto the small dock abutting the promenade at San Marco's. On her map, the water taxi driver drew a line that she was to follow from the square to Javier's apartment. She assumed that most Venetians put up with this chaos every year because of the tourist euros. She wouldn't have lasted two days if she lived here.

She passed the basilica and wound her way through the never-ending labyrinth that was the streets and passageways of Venice. She kept looking at the signs and crossed a narrow canal. The street name on the corner of the building matched the map. A light shone through a glass door covered by a sheer curtain. This looked to be a much stronger door than she'd seen almost everywhere on the island. She scanned the archway above it; a small inconspicuous camera sat high in the corner. The only identification was the brass number 17 above the door. No mailbox or apartment identifiers, just a single button. She pushed it.

"Ms. Polonia, I assume?" came the voice through the call box.

"Yes, Agent Castillo sent me."

"Of course he did," the voice said.

The door buzzed, and she pushed it in.

TUESDAY

Chapter 16

Sitting on the outdoor terrace of the JW Marriott, Attila Kozak read a copy of the world edition of Zagreb's newspaper, the *Večernji list*. A large glass of orange juice, half-gone, sat to his right. A coffee cup steamed in the early-morning daylight. Maja sat quietly to his left, wrapped in a heavy blanket. She carefully buttered a croissant. Two of his bodyguards sat at a nearby table. He watched as they wolfed down their breakfasts.

Good boys. Hard to find good boys these days.

He'd slept fitfully, thoughts of the next few days roiling around in his head. Last night he'd received word from the two men assigned to find Jurić that she'd taken both of them out, again—one thrown in the canal, the other's collarbone fractured.

Yes, it is hard to find good boys.

"I can't believe she was there waiting for me at the station," Kozak said.

"I think she was waiting for someone else," Maja answered, spreading strawberry jam over the butter.

"She was there—for me," Kozak said, pointing his butter knife at Maja. "I tell you, even before the failure of those fools last night, she is here to stop me or even worse. So help me God, I will make sure that she doesn't."

The manager of the hotel entered and stopped a short distance from Kozak's table. He coughed softly.

One of the guards set down his napkin and walked over to the manager, who said something in his ear.

The guard walked back to his boss. "The American is here."

"Excellent," Kozak replied. He signaled the manager and nodded. The man straightened his uniform and left the terrace. Kozak waved at the waiter. "Set the table for one more," he said in Italian. "And more coffee."

"Do you wish me to stay?" Maja asked.

"Of course. This fool has some business to discuss; then he is gone. You might find it both interesting and amusing."

The air drifting in from the lagoon tasted of rain and damp socks. An excellent hotel, this was, but he couldn't ignore the reality of it being in the middle of a swamp. It reminded him of mornings he'd spent in Bosnia and the bordellos along the Adriatic, especially Split. Those were the days, but today was important, very important.

The manager returned with a young man. They waited for Kozak's signal. The American was dressed in a dark-red leather jacket, black T-shirt, jeans, a bizarre black stocking cap, and, God forbid, cowboy boots. He carried a high-priced aluminum Rimowa briefcase.

Kozak waved the man over. When he approached the table, one of the bodyguards stood and placed himself between the American and Kozak.

"Sorry, but we must search you," Kozak said. "An annoyance, but necessary."

The man endured the indignity and then sat in the chair that Kozak pointed to.

"General Kozak, it is good to finally meet you." As requested in his preparation for this meeting, he did not offer his hand.

"And this is Maja Stankić, a friend and associate," Kozak added.

Maja just nodded and did not offer her hand either.

"Anything you say will be held in strict confidence."

"Ms. Stankić," the kid replied. He nodded to Maja, then focused on Kozak. "General Kozak, thank you for the time. I have heard so much."

"What you've heard is probably not all good." Kozak picked up a thin slice of toast and began to butter it.

"No, no. I don't pay attention to rumors, and besides, what they talk about was more than twenty years ago. I was just a kid in Omaha."

"Omaha? Where is this Omaha?"

"Nebraska. It's where my most important investor lives. I like to think he did it because of where we both have our roots. The vast Nebraska countryside can make you believe in big ideas."

"I've not heard of this Omaha. And remember, we all can have big ideas, no matter where you are from. You have asked for this meeting. As you can see, I'm eating breakfast. Hungry?"

"Thanks, but I ate on my plane, took a water taxi directly here. I'm scheduled to be wheels up at eleven. Coffee would be nice, though."

Kozak thought the kid had to be thirty years younger than he. Even at this hour, the American seemed nervous and on edge.

Good, it's nice to be feared.

"Now, what can I, a lowly servant of my people, do for you?"

"Good, right to the point," the man answered. "As you know, now that Croatia, Bosnia and Herzegovina, and Serbia have begun to settle—"

Kozak put his hand up. "Please do not mention those two pigs in any further conversation, understand? If you are talking with them, we are done." He waved to his guards.

"No, for God's sake, no. We are only talking with you. Please," the kid pleaded.

Kozak motioned to the bodyguards to stay, and the men slowly sat, like jackals lowering their haunches to the ground.

"Good. Now, what is your proposal?" Kozak asked.

"My international booking agency uses the latest algorithms—my design, of course—to search out and lock in vacation rentals across

Europe. We see big things in Croatia. Over the last few years, thousands of quaint rental properties have been built or renovated. As it was before the war, people want to return to Croatia to relax, drink the wine, and enjoy Croatian hospitality."

"True, that's all true. And the reason you think this is all happening?"

"You are affordable. You don't use the euro, the exchange rate makes it a bargain, and—"

"We are not a bordello to be used and taken cheaply."

"Oh no, no, no," the kid said. "It's just that with all the troubles in Greece, the crazy prices in Italy, and the impossible access to the coasts of France and Spain for the average traveler, Croatia is poised to be *the* place to vacation."

"So, why are you talking to me? I'm not a travel agency. There are government officials for all that."

One of the guards poured them coffee. Kozak took a long sip, his eyes never leaving the young American.

"People I know say that you have the inside track on the presidency," the American said. "What I want to discuss are the opportunities for my company to have an important role in accessing and managing these rentals."

"And you think I can help you in this matter."

"It is always good business to know people in government that have the interests of their people at heart. So, yes, of great help. If you become president—"

"Not if, but when."

"Sorry, *when*. For both of us it would be mutually beneficial to know that our interests are of the same mind."

"And that is?"

"To allow my company to be the sole point of access to all these rentals."

Kozak buttered another slice of toast. "Now, how could I manage that? There are thousands of these houses from Rijeka to Dubrovnik."

"That you do not have to worry about. That is my business. All I ask is that there are no impediments thrown in our path. Government bureaucracies can be so difficult to deal with."

"That is true. How much might be involved in such an opportunity?"

The kid unpocketed an envelope and laid a spreadsheet on the table. "Now, this is just a preliminary estimate based on ten thousand rentals, but we believe there are far more, and the longer there's peace in the region, the more vacation rentals that will become available."

At 20 percent Kozak's share would be enormous. "And my participation?"

"Would be deposited into an account of your choosing. Of course, none of this will happen if you don't win."

Kozak waved his butter knife at the American. "Now you insult me."

"No insult meant. In fact, this fine piece of German luggage is a token of our interest. It is yours, no matter the outcome, no strings attached." The American picked up the briefcase and set it near Kozak, where it landed with a heavy thud.

"I have watched your American movie *The Godfather* many times. I know there will always be strings. The person who pulls the strings makes all the difference in the world."

The American leaned back in his chair. "No strings, just a mutual agreement—nothing more than a handshake. I have done business that way my whole career."

"And that career, as you say, is now maybe six years?"

"I look young for my age. Ten years, actually."

Kozak laughed. "I have underwear older than that."

They talked for another fifteen minutes, and three times the guest looked at his Vacheron Constantin watch.

"Are we delaying you?" Maja asked.

"Sorry, I just need to be in Zurich by one o'clock."

"I'm sure you will make it," she replied sourly.

CHAPTER 17

Alex woke in a haze. Maybe it was the massive bed, or the suite. Maybe it was the knowledge that Albert Nox, ex-army master sergeant and concierge, was downstairs. Or maybe it was the two vodka tonics she had fixed for herself from the bar the previous night. She walked across the room to the bathroom and slipped on a white robe. She checked her phone. One text: *Good to hear that all is well, I'm trying to get on the afternoon train, will arrive at 5:00. I hope you slept comfortably.*

Her heart fluttered, then jumped. *What the hell was that? Am I falling for this guy?*

The room phone rang.

"I hope I didn't wake you, Ms. Polonia," Nox said once she answered. "What would you like for breakfast? Agent Castillo seldom eats in the unit. He prefers a pastry shop around the corner he refers to as—"

"Let me guess: *fabulous.*"

"Precisely. Happy to fix you something instead, though. An American breakfast perhaps?"

"Mr. Nox, don't you ever sleep?"

"I'm off duty at ten o'clock. It's a twelve-on, twelve-off shift."

"Brutal."

"It *is* Venice, ma'am."

"Tough duty. Breakfast would be wonderful. Give me forty-five minutes—that work?"

"In your apartment or the rooftop?"

"There's a rooftop?"

"Yes, take the elevator to the fifth floor, then walk up the stairs. Today you are my only guest. The view is quite nice. Bring a coat if you wish to sit outdoors. There is also a small enclosed glass house. The forecast is rainy this afternoon, and there is a cold front moving in. But right now, even if a bit chilly, it is quite nice."

"Mr. Nox, it seems that I do not have anything to wear. The dress is the worse for last night, and the heel on my shoe is bent. So . . . it will have to be my room."

"Outside your door is a bundle you will find helpful. I hope everything fits."

"Are you always this accommodating?"

"Agent Castillo suggested that a few things from the clothing locker might be useful. If you need something else, pick up the phone."

"That said, Mr. Nox, the rooftop."

"Yes, ma'am."

"Knock off the *ma'am* stuff."

"Yes, ma'am, knocking it off."

Javier's apartment was a lot nicer than her lovely room at the Aqua Palace. But then again, this was an offshore government safe house. If you were going to be safe, you might as well be comfortable.

The clothes in the bundle—slacks, sweatshirt, and tennis shoes—fit reasonably well. Going braless was surprisingly refreshing; she decided that at least until she returned to her hotel, she could suffer through wearing the same panties two days in a row. After dressing, she removed both the Makarov and Javier's small Glock from her handbag, wrapped them in a small towel, and headed for the elevator.

Coffee was waiting on a small buffet in the glass house, along with juice and cut fruit. She filled a dish and went out on the small terrace that faced west. Four tables with chairs were set across the red-tile floor. The building was taller than its neighbors, so privacy on the terrace was excellent. If it weren't for the fact that the observation deck of St. Mark's Campanile was looking down on her, it would have been the perfect place to see and not be seen. For now, she ignored the visitors standing in the campanile's windows. Surely, they had other things to look at.

Mr. Nox placed a breakfast of bacon, eggs, and hash browns on the table.

"How did you find hash browns in Italy?"

"My own recipe, ma'am. Enjoy." His eyes moved to her bundled towel.

"One item in the towel was a spoil of war, the other a loan from Agent Castillo. Please deal with them."

"Gladly, ma'am."

She gave up on the *ma'am* business; the man was so military. *Nice gig if you can get it.*

She gazed across the confusion of red-tile rooftops. Old TV antennas rusted and bent, modern satellite dishes all angled the same direction, and early laundry strung high over Venetian passageways told her one simple thing: this was also a town where people lived. While the costumes and masks gave it a Disney World atmosphere, she saw it differently from her perch high over the city. Venice was also a city of mystery and, after yesterday, international chicanery and underhandedness.

Her phone buzzed, and the numbers 007 displayed.

"Good morning. Is Mr. Nox treating you well?" Javier asked.

"I like your screen ID. Very Bondish."

"Some say I have a sense of humor, but you—are *you* okay?"

"Yes, all things considered. Having my own butler is a treat. But I refuse to ask him to do laundry. I need to get back to my room. My dress is a shambles, and I feel a little out of sorts in these clothes. The sweatshirt is overly large, but the army logo is a nice touch. That said, I may move in. What's the rate?"

"More than you can afford. Your temporary accommodations are an off-the-books thing between Mr. Nox and me. He's quite discreet.

He is off at ten. I'll ask him to walk you to your hotel. It's on his way home."

"I can take care of myself."

"No argument," Javier said. "And besides, after your little escapades from yesterday, there are two pissed-off bad guys out there. The next time they will be prepared."

"You better tell that to Marika. She is the one they are after—not little old me."

"I told her. She's glad that you are all right. When she told Ehsan, he offered to come to your aid. I said no. I'd rather not include my apartment in their address book."

"Understood. Mr. Nox would be fine. One of these mornings I'm going to finally become a tourist. That *is* the reason I'm here, or so I thought. I'm taking Marika up on her suggestion and going to Murano later this morning, then spending the afternoon with her."

"I talked to the water taxi people. The boatman's name is Roberto. We worked together in Afghanistan. He was with an Italian regiment assigned to NATO. Good guy. But I don't think he can take you to Murano. He said he has a tour this morning."

"The vaporetto will be fine. Thank you for this afternoon. Are we still on for dinner?" The tone of her voice, soft and expectant, surprised her.

"Of course. I will pick you up at eight."

"I will need a dress. Seems the one I brought has seen better days."

"Or evenings."

"Maybe Marika has an idea about shopping in this town."

"My guess is that she does. See you this evening."

"Did the information go out?" she added, wishing the call wouldn't end.

"Yes, now it's up to State. If they decide to denounce Kozak, the fireworks start. Not my problem and Marika is a big girl. She knows how to take care of herself."

"I can believe that," Alex said. "Mr. Nox is coming. Do you want to talk with him?"

"Already have. He'll be glad to escort you to your hotel."

"You assume too much, very Special Agent Castillo."

"It's my job."

Marika sat in the richly decorated dining room of the Ai Reali, looking out the large windows that faced the canal.

In two days this will be all over. The monster will be ruined. Two days.

Ehsan arrived and kissed his mother on the cheek.

"Good morning, Mother," Ehsan said. "I wasn't sure after last night whether you would be up this early." He waved to the waiter and pointed to his coffee cup.

"I'm fine," she said. "I've lived with that day for all these years. One more telling didn't make a difference. I slept well. Are you having breakfast?"

"Starving," he answered. "While dinner was excellent, after my workout in the gym, I'm famished."

He ordered when the waiter set the coffee carafe on the table. "You should eat," he said after his mother didn't order anything for herself.

"I had some fruit and a croissant. It's enough. Are you still meeting Asmir and Cvijetin?"

"Yes, they are coming in tomorrow morning. Asmir is taking the early train from Trieste, and Cvijetin says he'll arrive soon after. There are fewer trains from Zurich, and today being somewhat of a Christian holiday, the trains are full."

"I've told you many times that religious traditions are just that: cultural touchstones to our past. It is good you have kept your college friends. They are fine men. Good to have their support, considering their pasts are as difficult as ours."

"We all carry the scars, but I don't want to talk about that. Yes, it will be good to see them. Asmir tells me he was promoted. He's now head of the container division of the logistics company. Cvijetin just moved to a new position with Swissôtel as director of marketing to Muslim countries. Yes, good boys, smart boys, lucky boys."

"We were all lucky," she said.

"My luck is you," Ehsan said. "I've had a wonderful life because of you. Thank you, but I have said that so many times. It is too easy to become maudlin. Today is a good day for us, and in two days you will triumph. The killer will be destroyed; the world must see him as the monster he is. Your work—"

"Our work."

"Your work, Mother, will open a new chapter of peace for our homeland."

"I hope so."

"It will, Mother. It will." He poured himself more coffee. "Are you still going out this afternoon with that American woman?"

"Yes, it may be a pleasant diversion. As you said, it will be nice to get out of this room. Agent Castillo sent me a text explaining the taxi. It might even be fun."

"And Kozak's people?" Ehsan asked.

"They'll do what they do. I can't just sit here. Besides, the woman is a police officer."

"Oh really? Now, this is a surprise."

"Ehsan, I think between the two of us, we should be able to handle most anything that might happen."

"Kozak is quite resourceful, and after yesterday, I take him at his word. He has spies watching everything. The man is a murderer, and we will stop him."

"Yes, we will."

CHAPTER 18

Through the glass doors of her hotel, Alex watched Nox walk away. He immediately extracted his cell phone.

"Why am I not surprised?" she said aloud to no one.

She had told Nox she would be fine, then thanked him for all his help—most especially the breakfast.

"We are a full-service safe house, ma'am," he'd told her. "We have had many kinds of guests."

After returning to her hotel room, she laid out her clothes for the day, and then took a long shower.

"What can happen now?" she said as she carefully folded up the damaged dress. She placed it in the bottom of her suitcase; she just couldn't bear to throw it out. It would be a trophy of an extremely strange evening.

Now that she'd been mistaken for Marika twice and the clowns from the DEA were in town, the heft of the captured Glock in her handbag was reassuring—disquieting too.

At nine, she put her leather jacket over her arm and went down to the lobby. Sonia was at the concierge desk.

"Ms. Polonia, how can I be of assistance?" she asked.

"Good morning, Sonia. Someone suggested I visit Murano. What is the easiest way to get there?"

On Alex's map, Sonia showed the route to the vaporetto dock. The boat would make just one stop before reaching Murano. "The first stop is the cemetery. I do not think you should get off there. It's just a few minutes more to Murano. You will enjoy it."

"Thank you."

Sonia added, "The shops and glass factories are everywhere, and besides, it's an island. How can you get lost? You have a jacket, excellent. Rain is predicted for early this afternoon. Are there any other arrangements I can make?"

"No, but thank you. I'm touring the rest of the islands this afternoon with a friend I met last night."

"Your enigmatic Texan?" Sonia blushed. "Sorry, I didn't mean to ask."

Alex smiled. "Not a problem. No, she's a friend of his. The gentleman has asked me to dinner, though."

"He is beginning to sound less enigmatic."

"Sonia, I think he is," she said as she walked away from the desk.

The calli were almost empty. While there were some obvious tourists about, most of the carnival goers were sleeping off hangovers. She smiled when she thought about the Croatian thug she'd dumped in the canal. A quick shot of panic swept over her. She turned and studied the passageway behind her. Nothing.

Damn nerves.

She methodically followed the trail Sonia had drawn on her map, the same map she had used the night before as she walked from the train station. The red lines looked like strings of spaghetti. She double-checked the street names to the map and the signs posted on the corners of the buildings, and after passing a florist's shop that colorfully filled the intersection of two passages, she saw the sun reflect off the lagoon beyond.

She was quite proud of herself for not getting lost. A vaporetto was pulling in, the number 13 on the boat matching what the concierge had written on her map. She waved her pass over the machine and strolled on board the half-full vessel. In seconds, the boat pulled away and headed toward some islands across the lagoon. Alex walked to the bow and caught the wind in her face as the ferry gained speed.

Alex let the lagoon's air wash over her like a cold, cleansing breath. She tasted salt and a visceral richness she hadn't found elsewhere. Cleveland, with its decrepit waterfront and sterile beaches, had nothing like this. *Every waterfront in the world must be different, taste different, smell different,* she thought. Someday she hoped to find that out. Cleveland smelled of rust and creosote. *Maybe here it's no different. Maybe the Venetians think the same about their home as I do about mine. But it's all magic to me.*

The vaporetto slowed, and a dozen people queued up at the door. Alex stood to the rear and watched the three water taxis that had followed them from the island of San Michele. The first disappeared around the last of the three ferry stops; the others passed by on the port side. She walked across the barge-like dock, stepped onto Murano's stone paving, and headed toward a tall column that seemed to be the focal point of the landing. The few tourists shivered in the cold wind that had kicked up from the north, inspected their maps, and took photos.

Alex smiled when she thought about Sonia's comment. Yes, an island. Hard to get lost and hard to hide.

The cold front that Nox mentioned had arrived early. The temperature dropped as she crossed the lagoon, and now the paving began to spot as the first drops hit the stones. Wishing she had picked up an umbrella from the hotel, she turned into the first glass showroom and factory.

Inside, the temperature warmed significantly. Men busied themselves around three large furnaces, carrying long rods with globs of red-hot glass stuck to the ends. Mesmerized, she watched one artisan manipulate his molten bubble until it became a large balloon shape. At each step, a part was added: a handle, a spout, and eventually a thin thread of yellow glass as decoration. More magic. The heat radiating from the furnace and the rods the men carried warmed her, body and soul.

"American?" a small voice behind her said.

"Yes."

"We have a shop next door. Through the door there." The girl, not more than fifteen, pointed.

"Thank you," Alex said. She followed the girl out of the heat and into a shop filled with mirrored shelves of handcrafted glassware. The contrast between the two rooms astonished her.

"Can I show you something, signora? Maybe a lion, the Lion of Venice? We have many fine animals."

"Let me look around. Then I'll see."

"Yes, signora."

Alex studied the shelves filled with touristy knickknacks, small bowls melded into a million colors, thin goblets, cups with colored bands that matched the poles along the canals, even pendants and bits of jewelry. From the ceiling hung chandeliers and bell-shaped lamps. There was no end to the colors that filled the shelves and ceiling. She looked keenly at a neatly displayed collection of multicolored wineglasses.

She had felt the man's presence before she saw him. His face reflected in the mirror behind the wineglasses.

"So, Detective, where is the money?" Turner whispered into Alex's right ear.

Alex just stared into the mirror. Behind Turner stood Damico. "Go back to the hole you crawled out of, Duane, and take that moron with. I do not know where the money is—I never did. Hell, I didn't even know my husband was such a bastard until this whole thing blew up. Then you show up here! Just leave me alone."

Turner pushed himself even closer. "Damn, you smell good—for a cop. I'm running out of patience. I want to know where it is. That asshole of a husband of yours owes the government twenty million, and I want it."

"Damn you, Duane. You deaf or just fucking stupid? I do not know where the money is. You have to ask him." She pushed herself away and turned to face him.

"Signora, is this man bothering you?" the shopgirl asked. "I can have the men from the factory out here in a second. Is this man—"

"That's okay, we're cool." Turner raised his hands and backed away. "We were just talking. She's a friend I haven't seen awhile."

"Damn, Duane. Make her tell you, so we can get the hell out of here!" Damico demanded. "I didn't come all this way for nothing."

Two men from the factory stood in the doorway, each carrying an iron rod. One rod still had a glob of glass on its tip, and a long dribble of molten glass dropped onto the floor.

"*Cosa c'é?*" the older of the two demanded.

Alex watched as Turner slowly backed away, while Damico—a few feet behind them—stood his ground.

"Tell us where the money is, we know you're here to get it," Damico said.

"Bill, shut up," Duane said.

"These boys giving you trouble, lady?" one of the factory men asked.

"Stay out of this, asshole. It's none of your business."

"This is my house, no one tells me what to do." The two men, easily fifty pounds heavier than either Turner or Damico, tapped the rods on the concrete. Molten glass exploded across the floor.

"What the hell? This is United States government business." Damico bull-rushed the man to the right, but all he got was an iron rod over his shoulder. He crashed to the floor. When Turner spun back to Alex, she threw a punch to his jaw. The impact rocked him, and he fell back onto a glass case. It exploded, sending glass doodads and shards flying across the floor. Turner pushed his hand into the mess, and blood began to ooze between his fingers. Alex bolted out the door into the rain.

Ten minutes later and over two canal bridges, she was soaked. She walked down one passageway, then another, hopelessly lost. She kept shaking her hand, sore from Duane Turner's jaw. Laughing to herself over the thought, she soon found a small café at the base of the light-house that marked the island's southeast end. The weather had apparently sent most of the tourists back to Venice. Like the night before, she was again the only one in the café.

"Double espresso?" she asked.

"Sì, sì," the waiter said.

He addressed the impressive machine behind the counter and began the process. Alex removed her jacket and shook off the rain. The steaming coffee and the drumming of the rain on the entryway's canvas awning softened the racing of her heart and the surge of adrenaline. What the hell did Turner think he was doing? Why was the DEA here after her? She'd told them a hundred times she had no clue where Ralph had hidden the money. Now it was as if they wanted the money more than they wanted Ralph in prison. As far as she was concerned, every last one of them was an asshole.

She sipped the thick coffee. She'd never tasted anything this good in Cleveland. Her staple was Starbucks, but this was like a fine Bordeaux to Cleveland beer. What next?

Maybe Turner and Damico were now guests of the carabinieri in a Murano jail. Maybe those glassblowers beat the shit out of them and threw them in the canal. Maybe . . . Shit, too many maybes.

She took out Javier's phone and punched in 007. It rolled over into voice mail. She left a brief message to call her that said nothing about the DEA agents. Outside the wind had died down, but the rain continued. She could see the Murano Faro ferry stop by the lighthouse that stood off to one side of the piazza. She wasn't sure how Turner and Damico had found her, but it was certain that they had followed her from her hotel. She was, as they say in the spy business, burned. Who told them she was in Venice? She needed help now.

Help was a six-foot-tall retired army ranger that strolled through the door. He walked straight to Alex's table, sat, and said with a chagrined look, "Agent Castillo is very, very pissed at me right now. He gave me one job, and I blew it."

She smiled at the man. "And what would you have done, Mr. Nox? Shoot them?"

"The thought did occur to me, but by the time I'd caught up to you, you were already running up the canal, and the men were backing out the door, being prodded by two glassblowers with long steel rods. The guys promptly jumped in a water taxi, the one they arrived in. The taxi driver was not too happy, my guess they hadn't paid him yet."

"Figures."

"Are you okay?"

"Now that you are here, I'm better. How did you find me?"

"Your phone has a chip, special issue through Agent Castillo's people. When I called, he checked your location, then passed on the information."

"Not sure whether to be thankful or pissed. Right now I'm thankful."

"No problem. Do you want to head back or do some more shopping?"

Alex lifted her eyebrow. "One more shopping remark and I'll scream."

"Sorry, just asking."

"No, I'm pretty much over my need to shop, even with a bodyguard. Can we get back from here?"

"Anytime. There're two or three vaporetti we can take."

"After my coffee."

"No problem."

◆ ◆ ◆

Marika was sitting in one of the hotel's lobby chairs when Alex returned. When she saw the condition of Alex's hair and damp clothes, she asked if she was okay.

"I'm fine, just caught in the rain on Murano."

"Agent Castillo told me what happened last night," Marika said.

Having no desire to relive the last twelve hours, Alex said, "Yes, after leaving Agent Castillo at the train station, I discovered that Venice can be curiously strange for a gal from Cleveland."

"I could say the same for a girl from Zagreb. It seems that we both are out of our element."

"I could not agree more."

Alex excused herself to run up to her room to change into dry clothes and blow-dry the moisture from her jacket. She also managed to fix her hair, which she left down, so that it didn't look like a disaster. The few pieces of jewelry she put on—earrings and a stack of bangles on her left wrist—were silver. Marika wore her hair up and under a dark-red, floppy felt hat. Her jewelry was gold. When Alex returned to the lobby, more than a few people took a second look at the pair; neither took offense at the attention.

The two women then walked arm in arm to the campo and toward a waiting boat. Moored to the wooden dock fronting the Campo della Fava was a beautiful motor launch, its mahogany brightwork glistening from the light rain. Standing on the dock, the boatman, tall and lanky with a cap typical of every Venetian waterman Alex had seen so far, held the end of the line wrapped around the dock's wooden post. He waved at the two women as they approached.

"Roberto?" Alex asked.

"Sì. And you are Alexandra and Marika?"

"Yes, we most certainly are."

"Javier said that he had a surprise for me. Seeing the two of you is definitely that. You are sisters? He only gave me your first names."

"No, just friends," Marika said. "Our similarities are as much a surprise to us as anyone. So, Roberto, where do you want to start?"

"Signore, I have what I call 'Roberto's Tour Fantastico.' The rain has let up, hopefully for the day. From here we travel to the Canale delle Navi, past the cemetery on the Isola di San Michele, then around the Cannaregio neighborhood, then into the Grand Canal on the north end. Like royalty, we motor down this most exquisite and famous place in the world, then to San Giorgio Maggiore Monastery for the obligatory photo opportunity. Agent Castillo mentioned that Marika had a special stop planned, but I am not to say what that is. We have the whole day."

"A special stop?" Alex said, looking at Marika.

"Very special," Marika answered. "You will see."

"I thought that Piazza San Marco was the most famous place in the world?" Alex asked.

"To the pigeons, it is; but to a waterman, it is the Grand Canal. Are you ready?"

Roberto turned his launch into the narrow canal and slipped under the Ponte della Fava. A few tourists stood at the apex of the bridge and waved; behind them two separate pairs of men entered the piazza, stopped, and watched.

"That is the celebrated cemetery built to receive the dead from Venice," Roberto said as they passed the island that appeared more like a fortress than a graveyard. "Many famous people are buried there, but so too are my grandparents. To me, they are a lot more important than the others. Do you want to go to Murano, to see the glass factories?"

"No, Roberto," Marika said. "Another day. Alex has never been to Venice, so to the Grand Canal. And after lunch, we need to find a dress."

Alex looked across the water at the cluster of buildings. Yes, she'd had enough of glass factories.

They rounded the entry into the Cannaregio Canal and took the shortcut through the neighborhood to the Grand Canal. A vaporetto passed them to port; hundreds of boats lined the long walkways that fronted the canal. This long, straight portion of the canal reminded Alex of a street, but here the street was water, the cars boats, the sidewalk a promenade lined with pastel stucco houses.

"The Jewish ghetto is over there," Roberto said, pointing. "Long, sad history there. This is the neighborhood I live in, just off the canal there on the right. At night I can hear the trains at the Santa Lucia station coming and going."

From under the forward cabin's protecting canopy, Alex saw everything. Children in bright-yellow raincoats walked in groups, an old woman stared out a window, two young lovers kissed in a church alcove, men unloaded a barge near the ubiquitous white-and-yellow vaporetto stops—she missed nothing. They turned into the Grand Canal, passed a produce market, and soon confronted the Rialto Bridge. Hundreds of tourists filled the steps up and over the iconic bridge with its six arches leading up and six arches leading down.

Alex drew Marika to her side and pointed to the spot where Kozak's thugs tried to grab her.

"Good girl," Marika said. "Now they know not to mess with the Cleveland police."

"In some ways, my ex is like Kozak. He has his own agenda, and there is little room for anyone else. And like Kozak, people die around him. I'm incredibly disappointed, but it's the life he chose. Thankfully, it is a chapter of my life that has passed."

"You seem intrigued with Special Agent Castillo."

"He is intriguing," Alex answered. "Not sure what to do, but like a summer fling, there is the safe chance we may never see each other again."

"True, but life throws strange things in our paths. It's how we choose to deal with them that makes us who we are. Enjoy this fling— I think you need it."

"You may be right."

After a few more minutes, Marika pointed to another vaporetto stop. "Alex, that is where I will denounce the man on Thursday. That is the Campo San Samuele and the Palazzo Grassi, where the conference will be held. While I would like to have the Americans support my evidence, I am prepared to proceed without them. The world cannot have men like Kozak leading countries, not anymore."

The launch motored on through the dozens of boats and gondolas that filled the Grand Canal.

"On the right is the Peggy Guggenheim Collection, a wonderful art museum," Marika continued. "Roberto, please take us to the Gritti Palace hotel. There's a restaurant that overlooks the canal, and even on a dreary day like today, it can be comfortable. I've asked for a special lunch for the two of us."

"Is this your surprise?"

"Yes, I hope you will enjoy it."

"This day is definitely getting better and better," Alex said as Roberto slowed the launch and allowed the wind to push it against the hotel mooring, where nearby a dozen tables under umbrellas filled the terrace. A young man took the line and secured the boat. The women stood and slipped their handbags over their shoulders. As Marika and Alex moved toward the gunnel to exit, the boat lurched hard and almost tipped from the violent collision of another water taxi crashing into their starboard side. The women grabbed the rails to keep from falling. Roberto spun toward the attacking water taxi and froze. Three men jumped from the boat, guns drawn. Two of the men grabbed Alex and Marika and pulled them over the gunnels to two more men waiting on the other boat.

Roberto saw the syringes as the boat pulled away. In seconds it was traveling full speed toward the massive San Giorgio Maggiore Monastery.

Roberto grabbed his phone and punched in a number.

"Nox, they snatched the girls. I'm at the Gritti Palace. Tell Castillo, I'm going after them." He pulled away from the pier.

Roberto kept his eyes on the escaping water taxi. His launch was more powerful, and he gained on the fleeing boat. He called the police and yelled into the phone what had happened. The kidnappers' boat weaved in and out of the traffic on the Giudecca Canal. Horns blared across the water from the other boats. When Roberto was less than fifty yards from the taxi, his windshield shattered from a volley of bullets. He dropped below the console, hoping that the wood would at least give him some protection. A sharp pain from his right shoulder screamed otherwise. His launch lurched hard to starboard. He turned and saw smoke rising from the disabled engine. He was losing speed; the other boat was now a hundred, then two hundred yards away. He shut off his boat's engine; his craft slipped in a long slide before stopping. Roberto jammed a folded towel under his shirt to stop the bleeding; the pain was like a torch to his skin. Standing on the deck of his rocking launch, he watched the taxi disappear around the far point, with its massive monastery. His right arm, now limp from the wound, fell to his side.

He called Nox again.

"They're gone, Nox, they got the girls. Goddammit, who the hell are these guys?"

CHAPTER 19

"At least your morons didn't kill them," Maja Stankić said as she walked the room, a cigarette in one hand. She looked out the window. Venice floated in the distance. "It was a mistake to bring them here. You could have been seen."

"My men knew what to do," Kozak said with a laugh. "They brought them up the back stairs. They were not seen. And both are trussed up like pigs waiting for slaughter, they are not a problem. So, don't worry."

"How can you be sure? You are all idiots. We talked about this. We can handle the press and anything the Americans can say. And you, Colonel Vuković. I am surprised at you."

"Fuck you, you witch," Vuković answered. "With her missing, they have nothing."

Stankić ignored the man's insult. "You are all fools. Now they will come looking for her. The Americans will do everything to find her, and the first place they will look is here. And look, you ass, there are two of them. You don't even know which one is the real Jurić."

Both women were tied to separate chairs, gagged and blindfolded. Kozak grabbed the arm of the woman on the right and jerked up her sleeve.

"Nothing, see?" he said.

Then Kozak slapped the woman, who moaned.

"Here, on the other bitch, the dagger tattoo—this one is Jurić. I don't care who the other woman is. She's probably the one who threw our man into the canal. I'm sure Vladimir and Egan will want a little playtime—to get even."

"There's no time for that," Stankić said. "Get rid of her. All we need is Jurić. You think the American might be connected to that CIA agent?"

The slapped woman moaned, while a muffled cry came from Marika on the left.

"We'll move Jurić later tonight and hide her until after the conference," Kozak said. "Then you will see. Colonel, remove that one's gag. I have a few questions."

Vuković removed the gag. The woman said nothing—she just moved her head around, obviously trying to dislocate the blindfold. She was sweating profusely. With the gag pulled away, she took in a great gulp of air. Vuković tightened the blindfold.

"Now, my pretty little pain in the ass," Kozak said as he patted the woman's reddened cheek. "Speak up. Who the hell are you? We know you are not Marika Jurić."

"Try English," Stankić said.

He repeated the question. Even though the English accent was harsh, the woman reacted by rotating her head toward the sound. She still said nothing, pulling hard against the restraints and trying to free her legs from the chair.

"Spirited too," Stankić said with a laugh. "The other one."

Vuković pulled out Marika's gag; she spat on the floor.

"You are all assholes!" Marika yelled in Croatian. "Butchering assholes!"

Kozak slapped Marika, hard.

"How quaint," Stankić said. "Now, Ms. Jurić, what should we do with you? This little game you are playing is one you will not win. The people are behind General Kozak; they want a strong leader, one who can stand up against the elites and politicians in Europe. They are tired of being treated like ignorant children who must bow and scrape to Brussels."

"The people will have nothing to do with you and your fascists," Marika said. "They do not want a return to war. They are too smart to put a criminal in office."

Marika was slapped again.

"Never underestimate the people. They are afraid, they want order. The crush of Muslims and refugees is changing the country. We can stop that."

"With what? Walls and fences, camps like twenty years ago? Death squads, assassinations? They will never accept that."

Another slap echoed in the room.

"Stop it!" the other woman screamed. "Stop it!"

"I told you she is American," Stankić said. "Our imposter has a voice, a strong one at that."

The woman tensed and seemed ready for a fist to her face. When nothing happened, she asked, "Why did you kidnap us?"

"If you are to play the double," Kozak answered, "your government should have trained you better. The men in my army know precisely what is expected of them. No wonder your country is so incompetent."

"I don't know anything. I'm a tourist—that's all. Your people are making a mistake. You stupidly mistook me for her. She is just a friend."

"And that CIA agent?" Stankić said. "Yes, we know all about him. We know that the three of you are working together to subvert the election. If you are who you say you are, just a friend, did it ever occur to you that you are the one being played for a fool?"

The American waited, but Marika said nothing. "I'm just a tourist," she repeated. "In the wrong place at the wrong time."

"Sometimes, my dear," Stankić said, "we are all in the wrong place at the wrong time."

Chapter 20

After he had left Milan, Javier received word from Nox—the train could not reach Venice fast enough. Nox met him at the water taxi stand outside the train station, in the safe house's motor launch. They speedily crossed Venice and slipped into the garage under the rear of the safe house.

In the office, Nox pulled up one of several computer images the CIA's Milan office had sent five minutes earlier. This one showed an irregular chunk of land surrounded by water, with a large building on its right side and numerous smaller buildings scattered about the rest of the island. Lounge chairs and umbrellas encircled a rectangle atop the larger building.

"That's a rooftop pool," Nox said. "I am guessing that's the floor where Kozak is staying. We have confirmed that he and his entourage checked in yesterday."

"The women have to be there," Javier agreed. "No other option, for now. They will have to move them later. We only have a few hours."

"Unless he's killed them," Nox added.

"Right now they are worth more alive than dead—after the conference, I'm not sure. That's why it has to be tonight."

"The Italian authorities should not be brought into this. They are looking for a different boat than what the kidnappers escaped in. Roberto was deliberately less than helpful when he provided a description."

"I will thank him when this is over, and yes, nothing would be gained. Our strategy?"

For an hour the two men planned the recovery. The sun set in the meantime, and as eager as they were to act, they needed to wait until later in the evening. Hopefully, most of the hotel guests would be in Venice celebrating the last night of Carnevale. The two men would leave the safe house just after ten p.m. and wind their way through the canals and then across the lagoon.

Javier emphasized no guns. Kozak's people might go crazy, and the last thing he wanted was a gun battle in the hallways of a luxury hotel. Careers had been destroyed over less, and besides, it might not guarantee a clean recovery.

"Inside job," Nox said. "The only way. Stealthy and no guns."

Nox called the Marriott. "Money is no object," he said in Italian. "I'm exhausted. Just arrived. I'm at the airport. Anything would be acceptable." He wrote the price on a tablet on the desk. He hung up. "Pirates."

Three hours later they dropped one duffel bag and one expensive suitcase in the stern of the motor launch. The craft was unremarkable and looked like any of the hundreds of water taxis in Venice. Nox carefully motored the boat through the maze of canals until they reached the open water of the Grand Canal and lagoon. The earlier storm had finally cleared; a stiff, dry breeze now blew in from the Adriatic. Even from a thousand yards, the JW Marriott hotel was unmistakable. The windows blazed like a well-lit ship on the dark gloom of the water. Nox aimed at the center mass of the island.

The plan was simple: Nox—unknown to the Croats and Kozak— would enter the hotel as a last-minute guest and check in. Javier would drive the boat, to blend in like one of the local water taxi drivers delivering a fare. After leaving his bag in his room, Nox would walk the halls until he located or, at worst, guessed where Alex and Marika might be held. The giveaway would be guards in the halls or being refused entry to a particular area of the hotel. His ruse would be a hotel bathrobe.

"I'm sure no one would suspect a rescue by a man in a white hotel robe," Javier had said with a laugh.

"I'll call you when I find out," Nox said, tapping his earbud.

After Javier dropped off Nox, he would head back out into the lagoon and then motor to a nearby pier, adjacent to some ancillary buildings on the far side of the island. He would tie up and work his way back to the hotel. Always in contact on their phones' earbuds, they would coordinate their actions after that.

"Ever done this before?" Nox asked Javier as they crossed the lagoon. The cold waves bounced them about. They stayed out of the spray in the small forward cabin.

"Other than Afghanistan, once, about five years ago," Javier answered over the drone of the engine. "We had intel that a cartel big-wig was holed up in a condo on Fisher Island in Miami. Two teams were sent in to snag the guy, one from the land, the other from the water. It was a mess from the start, as is typical with any joint operation with DHS, DEA, FBI, and us. The only way on and off was by ferry. The two teams headed out; the land team missed the scheduled ferry. I was in a high-speed cigarette speedboat, some Homeland Security idiot's *Miami Vice* wet dream. They'd confiscated the yellow nightmare a few months earlier. We pulled up to a pier near the target condo building and waited until the ferry got to the team on the mainland side. Then we had to wait for them to arrive on the next ferry to the island in three ultrasinister black Tahoes—so macho, so typical, so stupid. Just as they landed at the dock and drove off the ferry, now an hour and a half late, we stormed in from the south and moved toward the mid-rise condo-minium. When we hit the front entry, we heard the whomp-whomp of a helicopter. It flew over our heads, landed on the golf course, picked up our guy, and disappeared. All we got was his mistress, who said absolutely nothing. Last we heard he was somewhere in Colombia. It's all about planning, Nox, all about planning."

"What does it say about this?"

"The screwed-pooch margin is huge."

They switched places at the helm just before entering the narrow, T-shaped private cove located in front of the hotel. Nox waited in the boat as Javier did a reasonably professional job putting the craft against the dock. An attendant tied the boat to the mooring. Dressed well in a dark suit, Nox stepped onto the dock and waved to Javier as he backed the launch out of the cove.

Javier, after moving down the shore of the island, gently slid the launch up against the piers of a short dock, threw one of the lines around a mooring pole, and secured the boat. He stripped off his taxi-driver striped shirt—worn over a thick sweater—and put on a black nylon jacket that covered his ballistic vest and shoulder holster. They were not going to storm the hotel like in some action movie, shooting everything in sight trying to find Alex and Marika, but he sure wasn't going to die executing this rescue. He also put on a black ski cap that snugly secured the phone earbud under the cap's double brim. He tightened the web belt that held flash grenades, a Taser, and duct tape. Feeling ninja-like, Javier quietly worked his way to the hotel and then through the mass of shrubbery at the edge of the garden, to the opposite side of the building. He looked at his watch. 12:05. Carnevale was now officially over.

WEDNESDAY

CHAPTER 21

Javier's earpiece buzzed. "Go. Status?" he whispered.

"I spotted what had to be two of Kozak's men in the lobby—as obvious as skunks at a bridal shower. They ignored me. I have an extra key card, room's not bad for a last-minute reservation. Maybe I'll stay the night."

"Funny," Javier said.

"I'm on the third floor, west end. Kozak and the women, I believe, are up a floor. Give me five minutes to change and gear up; then I'm out exploring. I'll call you."

A small grove of trees stood to the side of the extensive gardens flanking one side of the hotel, and walkways radiated diagonally outward from the building and disappeared in the dark. Javier stood in the shadow of the trees.

Chic. Nothing like it in Waco.

His earpiece buzzed again. "Go."

"East end of the building. I'll drop the key card."

Javier looked up the face of the building to a balcony on the third floor. A man walked to the railing.

"Got you. I'm below and to your left."

A small box fell gently from above and landed on the grass. Javier retrieved the box and slipped back into the trees.

"I'll keep the phone on—just looking like a poor soul searching for the spa."

"Take a selfie," Javier whispered. "Just love to see you in a bathrobe." There was no response from Nox, just the sound of elevator music.

Javier heard the elevator door slide open and a mechanical voice say *"quarto piano."* He then heard the door slide closed and the music stop.

"Walking the fourth floor," Nox said. "Nothing forward or to the rear. Double doors at the end of the hallway. Hold on—two men just walked out the double doors. I recognize one from the lobby. This has to be the suite."

"What you want?" Javier heard the guard ask in broken Italian. "Go away."

"Sorry, just looking for the spa," Nox said.

"Not here, pretty boy. Go away."

"That's cool, no problem," Javier heard Nox say. "You heard?" Nox asked. "I'm back in the elevator—holding. I've locked its doors."

"Not very friendly, are they?" Javier said. "West end, top floor. I passed a glass stair tower; the key card should get me in."

"Stair exits across the hallway from the double door. When you are at the top of the stairs, let me know."

"Almost there, three minutes," Javier answered.

Javier began to count from one; he needed to be at the top of the stairs at one hundred and fifty. He double-timed along the garden side of the building, to the far end of the hotel. The stairway, visible through the glass enclosure, zigzagged up the face of the building. *Twenty,* he mentally counted. He looked around a corner, toward the same plaza and cove where he'd dropped off Nox. Two launches were arriving. From the noise and singing, they were returning from Carnevale. He looked up the stairs—no guard.

"What's that?" Nox asked.

"Guests returning from Venice. Now or never. The key card worked—going up the stairs."

Javier took the stairs two at a time and stopped at the third-floor landing. "Nox?"

"Go."

"I'll check the door when I reach the floor, to see if the card works. If so, I'll tape the latch. Then the floor is yours."

"Roger that."

Javier took the last flight of steps, then slipped the key card in the door's lock. It clicked green. He pushed the door slightly open and placed a small square of duct tape over the lock.

"Done, go."

Seconds later Javier heard the voice over the speaker say *"quarto piano"* again, in a pleasant yet annoying voice. He heard the door slide open as Nox reopened the doors.

"Two guards at your end."

"Roger that," Javier answered.

"I told you, no spa," he heard a gruff voice say.

"I was told it was up here. What can I say? I'm going to take a look," Javier heard Nox respond in Italian. A few seconds passed. "Now," he told Javier.

Javier casually pushed open the stairwell door, walked up behind the second guard, and aimed his Taser at the man's back. When Javier activated his weapon, Nox swung his Taser up and fired. Both guards were quickly gagged, blindfolded, and bound with duct tape. They slid the unconscious men around the corner of the hallway, out of sight from the main corridor. Javier found a key card in one of the men's pockets.

"Now the fun begins," Javier said. "Quick peek. Ready?"

Javier pulled the pin on a flash grenade and held it tight while Nox slipped the card in the door and the light went green. Nox pushed open the door and took a look around. "Go."

Javier reached over Nox's arm and pitched the grenade into the room. Nox pulled the door tight. Instantly, a loud bang and a halo of light encircled the doorway.

"Go," Javier said.

Nox keyed the lock again and jerked the door open. Javier pushed past and scanned the room. Four men were down and rolling on the floor, their hands on their ears. A woman lay next to the men, her hands to her face. In the center of the room sat Alex and Marika, blindfolds over their eyes, dazed and pained looks on their identical faces.

Nox secured the four men's hands and feet with tape and placed a strip over their mouths. He assumed that two of them were bodyguards; all were regaining some of their confused senses.

Javier, after taping the woman's hands, feet, and mouth, cut Alex and Marika free. When he removed Alex's blindfold, she smiled.

"Took you long enough," she said, "but damn, you make a lot of noise."

"The cowboys to the rescue," Javier said. "We need to move. Nox?"

Nox was helping Marika to her unsteady feet. "Ready. We are out of here."

As they led the women out, Javier saw the hatred in Kozak's eyes. It was a palpable hatred. He now knew why Marika was doing what she was doing. He looked at Marika, who straightened herself, let go of Nox, and kicked the general in his side, driving the air from his lungs. Then she grabbed her satchel bag from the chair.

"Next time kick him in the balls for me," Alex said, pulling Marika away from him.

Javier and Nox led the women down the stairs and out into the garden. Javier set a fast pace through the tangle of shrubs and garden beds. Luckily, there was no one about.

When they reached the boat, Marika, exhausted, had to be helped into the launch. The others climbed in after her. Nox took the helm and aimed the boat at Piazza San Marco's illuminated campanile across the lagoon.

Javier took Nox's place at the helm as the sergeant slipped on jeans and a sweater from a bag in the cabin. The women sat facing each other on the long bench seats; neither said anything. Nox offered the women water, and they both emptied the bottles. He then handed out sweaters and jackets. Still, they shivered from the cold. The trip across the lagoon to the Grand Canal was slow, the rain had started again, and it took time to maneuver the launch into the narrow canal that led to the plaza in front of Ai Reali.

In the dark quiet of the canal, Marika said, "Ehsan will be frantic. Did you say anything to him?"

"No," answered Javier. "We wanted as little interference as possible. I'm not sure I knew what he would do."

"He will still be upset. He's probably called the police."

"Nothing has come across the scanners," Nox said. "Roberto kept a lid on it when he was towed in by the police. Said it was something about a labor dispute. He hopes that the police buy it. The police are looking in another direction and for a different kind of boat. The reports from those at the hotel are just adding to the confusion."

"Nice to have friends," Alex said.

"I've been through worse," Marika said. "And I don't think I have to worry about Kozak tonight."

"Yeah, last time I saw him he was tied up," Alex said. She wasn't smiling.

"Will I see you in the morning?" Marika said. "Will you have good news?"

"Yes, hopefully by late afternoon," Javier answered. "Then we will see what happens."

"Yes, then we will see your government's true face."

Marika climbed onto the small dock, then up onto the plaza. Without saying a word she turned and walked toward her hotel.

"I'm going to get those assholes," Alex said to Javier. "You said that shooting wasn't the answer. Right now it is." Alex shivered under the nylon jacket that Nox had slipped over her sweater. "I have no idea what they were trying to do. The woman with Kozak is a piece of work. I am sure she's the brains behind Kozak. He's nothing but a thug. She, on the other hand, had finesse. Marika? Now, that's one tough broad. We both took a few solid hits to the face. She spit at them."

"Get a name?"

"Hers was Magda or Maja, something like that, I think. Did not hear or understand a last name. The man was Kozak—that I'm sure of. She called him 'general'; he was the man who slapped us. Only when you pulled the blindfold off me did I notice the other man, who was in uniform."

"He is Colonel Oskar Vuković," Nox said. "Don't know the woman." He maneuvered the boat back into the Grand Canal. "Vuković and Kozak go way back, like old gangsters-in-arms. He was with Kozak in Bosnia. I'll check on the woman when I reach the house."

"Where are we going?" Alex asked.

"To your hotel," Javier said.

"No way. I'm staying with you tonight. You can't get rid of me like Marika."

"Marika will be okay, and so will you," Javier said. "Mr. Nox made some arrangements with a local security agency who are watching her hotel. She will be safe."

"And the same for me? Like hell, I'm sticking with you. No one kidnaps this girl, drugs her, and trusses her up like a pig. I'm with you, Special Agent Castillo, like it or not."

Nox leaned over and whispered into Javier's ear, "I like her."

"And you, Master Sergeant, are not helping." Javier looked at Alex. "It's your butt."

"Please . . . my butt's fine now, thanks to you," she answered. "Is this rescue all your doing, Mr. Nox?"

Nox didn't reply, and continued maneuvering through the canals.

Turning to Javier, she asked, "The driver, your friend Roberto, is he okay?"

"He was nicked in the arm by Kozak's men as they fled. He's pissed they shot up his boat. The repair bill will be significant. I'll try and find some account I can use to make it right."

"Not sure what he could have done. It was a sudden shock for all of us. Tell him thanks for trying."

"Will do," Javier said. "Marika seems to have come out of it all right."

"I don't know, there's something about that woman. Chalk it up to my detective skills. Something hinky."

"Hinky—that fits," Nox said as a panel door opened, rolling up from the surface of the canal. He idled the boat into its slip. The door slid silently down behind them, and overhead lights came on. "After I secure the boat, I'll meet you two upstairs."

When they reached the office, Javier poured two straight Boodles on the rocks. Nox entered, and Javier handed him a beer from the small refrigerator.

"Now I know why you have 007 on your phone," Alex said as she habitually reached for her handbag to retrieve her phone. "Damn it. They have my bag! In all the chaos I forgot to grab it. Phone, passport, money—dammit. I watched Marika grab hers but never thought of mine."

Javier stopped and thought for a moment. "You're burned now. This may change things."

"May? Dammit, Javier, I do not have a passport, no way off this damn island with its stupid thousand years of history. I can't even buy an espresso. They have my room's key card and my gun."

"If you need a gun so bad, I'll get you another. That's not a problem. The real problem is what they are going to do with it. They've shown their hand. They are now willing to do anything to stop Marika."

CHAPTER 22

"No, I am not moving. Ehsan is here. I'm safe." Marika lit another cigarette and walked around the room, her phone on speaker. "Agent Castillo, I am very glad you rescued me, but for right now, I'm staying here. You do what you need to, but until Thursday morning, I am not moving from here."

"There are two security people out in the passageways around the hotel," Javier said. "They will run interference. But I'm concerned."

"I want to thank you from the bottom of my heart for what you did tonight, but who said you have to protect my mother?" Ehsan said. He was sitting in a chair in the corner of the suite. "That is not why you are here. We have managed quite well for the last twenty years; it is not your job or the job of the United States to watch over us. We do not expect it and actually don't want it. Please remember the only request we have made of the United States is to support our claims that Kozak is a mass murderer and a perpetrator of crimes against humanity. This kidnapping just confirms that. With your government's support, we could go to The Hague and put this criminal in prison. The sooner they make their declaration, the safer we will be."

"This rescue was unofficial, off the books," Javier said. "No one will ever know about this kidnapping. That is the way it has to be."

"Never know about the kidnapping?" Alex asked, joining the conversation. "Can't we get the Italians to arrest him for that?"

"Ms. Polonia, legally speaking, what kidnapping?" Ehsan said. "There will be no police report, thanks to Agent Castillo. There is nothing to link Kozak to what happened. And I'm sure Kozak is not going to ask the authorities for help. It would be your story against his. And from what I've read about you, Ms. Polonia, let's just say your story would raise many questions."

"What the hell do you know about me?"

"I know about Cleveland, and I know about your ex-husband. What I don't know is why you are here. Maybe your government is involved with something that Agent Castillo has neglected to tell us. A professional police detective shows up in Venice, at exactly this time, who looks remarkably like my mother. All very suspicious to us—we who are suspicious of everything."

Shocked, Alex started to say something, but Javier put his finger to his lips.

"What I've told you is true," Javier said. "Everything is true. But Ms. Polonia is, against my own beliefs, a coincidence, a fluke, a strange accident."

"Thanks, a fluke?" Alex protested. "Dammit, Javier, I've been attacked three times and now kidnapped. Those were no accidents."

"And she seems to be a bit excitable as well," Marika said.

"Screw you, blondie," Alex said and grabbed the windbreaker off the chair.

Javier pushed the mute button. "Where are you going?"

"I've changed my mind, Javier. I'm going to my hotel."

"First you want to come with me. Now you want to go to your hotel."

"Yeah, I changed my mind. A woman's prerogative."

"Are you still there, Agent Castillo?" Marika said.

He released the mute button. "Yes, we are."

"Excellent. Ms. Polonia, I'm sorry we didn't have lunch. Maybe sometime soon."

"Really? That's it? Marika, I'm done with you and your political passion play as well. I am on vacation! I'm through with you and all this. Now, all of you have a nice evening. Ms. Jurić, good luck on Thursday. I sincerely hope your paranoia and the need for revenge doesn't bite you in the ass. And you, Special Agent Castillo, still owe me dinner."

She stormed out into the Venetian night.

Alex was far beyond being steamed; she was boiled, fried, and stewed.

Fewer than two days earlier she had been a carefree tourist, or as carefree as someone with her recent history could be. She thought of her ride across the lagoon from the airport and the cute water taxi driver in the striped shirt. What she wouldn't give to have a job as totally stress-free as that. Driving a beautiful boat around one of the world's great cities, meeting tourists as excited as she was to finally be here. Wonderful, fresh air, not Cleveland's heat and humidity or its counterpoint below-zero cold. Just the clean, sharp breezes off the Adriatic.

What's with that guy Ehsan? Calling me some kind of secret agent working with the Feds in some clandestine operation? What's that?

She shivered again, from anxiety, not the cold. She thought of a hot bath in her suite's delightful tub, then a long night's sleep. She rubbed the raw parts of her wrists, then her temples. Whatever they knocked her out with had left a nagging headache. When was the last time she had slept? The knockout drug had hardly relaxed her; she was tense, like a cat. She remembered the lost purse, phone, and passport. Javier had better come through.

For a long moment, she stood outside the glass door to the hotel, empty-handed. A small sign read, in both Italian and English, "After 22:00, please use your key card for entry." She pushed a buzzer below the sign and waited. She pushed again. Nothing. Nox's jacket and sweater were not nearly enough to fight the damp chill. She was now cold.

She cupped her hands around her face and pressed them against the glass door. She pushed the buzzer again, then moved back from the door. Reflected in the glass, two men stood on either side of her. Each grabbed one of her arms and pulled her into the center of the passageway.

"Where the hell have you been?" Duane Turner hissed, spinning Alex around.

"Good God, really? Not you two," Alex said, looking at the two DEA agents. She tried to pull Damico's hand from her arm, but he squeezed tighter.

"You are tough to find. After our little adventure on that fucking island, we watched your hotel and followed you until you got into a fancy boat with, I'll be damned, a woman who looks like your god-damn twin."

"Just leave me alone. I've had a bad day, and I don't need you creeps jacking me up. I know you tried to intimidate the woman who looks like me. She doesn't know anything—just like me. Drop all this and go home. And who told you I was here anyway?"

"The money, all we want is the money. Just tell us. We may even give you a piece if you tell us."

"Really, that's it? Ralph's money? I'm telling you, I do not know where Ralph hid the money." Alex looked at Turner and laughed. "Damn! It's *you* two who want the money, not your bosses. I should have guessed it when you interviewed me in Cleveland, you jerks want the money."

"Duane, she's bullshitting us. She knows where it is. Maybe she'll take a quick trip to Switzerland, stop at a bank, make a withdrawal."

"Jesus, you're both totally batshit crazy," she said, her impatience rising.

"Crazy as foxes," Turner said and pushed Alex hard against the alley wall, trapping her, his hand tight against her throat.

Alex tried to push back, but Turner was significantly heavier. He leaned in hard with his arm. She started to cough.

Staring into the man's eyes, all Alex saw was hatred.

"If I'm dead, you get nothing," she said, then saw a pistol pressed against the side of Turner's head.

"Let go now," Javier loudly whispered in his ear.

Turner released his hands, and with the muzzle still near the side of his head, he backed away. Damico, his hands up, stood a few feet away where Javier could watch both men.

"Good boys. Now, this is not how you talk to a friend of mine. Keep your hands where I can see them." He looked at Alex. "You okay?"

"Yes, but I certainly want to—"

The hotel's door banged open, startling everyone.

"Signora Polonia, you need help?" Signor Portero said.

That was the break Alex needed. She pushed Turner back with her hands. "Look, you shit. Believe me, I don't know where it is. Do you think I'd be here if I did? But if I ever find it, you will be the last person on earth to know. Got it? Just nod . . . good. If you come at me again, I'll make sure the Italian authorities know all about you and Billie boy. Capisce? And I ask again: How did you know I was here in Venice?"

Turner just smiled. "Wouldn't you like to know?"

"You be more respectful," Javier said, then pointed the gun at Damico. "Get this idiot out of here, and never come after Ms. Polonia again."

"Polonia?" Damico said, confused.

"Polonia," Alex said, reinforcing Javier's order.

"Ms. Polonia, can I help?" Signor Portero repeated as he walked toward the group. "Are you all right?"

"Never better, Signor Portero, never better. My friends are just leaving. Aren't you, Agent Turner?"

"You will pay for this," Turner said, rubbing the side of his head and staring at Javier. "I don't know who the hell you are, but you will pay for this."

"We'll give you until Thursday," Damico added.

"In your dreams," Javier said as he slipped his pistol back under his jacket. "Now get the hell out of here."

They watched the two men walk down the alley. Turner and Damico never turned around. Alex turned to Signor Portero, hoping he hadn't heard what'd been said.

"Who were those men?" Signor Portero asked.

"They were lost, asking directions. I told them where to go. I'm sorry to bother you, but my handbag was stolen along with my wallet. My passport and identification are gone, as well as my key card. I'm so upset."

"Did *they* take them?" He pointed down the alley, then looked at Javier, a question on his face.

"No, it was earlier. Signor Portero, this is my friend, Javier Castillo, with the American consulate. He is helping me with my passport."

"My pleasure," Signor Portero said and shook Javier's hand. "Sadly, this is not the first time it has happened to our guests. There are many Gypsies on the island that wait for just the right moment. It is an embarrassment. I apologize for my city."

"It was all my fault. I left my handbag on a chair, and one minute later it was gone. So stupid of me. The consulate has been helpful."

"Especially at this hour of the night, I'm impressed," Signor Portero added, still looking at Javier. "Let's get you a new key. I will deal with any credit card issues that come up. We will start there. American Express can be helpful when they wish to be." He led them into the lobby.

"Thank you, Signor Portero."

◆　◆　◆

Alex mixed Javier and herself a double vodka from the minibar in her room. The clock read 03:32.

"Why did you follow me?" she asked.

"There was no way, after what we just went through, that I was going to let you storm out of the apartment and cross half of Venice without looking out for you. And with Kozak's men now really pissed off, I wanted to make sure you arrived safely."

"Really? I can take care of—"

Javier stepped in close to Alex and, taking her face in his hand, slowly kissed her. It was a long, searching kiss—a kiss that she didn't refuse. She gently pushed him away.

"That was nice. Are you sure this is how you want the evening to end?"

"It's morning, and I can't think of a better way to start the day."

She kissed him again. "Give me a few minutes . . ."

"Only a few."

Alex kissed him again, then disappeared into the bathroom.

Standing in front of the mirror, she was shocked by how she looked. The long afternoon and evening had not been kind, and a slight bruising was developing on her face from the slaps and blindfold. Her lip was a bit swollen, and her neck was sore from the injection needle's pinprick. She thought of Javier. To sleep in the arms of a lover—there was nothing better.

She slipped the robe over her bare shoulders and returned to the bedroom. Javier had stretched out on the bed, his shoes on the floor, his head on the pillow. He was sound asleep. She smiled and, cinching the robe up, climbed into bed and slipped her head into the crook of his arm.

"Who the hell is this Alexandra Polonia?" Kozak demanded when he finished rifling through Alex's handbag. He'd found her passport and driver's license. "Cleveland, Ohio? The phone's worthless; it's locked with a code or something. The pictures in the wallet match Jurić. There are other cards, with Alexandra Cierzinski on them, an alias? How is this possible?" He held up the Glock. "This looks like Vladimir's weapon. I should shoot him with it."

Maja took the handbag from Vuković and found a black wallet in the front pocket. She opened it and found a gold shield and credentials. "She's a police officer, dammit. Attila, you see what we are up against. She's obviously working with the United States to undermine us. Now, after this foolish adventure of yours, they will be doing everything to stop your candidacy. You are such an idiot."

Kozak wandered around the suite, smoking and looking for something to kick. He'd downed three shots of vodka.

"Maja, you said these Americans have nothing. You said they don't care. As it was during the war, the Americans are only concerned about themselves, not the people they whined about, the Serbian scum, or the Bosniaks. Then they ran away when the peace was made. Now they make trouble."

"Attila, don't be such an ass. This is politics. This is what you wanted. This is the way to our fortune. After a few years, we disappear, new identities, money. All with our new friends, the Russians."

"I do not trust your friends. Those people know nothing of our culture, of our race, of our past. Besides, I think they like the Serbs more. They have meddled in our country for too long. Now, when we are being overrun by refugees, they decide to help, all because they cannot keep the peace in their own lands. This new vermin, these so-called migrants, are nothing more than opportunists from their broken countries. Croatia will be destroyed by these invaders, these new Turks."

"Attila, that war was fought hundreds of years ago," Maja continued. "The war we fight is now. These people are fleeing because their own countries are disasters. Fighting between the mullahs and the Sunni and the Shia—it will never be over. Those fanatics want to overpower us with this mass of depraved humanity being pushed in front of the mullahs' war machine. We are at the edge of this war. If it can be stopped, it can only be in Croatia. That is why you are leading our party. That is why you have the support of the people of Croatia. A few dollars won't be missed, but your chance at history is here, now. And my friends from the north will help."

"Like they helped the Ukrainians?" Kozak said and kicked back another shot of vodka.

Vuković looked up from his computer, a smile on his face. "The newspapers in Cleveland suggest that this Polonia may be a criminal, or at least in league with her ex-husband, who made drugs. Both are members of the local police."

"What?" Kozak said. "Drugs, criminals, police?"

Vuković tried to translate the articles he found when he did a search for "Alexandra Polonia Cierzinski Cleveland." Dozens popped up.

Intrigued, Maja and Kozak listened. Ideas began to spin in their heads, some good, most bad. All involved this imposter and American agent, Alexandra Polonia.

Chapter 23

Later on Wednesday morning, Ehsan Abdurrahman opened the door of his room at the Ai Reali to find his friends Asmir Fazlić and Cvijetin Radić standing outside. Both were dressed professionally, in dark suits, dark slacks, and open shirts. Each wore the light facial hair fashionable with young men. Ehsan looked up and down the hotel's corridor, then with a nod let them in.

"*Asalaam alaykum,* my brother," Asmir said.

"*Wa alaykum asalaam,* my brothers," Ehsan responded. "Come in."

"Your mother, is she well?" Cvijetin asked.

"These last few days have been hard on her. Yes, she is well. I told her you were arriving today, but I hope your past two days here have been worthwhile." He told them about the kidnapping.

"Allah smiled on her," Cvijetin said.

"And now the Americans are proving to be even more challenging. As you can expect, she is confused, and this CIA agent makes her even more so."

"Do you trust him?" Asmir asked.

"I trust no American," Ehsan said. "They only believe in themselves. This has been shown a thousand times. They are also naïve, as children. They come, they go, they rant, they blame. They take no responsibility. This Agent Castillo just believes what he is told or wants to believe. He is nothing. He will not stand in our way."

"Good," Cvijetin said.

The three friends sat around the small table. Ehsan offered them coffee, black and strong; they sipped from small cups.

"Tell me about the conference venue," Ehsan said. "Will our plans work?"

"We were given a tour of the facility yesterday," Asmir began. "Our ruse was the need for a future conference location for my company. The woman who gave us the tour was helpful. I left a business card. I'm sure she will not take the time to verify its authenticity. If she does, my assistant will only say that I am in Venice to prepare for a meeting. We walked through the various conference rooms. We were shown the electronics we could use. I told her they were all up-to-date and acceptable. She even showed us the room where tomorrow's conference is to be held. A long table was set up, no guards, nothing for the moment. Some of the usual propaganda was draped on the table and hung from the ceiling. All is like we thought it would be. There were no surprises."

"Excellent. The campo?"

"Everyone will come by boat. There is a landing area off to the side near the vaporetto stop. I asked the woman if this could be used for bringing our corporate leaders to the conference directly from the airport or the train station. She said yes and then described how it was set up for tomorrow's conference. A blue carpet for the EU will be laid out on the paving stones leading from the landing to the building entrance. This is where many of the dignitaries will arrive; they will then be directed into the palazzo. Off to one side, there will be a lectern with a microphone and speakers set up to make announcements and for the press to ask questions."

"Good, and the distraction?" Ehsan asked.

"Completed," Asmir said. "I tried the duplicate we were given last week, in a small lake in the mountains. The explosion was acceptable, just enough to confuse people in the piazza. The cell phone set it off as expected. The canal in front of the conference hall cannot be more than a few meters deep. It will not block the mobile-phone signal, and the explosion will provide more than enough of a diversion."

"You are troubled, my brother?" Cvijetin asked. "You seem concerned."

"A woman who looks so much like my mother she could be her twin," Ehsan said, "has mysteriously appeared, compliments of the CIA. Her presence, just as all this is coming together, is too much of a coincidence. She was abducted along with my mother. They were both unharmed, but my mother is not taking it well. We need to be vigilant. While I believe that our friends would not divulge our operation, we must be watchful."

"This woman, she is American?" Cvijetin asked.

"Yes, and her appearance, as I told you, is disquieting. Their similarities are too close to be a coincidence."

"And they did nothing about Kozak? File a police report?"

"No, it is all strange," Ehsan added. "If I did not know my mother, I would question whether it even happened. It could be something to confuse us. Therefore, we need to be extremely careful. I also believe that Kozak and that pig Vuković will now be even more suspicious and on guard."

"We are prepared," Asmir said. "Our diversion will be more than adequate."

"Excellent, my brothers, excellent. In the chaos, I will have more than enough time to kill the man who murdered our families."

Chapter 24

Javier's phone rang four times and went to voice mail. Soon afterward it started to ring again. Waking, he reached into his pocket, fumbled with the buttons, and said, "Hello?"

Alex's head popped up over Javier's arm. She had a quizzical look on her face. The clock read 9:01.

"*Hello?* That's all I get? What are you doing?" the voice said loud enough to be heard throughout the room.

"Mom? Is that you?" He looked at the clock. "Why are you up, it's two o'clock in the morning there."

"I know you are a very special government agent, and I shouldn't be calling, but you didn't call last night like you said you would. I was worried."

"My mother," Javier said softly to Alex. "I completely forgot to call her."

"Who are you talking to?" Javier's mother asked.

Alex smiled at Javier's exasperation. "You were busy. Should I talk to her, explain?"

Javier slowly shook his head. "I'm having breakfast with an associate."

"Do I know him?"

"No, Mom, you do not. And why are you up so late?"

"You didn't call."

"Yes, I'm sorry. They have me very busy here. I'm just fine. It's early here, and I'm in the middle of an important meeting. Can I call you later?"

"Of course, it's just that I was worried. Have you been to church yet? It's Ash Wednesday."

"No, but I will."

"Make sure. Call me this evening, your time."

"Love you, Mom." He clicked off.

"That was cute," Alex said, climbing out of bed. She cinched the sash tighter around her waist. "My mother can get like that."

"All mothers can get like that," he said.

Alex padded across the room and adjusted the blinds so sunlight streamed in through the slats.

"Thank you," she said.

"You're welcome. Sorry I fell asleep."

"There will be a time when we are both awake, I hope."

Before Javier could answer, his phone rang again and lit up. "Good morning, Sergeant."

She waited.

"Be right there." He clicked off.

He swung his legs out of bed and adjusted his jeans and jacket. "I hate falling asleep in my clothes."

Alex smiled. "I was going to do something about that, but there are rules."

"Sometimes rules are made to be broken. I need to get back to Nox. Stuff happening. Will you be all right?"

"Quit asking me that. I'm a cop, though I'm beginning to wonder after being caught off guard like that yesterday. That won't happen again."

"You will be fine."

Alex slipped into the massive bathtub, parting the thick layer of bubbles. She sipped from a tall flute of champagne and sighed. "Finally."

Through the bathroom doorway she could see the room-service cart. What remained of the breakfast she had ordered after Javier left was scattered across its white tablecloth. She was still hungry.

No matter how she tried, she could not push any of the last two days out of her head. Even in her troubled sleep, the dreams kept waking her. The utter sense of hopelessness, the inability to move, the restraints, the gag—mostly the gag. What dark hole had she fallen into? Her cop sense tried to sort through everything. Attila Kozak and his thugs, and the woman—who was she? Marika's violent attack on Kozak as they had escaped; the masculine body odors and tobacco that had permeated the men's clothing; the woman's voice, shrill and demanding; the stench of a perfume Alex could not identify; the rough hands; the pinprick to her neck. She rubbed the raw spot below her right ear. *Bastards.*

And the idiots Turner and Damico—what was their game? All this for the money? Millions of dollars will make you do stupid stuff.

The hot water eased the tension in her shoulders and back. She submerged herself beneath the bubbles, and for a moment—a brief moment—everything went away. Her eyes tightly closed, and her mind went blank; she relaxed, slowly rising up through the foam. She softly blew away the bubbles on her lips and took in a deep breath.

The room's portable phone rang next to the tub.

"Hello?"

"Signora Polonia, this is Sonia at the front desk. Signor Portero has contacted American Express, and they understand. Your credit is valid, but you will need to contact them. There is also an envelope for you at the desk. A tall, and if I may say so, very handsome man left it. He did not leave his name. Do you want me to bring it to your room?"

"Thank you, Sonia. That isn't necessary. I will be down in a little while. Are there any other messages?"

"Someone called twice. A man's voice. I told him you were unavailable. He did not leave his name but did leave a number. Shall I give it to you?"

It had to be Javier. Who else knew she was here?

"No, that isn't necessary, but would you be kind enough to return the call and forward it to my room? I am not in a position to take down the number."

"I understand, one minute."

She set the phone on the edge of the tub, refilled her glass, and drifted into reverie—Javier the focus.

The phone rang again. "Hello?" Alex said in a soft voice. "Good morning again."

"Alex? Bob Simmons here. Are you okay?"

Stunned, Alex carefully set the glass back on the tub's edge. *Why is my partner calling, especially at this time of the morning—this morning?*

"Yeah, I'm fine but—it's the middle of the night!"

"Good, I tried your cell phone but got some guttural answer in a language I didn't understand. Then they hung up."

She hesitated and thought for a moment. "My handbag with my phone and passport was stolen last night. My Cleveland creds and badge were in it as well. The captain will be pissed, but not as pissed as I am. Can you tell him?"

"Jesus, sure. I'm up early, the captain wants me in. But that's not all of it. The captain got some strange calls from the FBI Cleveland field office yesterday. They had a thousand questions. I thought you were on vacation."

"I am, or at least trying. What were they about?"

"About what your involvement was with Ralph. All very round-about—you know how the Feds can be. They also wanted to know why you were in Venice. Hell, the captain didn't even know you were in Venice."

"Some things are going on here. Did they ask anything else?"

"Only about your husband. His escape from prison has thrown all that shit back up in the air."

Dumbfounded, she paused. "Escaped? I don't know anything about his escape. What the hell are you talking about?" She was now standing, suds sliding down her body.

"I thought you knew."

"How was I supposed to know, Bob? What the hell?"

"He was knifed in the prison exercise yard late Sunday afternoon. They took him to the local hospital. The initial report came back that it was not as bad as it appeared. Sometime Monday night, when the guard went to take a piss, Ralph escaped. The CCTVs show him in an orderly's uniform. He went out the front, hailed a cab, and disappeared. There's a manhunt all over central Ohio for the son of a bitch."

"Goddammit, Ralph's escaped from prison?"

"Yeah, and with you out of the country, some of the people in Internal Affairs think you had something to do with it. Some think you set it up and are waiting for him."

"Me? I'm four thousand miles away. How could I be involved? *You* are the only one who knows where I am. I didn't tell anyone other than you; all I told the captain was that I would be traveling out of the country. My parents know—that's it, no one else."

"I haven't said a thing to anyone, but it will just be a matter of time. Alex, I'm not going to lose my pension over that husband of yours. If Internal Affairs asks, I'll have to tell them."

"I understand. You do what you need to do. Besides, the Feds know exactly where I am and what I've been doing. So, don't worry. Where are you?"

"In my car. I'm calling on a burner phone. But how the hell does the FBI know where you are?"

For the next fifteen minutes, Alex told him everything that had happened since she landed in Venice. While she talked, she ran a towel over her body and slipped on a robe.

"Jesus Christ, the CIA? Kidnapping, DEA jerks Turner and Damico, and Croatian criminals—are you sure you are all right?"

"I'm okay. But this has gotten all out of control." She looked at the clock on the end table. "What time is it there?"

"Almost four in the morning. I'm on my way in."

"Even if there was something I could do, there's nothing I can do from here."

"Don't worry. Keep out of this. Can you trust this Agent Castillo?"

"Maybe. I'm working on it."

"You be safe. Can you get to e-mail?"

"Yes, I have my tablet with me. Use my other, personal e-mail account; you know the address. When you can, send me an update. It's too risky for you to call again. If anything else pops up about Ralph, can you e-mail me?"

"Done. Not sure you're going to like what I find."

"Thanks, Bob. You be safe."

"Me? Dammit, Cierzinski, it's your ass on the line right now."

"Simmons, I go by Polonia now, remember?"

"Be safe, partner. Watch your butt."

She clicked off the phone, set it on the counter, and poured the rest of the champagne. *What a totally screwed-up day, and it's just ten o'clock in the morning.*

She dressed and called back down to the desk to thank Sonia for placing the call. She needed time, time she wasn't sure she had. She knew the Ohio State Police and her own Internal Affairs would be calling. She wondered if Javier knew. Is that why he needed to get back to the safe house?

At the front desk, she retrieved the envelope. She assumed that Mr. Nox was the delivery boy, after Sonia described the man. A note inside from Nox said that she would receive new credit cards and her passport the next day. If there were issues, she was to contact the American consular office in Milan. There were also a new cell phone and two hundred crisp euros. Thankfully, the man from Waco was true to his word.

Alex returned to her room, still fuming over her ex-husband and his escape. *One more fucking thing to add to this stupid trip,* she thought. *Leave it to Ralph to keep messing up my life.*

Nine Months Earlier, Cleveland, Ohio

"You are a complete asshole. You know that, don't you?" Alex said to her husband across the table in one of the interrogation rooms of Cuyahoga County Jail. "What the hell were you thinking?"

Ralph rubbed his hands together, and the handcuffs clinked on the metal surface. "You should not be here, Alex. They want to pin this on you as well."

"I have five minutes. The guard took a break. I've known him a long time."

"That is one thing about you that makes you a good cop: you know people, and you treat your friends well. Me? You are right. I am an asshole."

"Agreed. Why? Five years more and you could pull your pension. We talked a lot about the future."

"What future, living check to check? The pension is a bust; you know that. Getting pissed on by both the politicians and the public. However, you are right as usual—it's all fucked."

"My contacts in the DA's office say you left your partners out to dry?"

"Partners? They were opportunists, like me. I just jumped to the front of the line and got the deal. I was making good money, in fact a lot of money. Had I known how much, who knows, I might have started earlier."

Alex just stared at her husband. She noticed for the first time how old he'd become; his gut had settled into a middle-age paunch that the orange prison jumpsuit couldn't hide. The wire-rimmed glasses and the receding hairline added to the "going to seed" effect.

"They want the money," Alex said.

"No. It's mine. I worked hard for it. Someday I'll get it. Until then, screw 'em. Even my business partners don't know where I've stashed it. It was my insurance against them. They knew if they turned on me they wouldn't get a dime. I assume there are a few pissed-off people out there." *Ralph smiled.*

"Yeah, that's the rumor."

"But you see, I'm loyal too. I've protected you. The others couldn't stand the heat, that's why they took the easy way out. C'est la guerre."

"Don't be flip. It wasn't easy for Lockerby. His death was slow and painful."

"Told him to cover his butt," *Ralph said with a laugh.*

Alex could only stare. "You know there's a contract on your head."

"So I would guess. We handled a few of those contracts ourselves, sort of like urban housecleaning. I'll be fine. If I'm dead, no one will find the money."

Ralph smirked, looked at Alex, and squinted. "You look tired. You getting enough sleep? You need your sleep; it's extremely critical for good health. I try to get at least eight hours in here. Never could before. Schedules are easier in here. They plan every hour, you know."

"Bastard, your trial is in a month. From what I hear, there is zero chance of you pulling a not guilty."

"Most probably."

"So, what are you going to do?"

"I have no control over any of it. I do what they say. Maybe I'll plead guilty and throw myself on the mercy of the court."

"Dammit, Ralph, why the hell did you do it?"

"The money, lots and lots of money. Why else? Catering to people's needs is all we did. First-class product too. No complaints, good service, and we paid our distributors right on time. It is all a grand capitalist venture. Hell, *we were even asked to expand, go regional. I had some contacts in Miami who had contacts in Mexico and the Far East. We were thinking about it when the operation fell apart. Someone squealed—not sure who. I got away with an hour to spare. Too bad that I needed to sleep; I would have made it to Mexico. I paid a lot for that passport and the papers. I think they just might have worked."*

"Asshole."

CHAPTER 25

"I apologize for storming off last night," Alex said, her hotel room's phone to her ear. "It was all too crazy. I was tired. I was rude and tired."

"No, you weren't rude," Javier said. "My falling asleep and the call from my mother? Now, that was rude. Marika and Ehsan are a handful, as you can see. Especially Ehsan."

"What was that crack about my being some kind of agent?"

"He has become overly cautious and distrustful since our meetings in Milan, almost fearful. He was the initial go-between with his mother. My people say he's been seen at some pro-Islamic political rallies in Milan, and now he seems to be taking his religion more seriously. Probably means nothing, but we don't take anything for granted anymore."

"Paranoid is what I would say."

"There's that too."

"Javier?" she said after a few moments.

"Yes?"

"We need to talk. Something has happened in Ohio that may wreck what's left of my screwed-up vacation."

"What?"

"Still processing it. Can I buy you a beer?"

"Yes, a light lunch would be better. Completely forgot until Mom called—it is the start of Lent. Care to join me?"

"That would be nice."

"I haven't had a chance to receive ashes, so I'll pick you up."

"You are such a surprise. May I go with you? Still a Catholic girl at heart, and after the last few days, I need all the help I can get."

Lines of tourists and Venetians stood for twenty minutes waiting for the priest's blessing and the placement of the Lenten ash on their foreheads. Afterward, as Alex and Javier walked the block to the restaurant they'd eaten at two long days before, Alex could not help but notice that many of the people wore a smudge on their foreheads.

"I see less of this in Cleveland. Mostly older people and only a few of the younger generation take Lent seriously. Like many things in the States, the traditions are dying out, particularly the religious ones. Sad, I think."

"Yes, it is very sad. My mother is as devout a Catholic as one can find. She is proud to be from an old Texan family. She keeps the traditions. The family Bible is like a time capsule going back more than two hundred years, even before the Alamo. In my family, the women seem to be the caretakers of our history. The things Mother says about the newcomers, like the Bushes and the other carpetbagging politicians . . . Well, she does go to confession often."

"I think I would like her. Is that where you get your attitude?"

"My attitude is a combination of my mother and Texas."

They sat at a café table. He ordered a cup of bouillabaisse, she a croissant and a glass of Chardonnay.

"What happened in Ohio?" Javier asked.

She told him everything she knew. He could only shake his head.

"Incredible. Did he have help?"

"Not sure. Ralph is resourceful but trusts no one. Opportunistic, saw an opening and took it."

"They want you back?"

"Not sure. My partner will let me know."

The waiter soon arrived.

"That soup looks wonderful," Alex said.

"One of the best in Venice—light, low in calories."

"I draw the line at fasting," Alex said. "I found my hours were so screwy, it was hard to be a fasting Catholic during Lent. Made me ornery. My partners hated it. I eat when I can, mostly on the go. Not a good way to remain slim and sexy. Same with the church. After everything that's gone on during the last year, I should attend more often. Maybe all this is God's way of kicking me in the ass."

"We all need traditions and roots of some kind."

"Any word from the State Department?" Alex said, veering the conversation in another direction.

"No, and I don't expect any until late this afternoon or evening. Marika wants a lot, especially after last night. I've talked to her twice, trying to calm her down. The rumor from Milan is that the United States wants to stay away from this fight. But Marika has been very public about wanting our involvement, so we'll see what happens."

"Suppose they declare Kozak a war criminal. What then?"

"Marika also wants the international community to condemn the man and have him arrested and put on trial for war crimes. Her demands haven't been met with a positive reception by the European Union. It's not a fight they want either, especially now."

"Now?"

"With all the refugees and migrants fleeing the Middle East and Africa, the EU prefers to have a more malleable government in place in Zagreb. They want to ignore Kozak—wish he would just go away. I think the Europeans want the migrants to stay in the Balkans, not push on into Europe, and they want Croatia to be part of that wall. That's hard. The migrants want jobs, and with the financial difficulties in Greece and other countries in the Balkans, they know the best jobs are elsewhere. You can't stop this flood from washing over Europe without—"

"Bringing back old reminders of the past."

"The Muslims are called Turks in the Christian parts of the Balkans. The Ottomans were the dominant political and military power in the region for hundreds of years, until the end of World War I, when they lost much of their power and their empire. It didn't help that in World War II the Nazis formed a division of mostly Bosniaks that fought in Yugoslavia. The Bosnian War of twenty years ago was just one more chapter. Many historians believe this relative peace won't last."

"Kozak?"

"Yes, and others like him. Now, with all the anti-Islamic political rhetoric flying around Europe, Kozak is not alone. There's sympathy in France and even in the Nordic countries to keep the Muslims out. The political right wing is rising. Those countries have their troubles with the migrants and Muslims too."

Across the small piazza, three men strode out from a narrow break in the stucco-and-brick façades. Well dressed, they walked with confidence.

"Isn't that Ehsan?" Alex said, looking over Javier's shoulder.

He turned. "Yes, I don't know who the others are with him."

"Maybe those are the friends that Marika mentioned. Powerful-looking men. Almost have a military bearing."

To Alex's surprise, Javier pointed his cell phone at the men and took a series of photos. She started to say something, but Javier put a finger up, signaling her to hold her thought. He quickly typed a message into his phone.

"You are not sure about him either, are you?" she said.

"No. I'll see what Milan might have on the other two."

"You can do facial recognition?"

Javier smiled. "Yes, the wonders of technology and instant messaging. Probably nothing will come of it, but doesn't hurt to check."

At the far side of the courtyard, Ehsan stopped and talked with the men. All three looked around the piazza. Ehsan's friends went one way while he retraced his steps across the courtyard to the passageway.

"Something fishy's going on," Javier said.

"Your CIA spider-thing tingling?"

"I do not have a spider-thing, whatever that is. I use my intuition and years of experience."

"You're guessing."

"Yes, but I'm often right."

"Very Special Agent Castillo, are you thinking what I'm thinking?"

"Probably. Is that your spider sense?"

"No—ten years of chasing bad guys."

They hastily paid the bill, crossed the nearly empty piazza, and searched for Ehsan's friends. They glanced down the alleys that intersected their passageway—nothing. A few minutes later, as they neared the Rialto Bridge, they caught up with the men. Hanging back in the shadows, Alex and Javier watched as the men crossed the canal and walked into the San Polo district.

Alex and Javier followed at a discreet distance. Neither of the targets acted suspicious or nervous. Near the church of San Cassiano, the men stopped at a small building that fronted a narrow street. One knocked while the other nonchalantly acted as a lookout. The door opened, and a woman in a black hijab addressed the two. They said something in return, and she let them in.

"There are no mosques in the historic center of Venice," Javier said. "So, it's possible they're meeting up to pray."

They watched for ten minutes until two more men, Middle Eastern by appearance, walked up the street, looked around, and knocked. Each carried a large shopping bag. This time, a man met them at the door. As they entered the building, Ehsan's friends shook hands with the new arrivals at the door and disappeared inside.

Ehsan's friends walked out onto the street another ten minutes later. Each carried blue nylon duffel bags over their shoulders.

"Interesting," Javier said.

The men headed back toward the Grand Canal, taking a different route than earlier. They didn't speak and walked with an obvious purpose to their gait. Alex and Javier had to move quickly to keep up with the men's strides.

At the canal, they watched the two men expertly board one of the gondolas used to ferry commuters across. Javier waved at a gondolier and told the man in Italian, "Follow that gondola."

The small boat with Ehsan's friends crossed the canal and dropped the men near the San Samuele vaporetto stop. The station was on a small campo next to an impressive four-story stone building, the Palazzo Grassi. A towering campanile stood in the background. After leaving the gondola, the men stood in the piazza as if waiting for someone. They carefully set their bags on the stone paving. One man pulled out his phone, punched in some numbers, and put it to his ear.

"Damn, what's happening?" Javier asked.

"They look like they are waiting for someone."

From the bow of their gondola, Alex and Javier watched a woman walk out the doorway of the palazzo and head directly toward the men. She shook their hands and handed the man on the phone a large manila envelope; he nodded. The woman said something, then turned and walked back to the palazzo.

"What the hell was that?" Alex said.

"I don't know, but I'm going to find out."

Alex and Javier leaped from the gondola as it bumped against the stone bulkhead, and walked toward the men. Javier drew his pistol and held it to his side.

Tourists and Venetians strolled about the campo, taking photos, and a vaporetto with a dozen passengers stopped at the station. Alex guessed there were maybe thirty or forty people in the square. She looked at the bags, then the people, then Ehsan's friends. One turned, looked directly at her, and started to smile.

"Bomb!" she yelled. "Bomb!"

"Where?" Javier yelled. "Where?"

Alex, looking past him to the people in the campo, yelled again, "Bomb, terrorists!" She pointed at the blue bags sitting on the stones.

A woman screamed. *Bomb* sounded enough like the Italian word to throw everyone in the plaza into a panic. The two men just stood there staring at both Javier and Alex, totally nonplussed. The man who had been on the phone continued to smile at Alex. Both lowered themselves to their knees next to their blue bags.

Javier raised his weapon. "Alex, check their bags, slowly. Be extremely careful."

Alex looked at the men. Both were composed. The one had stopped grinning, which unnerved her. She grabbed the bags and dragged them away from the men.

"If these are bombs, Javier," she said, "there's a good chance they are booby trapped."

"I think they would have already set them off."

"Thinking, or hoping they wouldn't?"

"One and the same." Javier held his weapon with both hands. A commotion from across the campo caught his eye. Two Venetian cops were running directly at them. Dressed in dark-blue uniforms, with SWAT-type weapons belts and black boots, they yelled and waved their Berettas at the group. Javier lowered his weapon all the way to the paving and set it gently on the ground. He rose with his hands in the air.

"This is not good!" Alex yelled at Javier.

"No shit. What's in the bags?"

Taking a deep breath and saying to herself that she was glad she'd gone to church, she pulled the zipper on the first bag. Then she pulled the zipper on the second, slowly stood, and raised her hands. The police were shouting at Javier, and Alex did not understand anything being said. The agent said something that sounded like *"Americano, Americano, posso?"*

Ehsan's friends said something to the police. All she heard the police say in response was *"Chetate!* Shut up."

Javier carefully reached into his jacket, extracted his credentials, and handed them to one of the policemen.

The policeman's pistol remained pointed at the four of them. Alex smiled, but the man did not return the gesture. The senior officer looked at the photo ID and then Javier's face. A flurry of conversation in Italian began between Javier and the police. The senior officer spoke into his shoulder microphone. More Italian. From up the canal, Alex heard the wailing of a siren. Obviously, the officers had summoned reinforcements.

The two policemen told the men kneeling on the paving to stand. As they did, they put their hands on their heads. Two police cruisers pulled up to the vaporetto stop. In seconds the plaza was filled with police. If Alex were a bystander, she would have been impressed, but right now all she was sure of was that the two of them were in serious trouble. Across the piazza tourists held up their phones, clicking photos.

Javier, tense and exasperated, turned to Alex. "What's in the bags?"

"Laundry. It's their goddamn laundry."

Chapter 26

Alex and Javier weren't allowed to leave the police station until late afternoon. As they left down the steps outside, Alex turned and noticed the sign over the door, "Questura."

"'Questioning'? That was fun," she said.

"It says 'Police Station,'" he said.

"One and the same in my line of work."

At the bottom of the steps, an officer in a small police cruiser waved to them. They were to be escorted to Alex's hotel, just one of two options offered by the upset police commander. The other involved a night in jail.

"Just shut up," Javier said. "If you hadn't yelled '*Bomb!*' we would have been just fine. I had it under control."

Alex grabbed a handhold in the cruiser's cabin. She looked down the narrow canal as they motored; ahead lay the larger Grand Canal. "We were set up," she said.

"You think? I should have seen it from the beginning. You heard the police commander when he called the woman at the Palazzo Grassi. All they were doing was picking up information on the venue for a future meeting. That was bullshit. They wanted to find out if someone was tailing them and we walked right into it. That's why they were released—they were as innocent as lambs."

"Yes, it was bullshit," Alex said, brushing back her hair as the boat increased its speed. "But they are planning something, I feel it in my bones. Lambs? More like lambs wearing suicide vests. This proved it. Why go through this charade just to call us out? Because they *are* planning something."

"I'm going to catch hell from Milan and Washington. I can handle that. But Washington is going to want *you* a million miles from this thing. And I can't disagree."

"You never said anything to Washington about last night, did you?"

Javier looked out to the water.

"You have got to be kidding me. That's it, isn't it? They don't know about our little adventure with Kozak. The CIA wants to know everything its people do, and you have kept it from them. Don't worry; it is definitely a secret I can keep. Good God, I have a hundred reasons, that's for sure. And today? I went with you, remember? And after last night, it's the least I can do to keep you and Mr. Nox out of trouble."

"Me? I'm the one getting *you* out of trouble. You have been nothing but a pain in the ass since the minute you landed."

"Dammit, Javier. I'm the innocent bystander here. My crap is four thousand miles away, just waiting for the right moment to screw me over. My knight in shining armor . . ."

They were quiet for the rest of the trip as the rain started falling again. The police cruiser stopped at the landing near the hotel's front door.

"Are you always this difficult?" Javier asked.

"This is one of my better days." She turned to go into the hotel, then came back to Javier and kissed him. "You owe me dinner. I will be ready at eight. Don't be late—and pick a nice place."

Then she disappeared into the hotel.

CHAPTER 27

Marika stood at the window of her hotel room and watched the rain. For a moment, it obscured the view down the canal. Its sound, even through the double-pane glass, filled the canyon of brick and stucco. It was good to be with her son—their efforts left little time for the two of them.

She lit a cigarette and slumped into the chair. One more day and it would be over. She needed to move on. She knew that her obsession was taking its toll, but for now, there was no alternative. She was doing this for the dead; she was doing it for the survivors; she was doing it for her son. For her, twenty-five years seemed like yesterday.

Zenica, Bosnia and Herzegovina, April 1993

Marika and the boy scurried along Zenica's Kulina Bana Boulevard and into the Hotel Internacional. It was just past eight in the morning. The Bosna River, across the boulevard and full of spring runoff, cut its way through the heart of the ancient village. Sounding like thunder, rumbles from howitzer shell fire echoed and rolled from one side to the other across the valley.

"Does the bus for Zagreb stop here?" she demanded at the receptionist desk.

The woman looked at the two disheveled figures and shrugged. "Yes."

"What time?"

"Maybe three o'clock, but no one knows. He yours?"

She didn't have an answer. The question was always on the edge of her mind since she pulled the child into the woods and away from the execution squad in Ahmići. The boy? What was she going to do with him?

"Yes, he's mine," she blurted. "We were hiking and heard the artillery. Ended up here."

"Artillery? Where?"

"Over the hills toward Ahmići," she answered.

The clerk looked at the dark-haired boy and then at the young blonde woman. "You okay?"

"I'm fine," Marika said as she shifted the camera bag slung over her shoulder. Her small knapsack with a change of clothes was a memory, left under a tree somewhere in the hills above Zenica. She looked at the child. "Are you hungry?"

The boy nodded.

"Do I buy the ticket here or on the bus?"

"On the bus."

"Thank you."

She took the child into the women's restroom to clean his hands and wash his face, then cleaned her own. Afterward, feeling somewhat better, she led the boy across the lobby to the restaurant. She saw an empty table at the window, waved at the waiter, and pointed. He looked suspiciously at her and the boy, then shrugged.

The boy never fussed, never cried. He was maybe seven or eight, an age where every other sentence was a question, but he hadn't asked a single question since they left the valley. When she had asked his name, he said Ehsan. When she had asked how old he was, he only shook his head. During the long night that she had wrapped the boy in her coat to keep him warm, he never complained.

The waiter, a young man not yet twenty, returned with a menu, coffee, and milk for the child. As he stood waiting for Marika to order, three military vehicles roared past, and the building's windows shook. The waiter looked nervous, as every Muslim male in Zenica did.

Marika flashed her American Express card, and the waiter shrugged.

"What would you like for breakfast?" she asked the child.

He looked around the restaurant and then out into the street. Another short convoy of the military trucks thundered by, sporting a wolf's head insignia stenciled on the doors. The child's hands began to shake.

"It's okay. You will be all right. I'll protect you." Marika wasn't sure how she'd accomplish that after what she had seen the past day, but she was positive no one was going to get to this child.

They spent the rest of the morning in the hotel's lobby. Gunfire could be heard in the hills. The child shook whenever a howitzer shell exploded. The bus arrived at three thirty; they had to stand in the aisle. The driver, an impatient Croat, demanded kunas. He looked down at the boy, then her. She paid three times what she thought their fares should be.

As the driver drove uneasily along the two-lane highway, dozens of military vehicles passed them, heading into Bosnia. Their luck held. They were not stopped until they reached the newly established and very fluid Croatian border. The passengers were ordered off the bus. The guards casually glanced at the papers Marika offered, a two-hundred-kuna note folded underneath. When one of the guards asked about the boy, she said he was hers. He nodded and then stopped at two young Bosnian men who nervously offered their papers.

The sergeant looked at the papers, then the men. "Over there," he ordered. "These papers are false."

"No, they are good, see, they are stamped by—"

"I don't give a damn who stamped them. Stand over there, Turk!" The sergeant looked back at the rest of the people standing against the bus. "Welcome to Croatia. You can get back on the bus."

175

As they left the checkpoint, Ehsan climbed into a seat that a young Croatian man had offered Marika. The boy put his face against the window and, with Marika, watched as the soldiers escorted the two young Bosnian men toward a corrugated-iron building. She lost sight of them as the bus made a wide turn into the road.

They arrived in Zagreb late that night and went straight to her apartment. While the boy took a bath, she made a late meal of eggs and potatoes. Dressed in one of her T-shirts, Ehsan crawled into the bed she'd made on the couch. She sat drinking tea as the exhausted boy fell asleep. Soon she also fell asleep.

Marika learned later that after they had escaped Zenica, a mortar shell fired by Croatian HVO forces fell in front of a department store, killing sixteen civilians and injuring dozens more. The shelling began a year-and-a-half siege of Zenica by Croatian forces. During that year and a half, hundreds of trapped civilians died from bombardments and starvation. A couple of years later Ehsan asked Marika what had happened to the two men who were taken off the bus—she had no answer. More than a decade would pass before the historic village of Zenica would recover from this ethnic cleansing.

Marika raised the child as her own. Once he was situated at a Catholic boarding school in Zagreb, and her software business was doing well, she attempted to discover his family name. A nervous peace had been established in the devastated region of the Lašva Valley, but still no one trusted anyone. She talked with an old woman in the rebuilt village of Ahmići, the small community of stucco homes and red-tile roofs a short walk down the hill from Ehsan's home. The woman looked questioningly into Marika's blue eyes.

"Why would you want to know?" the woman said. "Leave this all alone. Go away."

Marika persisted. "They lived up there." She pointed, the scenes as fresh in her memory as if from yesterday. "A small cluster of homes and outbuildings. The road ends a little farther on after it."

The woman shook her head. "No, nothing is to be gained. The worthless Blue Helmets came through here sometime after the soldiers left and long after the bodies were buried."

"The United Nations . . ."

"More like fools and asses. Worthless. No one said anything to them. We knew nothing would be done. This has happened before, many, many times. Why? We have done nothing." The woman started to walk away.

"Please, all I am trying to do is find the name of the family for this boy." She held up a photo. "I helped him escape that morning."

The woman spun on her worn black shoes. "You took a boy? An eight-year-old boy?"

"Yes, he was about that age. The soldiers were killing everyone. The boy escaped out the back of the house, just before his family was—"

"Murdered," the woman said. "We looked everywhere for the child. Eventually, we believed he was dead, lost in the fire that consumed their home. He was my grandnephew. His name is Ehsan Abdurrahman, an old family name that goes back to the time of the great Suleiman—it means 'servant to the mighty.' My heart breaks when I think of that day, that time. Many were murdered, and many were to die later—shot by cowardly snipers. The worst were the children who starved. This valley became a prison . . . I must go. I beg you, please bring our child back to us—to visit. There is nothing for him here now, but a man must know his roots and his history."

Marika looked up the stony path that led to a cluster of newly tiled roofs at the edge of the forest. "Yes, I will bring him back."

After dumping the almost-full ashtray in the trash, Marika lit another cigarette and sat back in the chair. She was still sore from the manhandling by Kozak's men, and the side of her neck, where she had been injected, was swollen. If there was one thing she would do before this was over, she would make the son of a bitch pay—pay for what he did to the Bosniaks, what he did to the people of Croatia, and what he did to her.

She would never forgive the authorities for not bringing Kozak to justice. The same authorities who'd given her hell when she'd first brought Ehsan into Zagreb. When they'd asked his name, he said "Ehsan," and that's when Marika had first seen brightness in the boy's eyes, a deep-blue brightness—cerulean windows into a sharp mind. She had been surprised that he did not ask about his parents or what had happened. It would be two years before he would inquire about his family, or why he was different from the other children in his school, or why his name was different from Marika's. When she had told him, all he said was that he understood.

Since then, they'd talked about that day many times. He'd grown into a strong and handsome man. He had learned languages, and to many he looked Italian, from the northern part of the country, where blue eyes were common. He seldom said otherwise or corrected the assumption. That is, until they heard his last name, Abdurrahman. One moment a business acquaintance, a potential friend; the next a Muslim—one of those causing trouble in the world.

In time, he left his mother for Oxford. Soon after Marika sold her software business, Ehsan finished his law degree in Milan. He helped with the legal aspects of the sale. His shares of the company allowed him, even with his excellent job, more freedom to pursue other interests. Over the past few years, he'd explored dozens of ancient Muslim sites throughout the vast Ottoman Empire. Marika was pleased that he had found another outlet for his curiosity, though she was uncomfortable with his enthusiasm. There was in her heart an uneasiness growing about Ehsan.

After the sale of the business, she returned to journalism. She wrote for travel magazines, about the old country of Yugoslavia, about Slovenia and Croatia. She added stories to her own photo spreads on

Dubrovnik and Split that showed the beauty of the beaches and the mountains. Her feature on the vineyards of coastal Croatia made the travel section of the *New York Times* and was picked up by a dozen other international papers. People wanted to read about the magnificence and splendor of the Balkans. But when she wrote of the mass graves, the dead Bosnian Muslims, the Croatian corpses dug from the dark valleys, no one wanted those articles. It was all in the past. Nothing could be gained by embarrassing the people of Croatia, Serbia, and Bosnia and Herzegovina. She even received death threats.

One morning, while composing an article about the rebuilding of Croatian Catholic churches along the Bosnian border, she found herself studying the photos she had taken the day she saved Ehsan. In one photo stood Colonel Attila Kozak—now presidential candidate—next to a Croatian HVO Humvee. The Humvee was stopped on a narrow lane in front of a burning house with three bodies lying on the ground. Kozak was pointing at the next house. A puff of smoke rose from the soldier's rifle that was pointed in the same direction. When she followed Kozak's finger and the tip of the soldier's rifle, it stopped at a man with his arms raised, a portion of his face obliterated.

CHAPTER 28

Alex quickly loaded dozens of e-mails on the phone Javier had given her. Only two were from Bob Simmons, which had come in during the last hour. She called Simmons and let it ring.

"Anything new?" she asked once he picked up.

"Why are you calling me?" Simmons asked. "I thought we were going to e-mail."

"This is quicker, and the phone is untraceable. Any news?"

"Nothing, not even a half-assed sighting. Didn't you get my e-mails?"

"Yes, that's why I'm calling."

"Your ex even has the weather on his side. It is supposed to turn to crap later today, which will make it even harder to find him. Maybe he's wandering in the woods. Maybe he'll freeze to death and save the state a bunch of trouble. The captain figured I knew where you were. You need to call him."

"Is he there?"

"No, he's meeting with the state troopers, who are taking the lead. He said he wants the department—and you—to stay as far away from this as we can. He said it isn't his problem if the state can't manage their prisoners. He's got his own problems to deal with."

"He hasn't changed. Tell him I called. And that I have not heard from Ralph and hope to God I don't. I do not want to get involved—tell him that too."

"The guy from the Cleveland FBI field office mentioned that your CIA friend is quite the ladies' man."

"And what do you mean by that?"

"Oh nothing, just after the past year . . ."

"It is a lot more complicated than I want, and I didn't want any of this. By the way, did the captain get a call from the Venice police?"

"Now, why would . . . Alex, what the hell are you into?" Simmons asked.

"Why?"

"Let me think . . . the CIA, FBI, DEA, Muslims, Venice, and a budding romance in the air."

"Shut up, Simmons. It's winter, it's raining, and it's cold. And it's none of your damn business."

"Thought so. You're falling for the guy."

"Stay out of this, Simmons. You know I can hurt you."

"Just saying. So, have a nice time and stay out of trouble."

"It may be way too late for that."

Agent Castillo sat in the safe-house office, feeling less like a special agent and more like a fool who had been tricked into blowing a simple job. He'd been trained not to do this. He'd been on dozens of operations where this did not happen. The post-op review was written out, all neatly formatted on the computer. All he had to do now was push the "Enter" key.

Nox stood in the narrow doorway. "Does it need to go out right now? A day won't make a difference."

"It might, Master Sergeant."

"To what end? There's a lot of other crap going on here, and my learned experience says we should wait until all the cows come home."

"Really, cows?"

"I was raised on a dairy farm in Iowa; cows come naturally to me. Nonetheless, you see my point. Those two led you to the Palazzo Grassi for a reason—to find out if there was a tail. You confirmed it. It will change how they act, but there's still something going on with the conference. There's more than a discussion of the euro in Croatia going on here."

"Yes, with Kozak and his people in town, it's politics more than economics."

"They are often the same thing, flip sides of the same euro, you might say."

"Anything on that woman who was with Kozak?"

"One sec." Nox left the doorway to walk down the hall to his office, where soon a printer could be heard.

Nox returned, his eyes on the printout. "Washington says her name is Maja Stankić, Bulgarian. Runs a public relations firm in Budapest, mostly for politicians—right-wing politicians. Also says she has a string of fancy escort operations in Budapest and Zagreb. Some of her clients, when they are in town, are Russian oligarchs."

"High-class hookers and low-class millionaires?"

"Maybe not so high class. She's forty, arrest record for minor infractions, mainly dealing with solicitation and prostitution. Most of those were more than fifteen years ago. Kozak is listed as one of her PR clients; she left Croatia earlier this week on a train from Zagreb. Her passport was scanned on Monday when they entered Italy."

"I assume that Kozak was also listed as entering the country then?"

"Does not say, but we can assume that. She has been advising him on his presidential campaign."

"Wonderful. What a tangle of snakes."

"Stankić's connection to Kozak goes back almost ten years. She's provided legal assistance through a firm in Budapest. Its lawyers are mostly Croats, Slovenes, and naturalized Italians from the old Yugoslavia."

"As I said, snakes. What is the connection to Jurić?"

"Not sure," Nox said. "But since Jurić lives in Zagreb now and has a reasonably high profile fighting these people, this firm may provide some of Kozak's legal muscle challenging her. Jurić comes across as a pretty tough woman."

"Yeah," Javier said. "I got that from the first time I talked to her. With what we know about Kozak and Colonel Vuković, they are here to shortstop anything that might pop up regarding Washington's stand on Kozak's criminal past. Especially anything that Jurić comes up with. And this Stankić woman only adds spice to the mix."

"I agree, but it is way out of our jurisdiction—your jurisdiction. That's something for the Italians and Interpol—should they decide to intervene."

"I don't disagree, but Jurić is my responsibility, or is until this all shakes out tomorrow. I've been ordered back to Milan on tomorrow night's train. I'm already behind on my paperwork."

"See, that's why I'm just a cook and housekeeper—no paperwork."

"Right, and I'm the agency's director."

For the next two hours, Javier and Nox went over the setup for the Palazzo Grassi conference, then called their counterparts in Europol and the Italian police who were in charge of security. Javier's activities earlier that day had already reached the ears of Europol. They were not amused by his confrontation. An offhand remark about American CIA meddling brought a smile to Javier's face. He was beginning to understand there was a lot more to this conference than what showed on the surface.

As they were wrapping up their review, Javier's phone rang. He looked at the number. "Washington," he said to Nox. "Castillo," he answered. He listened for the next two minutes, saying "yes, sir" three times, then hung up.

"Langley isn't happy?" Nox asked.

"Correct, Langley and the State Department are not happy. They also said no to Marika Jurić and her whole exposé. They have demurred for now. In fact, they are not going to go public with any of this, and according to Langley, the paperwork never arrived. The Secretary of State is stopping in Zagreb in two weeks to show support for the Socialist candidate as well as issues dealing with the refugees and migrants. They want nothing to do with Kozak. By ignoring him, they hope he'll just disappear."

"Marika won't be happy."

"And I have to tell her not to say or do anything that might cause a problem."

"That, I'm sure, will be impossible."

"No shit."

CHAPTER 29

Maja watched as Kozak fumed and banged around the hotel room. Two empty bottles of Croatian Akvinta Vodka stood on the bar; two more waited their turn.

The bill for damaged furniture and knickknacks will be substantial.

"This cop Polonia, she's unimportant," Maja said. "I know her kind. Hell, I've bribed her type so many times, I know she's not worth the effort. Forget her. The real problem is Jurić and what she intends to do. Obviously, the Americans want us to think that they are not involved, but it's apparent they want to substitute this woman for Jurić, make her a stand-in. Why, I don't know. That's where the real problem lies, with the Americans. Attila, just sit down. We will work through it."

Kozak just stared at Stankić, took another shot of vodka, and then threw the glass at the fireplace.

"Feel better?"

"Fuck you. You got me into all this, you and your Russian friends. I was quite happy in Split until you arrived and waved all these wonderful things about."

"Millions of euros are a lot more than wonderful things." She pointed to the aluminum briefcase. "We needed you to pull the opposition together, and it is happening, particularly with these waves of invading Muslims. The people now understand that they need a strong leader to turn these refugees away. That is why they want you."

"To hell with the millions of euros. This is all falling apart."

"The Americans will stay away. It is not in their interest to take Jurić's side," Maja continued. "They will make an effort to show how supportive they are of the Socialists, but it's all bullshit. I know them; they wish we would all go away. They play big-boy politics. We are nothing, which is why we have the advantage. The people want a strong leader. You, Attila Kozak, are that person."

Kozak unscrewed the top of the next bottle, retrieved a glass from the bar, and poured another glassful.

"You know what I've said about your drinking," she continued. "It is not appropriate for the next president of Croatia to be a drunk. Set the glass on the bar and come to me. You need your rest. Tomorrow is a big day. The future of Croatia will be determined before the sun sets, and you need to be ready. I've laid out your suit, the English one; your shoes are polished; the tie from Savile Row is in our national colors—subtle but patriotic."

Kozak took a deep breath, set the glass on the bar, and dropped onto the couch where Maja sat, her legs curled under her. She took his unshaven chin into the palm of her hand.

"See, that was not hard. Now just relax. When Colonel Vuković returns, you can sleep. I will make sure you are up in time. The launch to take you to the conference leaves here at nine thirty. The press will meet you at the campo." She stroked his thick, gray-streaked black hair. "There will be time to review your statement in the morning. It will all go as I planned it."

The liquor had worked its way into every synapse and muscle. Kozak's eyes began to slowly close.

"That's it, just close your eyes. Tomorrow will be a day to remember."

She waited until Kozak's heavy breathing turned to a soft burbling, then laid his head on a pillow and covered him with her shawl. She walked to the bar and shot back the glass that Kozak had filled, then retrieved a phone from her pocket, scrolled down the address book, and selected a number.

"He's out for the evening. I have about two hours before he wakes and I have to put him to bed . . . Yes, I understand, it is exactly like I told you . . . You do not trust me?" Stankić waited for a reply. When none came, she said, "Of course you do, that is why you hired me. He will be there, you can be sure of that. But can your people do what is intended—what is necessary?"

Chapter 30

Alex ran her hand over her right hip and smiled. Just an inch above her panty line was a tattoo of the Venetian lion of St. Mark. She'd had the mark inscribed when she was in high school. It had faded, but every time she took a shower, slipped on a bathing suit, or slid her bottom against a lover, she saw it.

Standing in front of the hotel room's mirror, she looked at the smudge—now almost a birthmark—that reminded her of why she had come to this confusion of a city sitting in the middle of a lagoon at the north end of the Adriatic Sea. That tattoo was indelibly etched into her heart as well as the soft white skin of her hip.

She slipped on a black sweatshirt, "Rock & Roll Hall of Fame" stenciled on the front, the last world tour of Led Zeppelin listed on its back. The sweatshirt was long enough to hide her tattoo. It was the same shirt her ex-husband had bought her the day they toured the museum, and it was the same shirt she had on the morning her house was raided.

At least they had knocked.

Fourteen Months Earlier, Cleveland, Ohio

When she opened her front door, a small army of men stood on the front porch and down the steps. Other than the three men in suits at the door, the rest of the officers were dressed in black SWAT uniforms and carried MP5s. It was snowing.

"What the hell is this, Lieutenant?" she demanded. "What the hell's going on? It's six in the morning."

The lieutenant waved a folded paper. "Sorry, Alex, can't tell you. We have to search the house."

For the next three hours, they completely ransacked her home. They pulled out and flipped over drawers, pulled furniture away from the walls, tugged up corners of the carpeting, inspected every inch of the closets, and even melted the boxes of ice cream in the freezer. They spent an inordinate amount of time in the office she and her husband shared in a front bedroom upstairs. They piled records from filing cabinets into legal boxes that mysteriously appeared, and placed the two computers and one laptop in another box; and every thumb drive they found went into plastic evidence bags.

Afterward, they took her downtown, and for the next four hours, she was grilled by Internal Affairs, the Cleveland police drug-investigation unit, and the district attorney's office. Not once did her husband's name come up. From the sounds of it, she had been implicated in some type of drug-manufacturing operation as well as something to do with three drug dealers found dead in the past two months. She knew about the dead dealers. In fact, she and her partner had covered the second murder: a Felicidad Lopez found dead in an alley under Interstate 80, shot in the back of the head, execution-style.

"He was one very bad actor," she told the DA. "We found nothing else. No shell casings were discovered. His sheet was long, the usual gang history and involvement with the Easterlies, the local connection to a Mexican cartel."

"Nothing else?"

"Nothing, we wrote it down as a retaliation."

"Did you discuss the case with Ralph?"

This was the first mention of her husband.

"No, we make it a point to never discuss our cases. We seldom even bump into each other on the street. I'm here—my desk is downstairs—but then you know that."

The DA made a note in his book. "Do you know where your husband is?"

"No, he left late yesterday, mentioned that he'd received a call."

"About what?"

"I haven't a clue. Screw you."

"Detective, please keep this civil."

"You have got to be kidding me. Civil? After this morning? Not going to happen. I want my union rep, and I want him now."

The DA and his assistants left the interrogation room. She stewed for an hour before her union legal beagle arrived. Except for a stack of folders under his arm, he was alone. She was pacing the room when he walked in. The officer outside let him in, then closed and locked the door.

"Detective, I'm Walter Slatkin. I'll be your representative through all this, until you find appropriate counsel."

"Why the hell do I need counsel? What the hell is this all about?"

For the next half hour, Slatkin explained everything he knew. When he was done, Alex recognized that her world, the life she'd lived for the past fifteen years, was now an unmitigated disaster and sinking faster than a brick flung into Lake Erie.

They found Ralph Cierzinski at a Tennessee rest stop. He was asleep when the state police knocked on his car window. He put up no fight. The extradition was a mere formality—he waived his rights. Alex saw him for five minutes as he was charged with running an illegal drug-manufacturing operation and employing unnamed men in the killings of three members of the Easterlies. Two other defendants were also charged, both cops, cops she'd known for twelve years. Cops she'd made dinner for, cops that had sat in

*her living room watching the Browns and the Cavaliers, cops she'd trusted
with her husband's life.*

*She was eventually cleared of any connection to her husband's opera-
tions and actions. Most of the exculpatory evidence came from her husband's
testimony. When the DA dropped the charges, she didn't know whether to
be relieved or just pissed. She stuck with pissed.*

*Even when she went back to work, she knew she was marked. The only
man who would talk to her was Bob Simmons. He told her he had her back.
When she said he should get a new partner, his comment was simple and
straight: "Not a chance in hell." Regardless, she was pulled off the street and
given a desk and a two-foot-high stack of folders for follow-up interviews
on unsolved but active cases. And Bob Simmons was given a new partner,
a troubled kid a year out of the academy.*

*This continued until the trial ended and she and her husband agreed
to a divorce. After the papers had been signed, she did two things: booked
a ticket to Venice and got drunk. She would decide on her career while in
Venice, someplace a half world away from all the confusion and chaos that
had totally taken over her life.*

Alex mixed a gin martini, took a sip, and looked at the clothes she'd
packed. She wished she'd brought at least one more full suitcase. Being
kidnapped had put a serious crimp in her shopping for a replacement
dress, not to mention having quashed her date with Javier. She laid out a
fresh blouse, her best pair of slacks, and underwear. At least she did not
have to wear nylons. She had one pair of black high-heeled dress shoes
that she also set on the bed; they would work with the slacks. She would
wear the only coat she had brought, the long black polished-poplin one.

When she was done, the martini was history. She thought about
making another but decided it would be better to not be tipsy when
her date showed. She rearranged her hair, pulling it up into a tall, full

confection, and put on her makeup. In her limited case of jewelry, she located a pair of diamond studs that would fit the mood—her mood—as she anticipated the evening. She opened her black patent-leather clutch and put the euros and the phone Javier had given her into it. She missed her large handbag, and she missed, even more, her wallet with her old pictures and credit cards. The thought of her bag sitting in Kozak's hotel room and being searched by that Maja woman annoyed her.

The mask Javier had given her Monday night sat on the dresser, seeming to smile at her. For the first time in more than fifteen years, she looked forward to going out on a date.

A date, a real goddamn date with a good-looking guy—how my world has changed in three days.

The room phone rang at exactly five minutes to eight.

And prompt.

Once she reached the lobby, she found Javier dressed in a dark suit, black shirt, and black tie.

"I love a man dressed in black," she said. "With the right hat, you could pass for a river gambler."

"And you look breathtaking," he replied, his cheeks brightening. "And a gift." He held up a small envelope. "The State Department came through. Your passport. And your American Express card as well, nice service when there's a little pressure from Uncle Sam."

"Thank you, my liege."

He took her coat and helped her put it on.

"Is it chilly?"

"A bit, but the restaurant is not far. I think we can make it without freezing."

"I'll snuggle."

CHAPTER 31

The walk was short, maybe four meandering and crowded Venetian blocks. A light drizzle had begun by the time they reached the restaurant, a narrow storefront not much wider than the two front windows flanking the door. After a warm greeting, Javier and Alex were shown a table in the far corner.

"This is a little more private than up front—safer too."

"It is nice to be on the arm of a man with influence," she said. "Not sure if safer is what I look for in a restaurant." She inhaled deeply. "The aromas are scrumptious."

"It reminds me of an *osteria* in Washington, DC—simple and delicious."

He waved to the waiter, who stood off to the side. "Hugo, a bottle of Chardonnay from the Alto Adige. I can't remember the name."

"I believe it was Baron Salvadori," the waiter said.

"That's the one, thank you."

After all the usual wine-tasting formalities, Hugo poured Alex's glass, then Javier's.

"Salute," Javier said as he raised his.

"No, you don't. I get to make the toast. This may be your town, but I'm the guest. I'll make the toast." She paused, her glass high, and said, "To our futures, may they entwine for a hundred years."

Javier smiled. "I like that. *A noi,* to us."

The restaurant was comfortably full yet quiet enough to carry on an intimate conversation.

"Did you hear from Washington?" Alex asked.

"Yes, they said no. The reasons were muddled, but, as I thought, they want to stay far away from Kozak. Marika's efforts would force them to get closer to the issue."

"Marika?"

"She expected it when I called her. She didn't seem as disappointed as I thought she would be. Strange."

"Especially after everything that's happened. And Ehsan?"

"No idea, I don't think he was there. He and his two friends seem to have disappeared."

"Anything else on that Muslim house?"

"Nox heard that the Venice police knew about it. They are watching the house, but the holiday had pushed their priorities elsewhere."

"Typical bureaucratic response," Alex said. "So, Waco, Texas? South of Dallas, if I remember? I attended a couple of conferences in Dallas. A lot different than Cleveland."

"Not partial to Dallas, too big. I like the smaller Texas towns."

"Like Houston?"

"Not smaller. That city just goes on forever, and after the flood, it will be a tough place to live for a while."

"And you ended up in Milan. It is somewhere on my list, after London, Rome, and Paris."

"Someday I'll show you around."

"A man of the world . . ."

"My family is old Texican, Spanish and Indian long before the Alamo and the Republic. I was raised proud and nonapologetic. My mother, Maria, is one of the grandest and loveliest people you will ever meet, and she instilled her sense of duty and respect in us five kids. My father owned a bakery in Waco until he retired a few years ago. Now he plays golf and takes care of my sister's kids when she's working. As you can tell, nothing tragic or mysterious."

"And I know she likes to keep tabs on her children," Alex said with a smile. "And is there a Mrs. CIA Agent in a nice bungalow in Waco?"

"No, single and dedicated. Someday, who knows?"

"How did you get into the CIA?" Alex asked, intrigued.

"ROTC at Texas A&M, two tours in the army—the Middle East and Afghanistan, nothing remarkable. During my last year, the CIA recruited me. They discovered my language skills and offered me a job. I'd be in some back-water office in Nicaragua if it weren't for my mother demanding I be more fluent in languages other than street Spanish. It has come in handy quite a few times during the last few years. That's why I'm here; Italian wasn't too hard after proper Spanish. You? How did you get into the cop business?"

"My family's from the near south side of Cleveland, a romantic burg called Parma," Alex said. "Both parents alive and well, two younger brothers, Catholic school, Ursuline nuns, absolutely nothing remarkable. I received my BA degree from the local college, and I lived at home until I became a cop. I am serious about this being the farthest I've ever been from Cleveland. My language skills are enough to tell a Mexican gangbanger to drop to the floor and put his hands on his *cabeza*. Grandfather and an uncle were cops, both retired. Sometimes the job was exciting, sometimes drudgery—even with all that, I never fired my gun. Vacations were always on the lake. My marriage to Ralph put many things on hold. Dedication and all."

"You need to get out more."

"After what I've been through the last year, I'll probably get the chance. First guess: the option of an early pension."

"They put a serious squeeze on you, or so I've been told," Javier said.

"I assume you made some calls; I would have. Yeah, it was more than a squeeze—it was a meat grinder. There's a guy at the FBI Cleveland field office, Rodrigues, you know him?"

"Actually, yes, a friend. Gave you a passing grade."

"Passing grade? All I get after the last three days is a passing grade?"

"He said a lot of nice things, and just to let you know, he believes you."

"That's nice. He is one of the few. Next time you talk to him, tell him thanks."

"Let's order. The sole is amazing, and I need to improve your mood."

Alex contemplatively swirled the wine in her glass. "Sorry, still sore and edgy. Of course you'd check on me. Wish I could check you out, but my resources are not as readily available. Maybe later—a follow-up, in-depth, and personal interrogation, so to speak."

"I'll be available."

She ordered the sole and he a casserole of shrimp and scallops. He suggested another bottle of wine.

Later, after the waiter had brought two dessert brandies, Javier asked to be excused.

Alex retrieved the phone from her clutch and scrolled through the e-mails. Nothing new from her partner. She began to delete e-mails until one subject line caught her eye:

GL, Remember, Sandy?

"You have got to be kidding me," she said to herself.

When she was dating Ralph, they had spent a few weekends in the summer resort community Geneva-on-the-Lake, about fifty miles east of Cleveland, on Lake Erie. During one evening of gentle ribbing, he had called her Sandy from the musical *Grease*, mostly because the character's last name was Polish, Dumbrowski. She had chided him for his middle name, Danny—Danny Zuko from the show. Only one person in the world knew that—and this e-mail could only be from that one-and-the-same singular asshole: Ralph Daniel Cierzinski.

She took a deep breath and opened the e-mail:

Good morning, Sandy girl, from Geneva-on-the-Lake. You should know my situation by now. Had an uneventful trip north from the state-run hotel. Lucky that old pickup I borrowed still worked. I guess it was quite a shock to the other guests of the state when I checked out. Here in GL, my aunt's place still had the key where I left it. Lucky for that—might have frozen my ass off trying to find another way in.

Sorry I left you in such a shitty spot. As I said when we last saw each other, I'm a seriously fucked-up asshole—why you put up with me all those years is still a mystery.

I'm fairly certain no one knows about Aunt Pat's place here. So, for the time being, I'm okay. The laptop I have is clean, and the e-mail address is clean as well. Will be damn hard to follow this e-mail trail—assuming the geniuses have a clue how to do it anyway. I assume you went to Italy? You never told me where you were going—but knowing how much you love Venice, I hope you have a chance to visit. Still love that tattoo.

It's damn cold here, and a foot of new snow fell yesterday as I drove north. I'm going even farther north. The lake is frozen solid—thought about taking a chance with the snowmobile and crossing it, but contrary to what you think, I'm not a total idiot. I can hunker down here for a while. All the other nearby places are closed up. Remember that Christmas we spent here?

BTW, there was a rumor in the joint that a couple of DEA guys are looking for the money. Do you think I would leave my profits someplace easy to find? Really? If you get the chance, shoot them.

Got to go. If inclined, send me a note.

Danny

Stunned, she just stared at the e-mail. *Inclined? A note? Dammit, now what am I supposed to do? He's told me where he is. Now I have to tell someone, or I'm aiding and abetting the bastard. Shoot someone? How about starting with you, Ralph.*

It took every ounce of willpower not to pound out an e-mail and tell him he had ten minutes until she called her captain.

Why ten minutes? Maybe I'll just call Simmons now, that'll show him.

"What's the matter?" Javier said. Alex noticed that he'd returned and was studying her. "More from your partner?"

"Worse, Ralph just sent me an e-mail. He said . . . Oh hell, read it." She handed the phone to him.

A few minutes later he handed it back. "I can't believe the nerve. What does he expect you to do? He knows damn well that you have to report him."

"I know, but there's something else about this. It's too strange. It's almost a taunt, bragging. Damn the son of a bitch."

Javier's phone buzzed. He looked at the screen. "Milan." He put the phone to his ear. "Castillo." He listened and didn't say a word, then hung up without saying anything.

"A follow-up from Washington. Not only are they walking away from all of it; they also pulled me off the detail. I'm heading back to Milan tomorrow night. The Venice police have been talking to my boss. I'll stay through the conference. It starts at ten, runs for two hours, then there's a two-hour lunch, then they go for two more hours—all done by four o'clock. Marika says she will be there in the piazza that fronts the palazzo just before ten o'clock. I'll take the last train, the same one I took Monday."

"These bureaucrats do know how to live."

They strolled back to Alex's hotel, their evening cut far shorter than either expected, the mood evaporated. They stood in the soft light of the lamps outside the hotel; he took her in his arms and kissed her.

"I have no idea where all this is going," Javier said, pulling her close. "But for the first time in God knows how long, something has clicked. You are an unexpected gift, and to be honest, I am not sure how to open it."

"I won't break," Alex answered. She kissed him, a soft, lingering kiss. "After you see Marika, come back. It's early."

"No promises, it will be difficult. Breakfast tomorrow?"

"I understand. We could have breakfast in my room."

Javier pulled her tight and kissed her again. "As I said, no promises."

"Don't take too long." She turned toward her hotel.

"Alex?"

"Yes," she said, looking back.

"Take this, you may need it." He handed her the small Glock he'd given her two nights earlier. "Just in case."

Later, Alex looked out the window into the dark canal below. Even in the cool of a late winter evening, a gondola drifted slowly by. Two lovers, wrapped in a red blanket, snuggled together as the boatman slowly sculled his oar through the black water. She thought she heard an Italian aria drift upward. She went to look for another vodka.

Chapter 32

Ehsan sat at a small marble-topped table in a coffee shop in the corner of the Campo Santo Stefano. There were few tourists out this late in the evening. Across from him sat Asmir and Cvijetin, both smiling.

"That CIA agent was surprised," Asmir said as he sipped his coffee. "The whole charade could not have worked out better. A wonderful idea, Ehsan."

"And that woman, this is a mystery," Cvijetin added. "She must be working with him. She does look like your mother. Why did they select her?"

"A mystery we need to solve," Ehsan added. "She's here for a reason, one I can't see." He sipped his coffee. "Is it positioned?"

"Later tonight. There were still police walking the campo. It will be properly placed when the police leave. Tomorrow, all we will need is your signal. The diversion will cause all the chaos we will need."

"Excellent, I will be ready."

Ehsan's friends stood, said good night, and disappeared across the campo. As he watched them leave, Ehsan raised his right hand an inch off the tabletop and studied it. It was calm and steady. A day from now it would all be over, and, Allah willing, he would be free of this weight he'd carried since childhood. The memory of his home was a shadow, a shadow burning with fire. He still remembered the cold, wet ground, the stranger who took him from his mother, the strangeness of everything.

One day he was playing with his sister; the next he was walking with a tall woman. There was a bus, then large buildings, then food he did not like, and a bed that felt as cold and foreign as the woods. The lady was nice, talked softly, smoothed his hair. But he mostly remembered wanting to go home.

For many years, he had held this emptiness in his heart. When he was old enough, Marika had told him about his family and what happened. He met classmates who had also lost a parent or more during the war. Catholic and Orthodox children became his friends. They shared much, their memories his memories.

By the time he was about to go to college, he thought he understood. He also hated everything Croatian. While he loved Marika, as a child loves their mother, there was always a chasm between them. When he chose to return to the religion of his family, she supported him. When he told her that he'd gone to the Lašva Valley and visited his home, said a prayer over his parents' grave, and spent time with his relatives, she said she understood. She said she hoped it gave him some closure. At the time, he did not recognize what she meant; but over the years, he began to understand. Closure was what he wanted, what he needed. What he ended up with was a drive for vengeance, a visceral desire to kill the man who had destroyed his life and his family.

When Marika showed him the photographs she'd taken the day of the massacre, his heart throbbed with pain. It beat fast, too fast. When he recovered from his faint, she was caressing his cheek.

"I understand," she said. "Take your time. Breathe slowly. This man cannot hurt you now. I'm sorry I showed you these—it was foolish."

"I'm fine," Ehsan said. "I guess it was just the shock of seeing things I'd been watching in my head for years. Mother, please, do not worry."

"I hope to never cause this pain again. I will always take care of you."

He looked for the photos, but she had hidden them. For a time, he put his horrid past behind him.

His mother knew that day in Lašva Valley as a dark shadow she could not escape. For ten years, she put her heart into raising him and developing her company. Every waking hour was focused on its growth and profitability. The small investment made by a European investor was repaid. The company's stock, held by a few devoted friends, grew exponentially. When Attila Kozak announced he was running for the presidency of Croatia, Ehsan watched his mother remove photos from the small safe in the apartment and stare at the faces. The shadow now had a face, a face she had pushed out of her mind.

"What are you looking at?" Ehsan asked.

His mother turned the photos over. "They are nothing, something from my days at university."

"Are those the photographs you showed me?"

She paused. "Yes."

"May I see them?"

"I wish you wouldn't. I have tried to protect you from these. They should not be seen."

"Mother, I am a man. I know what is behind those photos. I know what they mean to us."

His mother, at the urging of her stockholders, sold the company. She didn't protest too strenuously; it was a company whose time had passed. And the pressure from other companies would soon make her decision moot if she didn't sell. They made millions of euros. Ehsan understood why she sold it. He supported her explanation about new paths to follow, a new future with new opportunities. But he did not understand why those opportunities now involved digging up the painful past. He argued to leave it all alone, to set it aside. As Croatia settled into the European Union and the wounds of the war seemed to have healed for its citizens, she became even more involved in its past.

"In time, Ehsan, I will leave this," she said. "But now the murdered need a witness. I can be that witness. I can bring these killers to justice."

"You cannot bring the dead back," Ehsan said. "Justice will only make those alive—those that survived—feel like they did nothing to stop the slaughter. It is about their guilt for not doing something when they should have. I want no part."

In time, he did play a part—an important role, in fact, that helped his mother find lost truths and lost souls and even reconnect lost children. With the expansion of international business interests on the Arabian Peninsula, Ehsan prospered, his talents in great demand. He held excellent positions in international firms and traveled extensively. He eventually took the NGO position in Milan. Yet behind his outward European appearance, a dark past followed him.

It was Marika's photographs that made the difference. Ehsan saw in those photos the face of the man who murdered his family—the man who would die by his hand.

Ehsan's cell phone buzzed. He looked at it as he set his coffee on the marble table.

"Mother?"

"The United States turned us down," Marika said. "Agent Castillo left an hour ago. He explained that they will say nothing about Kozak or his crimes. They want it all to go away."

"We talked about this," Ehsan answered. "I said this would happen. They are not who they pretend to be. We could never trust them. We will have to take matters into our own hands."

"I just talked with some journalists who appreciate what has happened. I have invited them to our morning press conference at the Palazzo Grassi. There I will make my points."

"Do you think that's wise? Kozak may be there. He may be a problem."

"He's a buffoon and a murderer. There is little support for his kind here—that's what my friends have said. I will embarrass those who will not see what must be done. The press can be a powerful tool if properly wielded."

Ehsan paused and gazed across the campo at the few tourists bundled in their shiny puffy jackets, walking back to their hotels.

"Ehsan?"

"Yes, Mother. Tomorrow will be an important day. Maybe, for one day, the world will understand what happened to our countries when they were seized by madmen."

CHAPTER 33

Asmir and Cvijetin walked arm in arm down the alley near the house they had visited earlier, looking for anyone that might be a cop or watching. They and the people inside understood that the house was probably under surveillance. Two tours around the block had exposed nothing, but they understood there were limits to their observations.

Asmir tapped lightly on the rear door off a narrow, dark alley. Above, a small CCTV camera watched them. He held up two fingers, heard the door unlock, and slipped inside. It closed silently behind them.

"Are we safe?" Asmir asked.

"Yes, no police," was the answer from the woman who opened the door.

The walls of the narrow corridor were bare stucco, and the floor was covered with a long, threadbare Oriental rug. The woman led them to a small room in the rear of the building. No additional words were offered, or responses made. Everything had been said earlier that day.

On the floor of the room was another nylon athletic duffel bag identical to the ones that had carried their laundry. Cvijetin unzipped the bag, removed a cell phone taped to the top of a plastic-wrapped box, and slipped the phone into his pocket. He then removed the package;

it was about the size of a large shoe box. It was encased in a rubberized compound, making the interior mechanisms waterproof. For its size, it was heavy. Wrapped around its middle was a nylon strap; a large steel ring was secured to the center of one side. Also in the bag was a length of thin, black nylon rope, a stainless steel clip attached to one end. He zipped up the blue duffel bag.

Cvijetin looked up at Asmir and nodded.

Asmir turned to the woman. *"Shukran."*

The woman nodded in acknowledgment of his thank-you and replied softly, *"Allahu Akbar."*

The two men then left the building and walked through the cold alleys of the Dorsoduro district to the Ponte dell'Accademia, one of the bridges that crossed the Grand Canal. After crossing the bridge, they headed north to the San Samuele vaporetto stop, by the Palazzo Grassi. They talked about soccer and who would be in the playoffs. To any bystander, they were two good-looking men out on the town or coming home late from the gym.

At the San Samuele vaporetto landing, they took seats in the waiting area of the floating dock, as if expecting the next boat. They knew this late at night the stop was closed. Asmir unzipped the nylon bag as Cvijetin watched the empty campo. They had thought there might be guards, but as with most cash-strapped Italian agencies, the guards that had been stationed at the campo several hours earlier had been recalled.

Cvijetin tapped Asmir on the arm. Asmir reached into the bag and secured the rope to the ring on the package. Then he took the bag, exited the open door on the canal side of the dock, quickly secured the unattached end of the rope to an iron ladder built into the dock's side gunnel, and in one movement removed and then dropped the heavy waterproof package into the canal. It was quickly swept under the structure. He watched as the line jerked tight, then changed its angle as the package sank to the bottom of the canal. It was under the stop and would not be lost to the canal's current or the backwash of the vaporetti that would resume their stops in the early morning.

When Asmir returned, Cvijetin slipped the bag over his shoulder. They walked through the campo, past the Palazzo Grassi with its large sign proclaiming the European conference the next morning, and disappeared into the labyrinth of Venetian alleys.

CHAPTER 34

The clock radio next to Alex's bed read 23:25. She did a mental calcula-
tion: 5:25 in the late afternoon in Cleveland. It had been two hours and
twenty minutes since she'd read Ralph's e-mail. Two hours and twenty
minutes of torture. It wasn't that she would not call; it was what she
would say when she did.

Only a few minutes had passed since Javier called and said he'd see
her at breakfast in the hotel's small dining room. She was disappointed—
she would have preferred her room—but understood and agreed. He
needed to report back to Milan and Washington about everything that
Jurić had said. He'd asked her what she was going to do about Ralph's
e-mail. She had said she would call her partner and tell him.

"Dammit, Alex, I told you not to call," Simmons said. "You miss
me that much? I'm sure this phone is safe, but you never know."

"Where are you?"

"Driving home. There's another massive storm coming in. The captain
sent some of us home early. I'm bushed, it has been a long day."

"Lucky you. Did you talk to the captain?"

"Yes, he told me not to talk with you. He said he wants you where
you are. You can't cause any trouble from there."

She paused, trying to compose her thoughts.

"Alex, you still there?"

"Bob, I have a serious problem." She told him about the e-mail from Ralph.

"Why would Ralph risk contacting you? He knows you'd tell someone."

"Yeah, and that someone is you. I'm totally at a loss about what to do. And even though he tells me he's in Geneva-on-the-Lake, he could actually be on the far side of the moon. Damn, I really hate that man."

"If he's at this Aunt Pat's house, I can have a team there in less than two hours, full Special Response Team. This will then be over, no looking over your shoulder. The escape cost him the twelve-year sentence. Now he'll never see freedom."

"In case you've missed it, Simmons, he's tasting freedom now. My guess, he's not going to give it up. He's prepared. He may have stashed guns, clothing, everything he needs to disappear. What he didn't count on was getting caught so early in his game."

"You want me to send a team?"

"It is not my call," she said. "Pass it on to the captain. He wants me here, not there." She took a deep breath and thought for a few seconds. "If it were me, I'd drop a bomb on him. I remember the house; it's a block off the main drag, at the east end. The building backs up to the lake. That's the best I can do. Can't remember the address."

"I can work with that. I'll check with the locals. By the way, there's a goddamn blizzard here. On the east side, they may get two feet of snow. You are not going to have many friends, throwing the SRT people and the troopers out in this storm."

"You know this can't wait, but be careful. That son of a bitch is up to something. I know it."

"I know. And you?"

"I should have stayed home," she lamented. "Venice has not been fun, really. Call me after this goes down. And by the way, thanks."

"Thanks? That's all I get? It's freezing here, and I have to go find some asshole in a snowstorm. You owe me big time, Cierzinski."

"It's Polonia. Remember?"

She clicked off, rummaged through the minibar, and discovered a few gin bottles and a can of California pistachios. Thankfully, they weren't the ghastly pink color. The clock said 00:52 when she crawled into bed. She didn't know what time it was when she finally fell asleep.

THURSDAY

CHAPTER 35

The bedside clock read 05:45. Alex's cell phone would not stop ringing. It rang four times and went to voice mail, then started all over again.

"What?" she yelled into the device. No ID showed on the screen, just "Anonymous." *This had better be good.* "You know what time it is?"

"Yes, I fucking do know what time it is!" Bob Simmons yelled back. "It is the end-of-the-fucking-world time, dammit."

"What?" she repeated, dragging her brain into the present.

"It's all screwed up here, upside down, in the fucking ass, fucked up."

"Simmons . . . Bob? What is happening?"

"The house, it exploded all to fucking hell. I have one dead SRT member and three others severely burned or injured. The house, well, it exploded all to fucking hell."

Her hand shook as Simmons told her what had happened.

"After our conversation, I turned the car around and called the captain. When I told him what you said, he told me to meet him at the station. By the time I got there, a BOLO was focused on the north end of the state, and Cuyahoga and Ashtabula Counties had been broadcast to look out for Ralph Cierzinski. He also told me that Cierzinski had been spotted by a Geneva-on-the-Lake cop at a grocer on the east side of town. The cop had tried to arrest him but was wounded in the leg when Cierzinski pulled a pistol and opened fire. Cierzinski took the officer's weapon and escaped in a blue pickup truck. The captain was already in contact with the Cleveland SRT and the Ohio State Patrol's SRT when the shooting in Geneva took place. A half hour later, the local sheriff for Ashtabula County reported that the truck had been spotted at a house just east of the city limits."

"Dammit, Bob. Couldn't they wait?" Alex said.

"One of their men was down, they wouldn't hear of it. I also heard that county records made a family and ownership connection to Ralph and the house where the pickup was parked. It would be a full SRT operation. It was snowing like hell."

"Don't tell me they tried to take the house?"

"Yes. I arrived at about 9:30. Traffic was the shits. SRT and the sheriff were set up like a military operation. The pickup had stolen plates on it from near the prison. After the search warrant had arrived, they stormed the house. All hell broke loose from the inside, automatic gunfire shredded the door. Then the house exploded. The SRT team on the front porch was tossed into the air and the ones at the back were hit with shrapnel."

"Jesus Christ."

"The gale-force winds pushed the flames toward a nearby house. The smell of propane gas mixed ferociously with the snow, now blowing almost horizontal off the lake. By the time they were able to get to the injured officers, one was dead, one severely burned and bleeding internally, the others had been cut by wood shrapnel embedded in their legs and lower torsos."

"This is wrong, so wrong."

"You telling me? The fire died down when the fire department found the propane tank that was feeding the fire, and shut it off. The debris from the upper floors that had fallen into the basement became a sea of black slush. By morning this will become hell's own frozen swimming pool."

"Is Ralph dead?" Alex asked.

"I have no idea, no one came out. I hope the son of a bitch is frozen in a block of shit in the basement of that house."

"Goddamn, Bob, I'm so sorry," Alex said. "So, they think Ralph's dead?"

"Yeah, looks like it. No one got out of that house. We know there was gunfire from inside; in the after-action search, we found two rounds that hit one of the perimeter vans, could not have been from our team. It's still snowing here, now more than two feet. We won't be able to find anything for days. The blue truck's owner has been missing since Monday. He also lived in Warren, near where the plates had been stolen. Had to be Cierzinski. This is all so wrong."

"I'm coming home tomorrow. Everything is so screwed up here."

"Look, there's no reason for you to come back to this shitstorm. Stay away; this will be the final reason they need to fire you. They will want a head, and your pretty one would suit them fine. Stay there, and don't give them the satisfaction. Your info was good—I know it. It may take a few days to figure out, but it will get there."

"Thanks, Bob. I'll let you know later today. It would be difficult to get a plane out anyway, and besides, it would cost me a fortune." She paused. "Bob, don't tell anyone we talked, but between you and me, I know that Ralph's not dead—I just know it. He's too clever to be caught like this. I think this whole thing was a diversion to buy himself time. He could have set this up more than a year ago, just in case. He walked me right into it. It smells exactly like something that shit would do."

"I'll keep this between us as long as I can. Let me know what you decide."

"Good night."

"There is nothing good about this night." Simmons clicked off.

Alex and Ralph had each come to their marriage late in life—relatively speaking. In a time when most of Alex's friends were getting married in their twenties, she didn't find Ralph until she was thirty-two, he thirty-five. They had been stationed in the same district, but never as partners. The rumor around the station was that the two officers, both of Polish background, deserved each other. Alex wasn't sure what was meant by that remark. Ralph had his sharp edge, she knew that, but his biting humor was something she liked.

She had never been one for all the touchy-feely New Age police programs being rolled out of command, downtown. The street was a lot more dangerous than what was talked about at the training seminars. Cleveland's streets were a battle zone between gangs and cops. The job was never easy, particularly for a woman. When they both passed the detective exam, they had celebrated by going to Geneva-on-the-Lake, and for three days they had thought only about each other. *That was the last time we actually spent more than a weekend together.*

She considered herself smart, not book smart or test smart, but street and people smart. She called it her cop instinct, and more than once it had served her well. But the last year had turned it all upside down. She should have seen what was happening; she should have seen the signs. Driving the city streets she could spot dealers and pimps; she could see the drugs and the fear; she knew the boundaries between safety and danger. And she could see people on edge. For some reason, she did not see Ralph walking that line.

She knew that Ralph was alive and this was all an elaborate setup to give him time to escape. The man had twenty million reasons hidden, but where? How? The snowstorm raging in from Lake Erie had been about as good a cover as anyone could wish for. She thought it wouldn't have been a surprise that Ralph had waited for such a storm. Every hour since the house explosion, Ralph could have been forty miles farther away; several hours from now, he could be four hundred miles clear of Cleveland. Chicago was fewer than four hundred miles away; New York City and Charlotte, North Carolina, around five hundred. They all fit in the time window. After all, he'd been caught heading to Mexico, so maybe he would try that route again. Too many options and too much time.

At this point after the prison break, the only way Ralph Cierzinski would be caught would be by doing something stupid. She was certain that, at least for the next few weeks, he would retreat into a cocoon somewhere and wait. He had time, and he had means, and he had something she didn't—a future that he controlled.

CHAPTER 36

Later that morning, her head hurting from lack of sleep, Alex stood in the shower, trying to wash away everything that had happened. She knew it was hopeless. Ralph was all she could think of. Ralph in a truck, driving through a snowstorm with a big fucking smile on his face. Damn, she hated that man.

After dressing, she removed the Glock from the safe, checked the magazine, found it fully loaded, and slipped it into her backpack. She found Javier waiting in the lobby. She tried to smile, but the look on his face told her that she didn't pull it off.

"Coffee" was the only thing she said, and steered him toward the small dining room off the lobby.

"What happened?" he asked.

"Give me a minute," she answered and watched as the waiter filled her cup. She looked at Javier over its rim; a tear ran down her cheek.

"What happened?"

She told him.

"My God, and the state police think he's dead?"

"Yes, but I don't believe it. It will be days before they confirm anything, because of the storm." She drained her coffee, waved to the waiter, and pointed to the cup. "I am so hungry."

They ordered breakfast. Alex had scrambled eggs, Javier a cheese omelet.

"Better?" Javier asked as she finished.

"Yes, some." She looked at Javier, her eyes moist. "This is all wrong. I know Ralph planned this from the beginning. The son of a bitch probably had himself stabbed just to escape." She paused and took a long, deep breath. "What's the latest with Marika?"

"She's holding a press conference in the campo outside the Palazzo Grassi at nine thirty. She has journalist friends who will give her a fair hearing." He laid a manila envelope on the table, opened the end, and extracted a couple of pages. "These came in during the night; dossiers on Ehsan's two friends. Seems they have traveled quite a bit during the last few months, both separately to Saudi Arabia, as well as Dubai and Cairo. The reports also say they met with Wahhabi religious clerics while in Riyadh."

"Wahhabi?"

"Ultraconservative Saudi sect of Sunni Islam. During the Bosnian War, they sent fighters to oppose the Croats and Serbs. Many young Bosnian men were radicalized and trained in military operations by Saudi missionaries. Not too great a leap to think that Asmir Fazlić and Cvijetin Radić are in the Wahhabi camp. Those are their full names."

"Ehsan?"

"Maybe—his travels, the ones we tracked, are not so radical. He even went to moderate countries, including Turkey. All for business reasons, according to Italian passport controls. But there are a hundred ways around that. Just ask Marika."

"Marika? Why?"

"There is no record of her entering Italy from any country during the past week. It's my belief she slipped in, maybe by boat across the Adriatic. That way she avoided customs or passport controls, as well as any of Kozak's people. Why, I don't know."

"Like the thousands of refugees trying to cross into Italy?"

"My guess, she had better connections and accommodations. Nonetheless, she shows up here with documents on Kozak, then Ehsan added his, most particularly the film. I received an e-mail on Saturday, while I was in Milan, that she was on her way. We couldn't trace the e-mail back to a specific location."

"All this to get someone to arrest Kozak?"

"Yes, but there is something else going on now, especially after yesterday's fiasco at the campo. These friends of Ehsan make the whole thing, to use your term, hinky. Very hinky."

The walk from the hotel to the Campo San Samuele and the Palazzo Grassi was one of the first opportunities that Alex had had to actually walk the historic passages of Venice. On the way there, Alex turned to Javier, took his arm in hers, and said, "I'm glad you know where you are going. I have no idea where I am. I'm enjoying it, but lost would be an understatement."

"The Piazza San Marco is that way." He pointed. "The Grand Canal is that way. You can see the boats at the end of the campo. It is also that way and that way. It almost surrounds us here. We are in the Campo Santo Stefano. The Palazzo Grassi is that way. Five minutes tops."

"Sure we are," Alex said. Her phone buzzed. "Give me a minute."

She walked away, her phone to her ear.

"No good deed goes unpunished," she said to Javier after she hung up. "My captain wants me back in Cleveland as soon as possible. He is pissed. The state police are already setting up a press conference for later this morning—their time. He wants to know if it was a trap, if Ralph set me up."

"It sounds like it was," Javier said.

"Yes, probably was. I'm caught between the proverbial rock and a brick shithouse. They want a copy of Ralph's e-mail. I need a few minutes to get it off my phone. Is there somewhere to get coffee around here?"

"Follow me."

Alex finished her e-mail and the last drop of the cappuccino. "Okay, cowboy, which way do we go?"

"This way."

"It is beautiful," Alex said. "I think it's the contrast to everything else I know that makes it so stunning. There is nothing like it."

Using an arched bridge, they crossed over a canal. The narrow waterway below was surprisingly full of gondolas, and the songs from a dozen voices filled the tight canyon of stucco and brick. Beyond, on a corner of a building, a sign read "Pal. Grassi" and had an arrow below it. Javier led on.

They turned a corner. Standing against the façade of the church of San Samuele were Turner and Damico.

"What the hell are they doing here?" Alex said as she walked toward them.

"Leave them," Javier said. "They are nothing. We need to get to the palazzo. It's just down the passage. Forget them."

"If it isn't Detective Cierzinski or Polonia or whatever the fuck you call yourself," Turner said and turned to Damico. "I told you they would be here, didn't I? When I saw the picture of that Marika woman on the TV this morning, I said, 'Damn, she looks like our old partner Ralph's ex, Alexandra Cierzinski.' So, Bill here says, 'Where one is, maybe the other will show up.' And here you are, and you have brought your boyfriend. I wonder if old Ralphy knows."

"Maybe we should tell him," Damico said with a laugh.

"Good idea. So, after the other night, I figured out that your boyfriend is the one that's been taking care of the money. That's what I've been thinking."

As Alex walked up to Turner, she loosened the flap on her bag and placed her hand on the butt of the Glock, just in case. "You? Thinking? You are the two stupidest people I have ever met. The money is gone, and if I were you, I'd be careful. Ralph's escaped from prison, killed some people, and is now in the wind. My guess, when things settle down, he'll come looking for you two, and when he finds you, you'll end up like his business partners."

"That asshole's escaped?" Turner said, staring at Alex. "You are lying."

"Yeah, as in gone, flew the coop, big-time fugitive, and every cop in Ohio is looking for him. Get it, Turner? Can you get it through that thick skull? Javier, you are a United States federal officer. Is there a chance I can shoot them and claim self-defense? I'm so tired of this."

Javier smiled. "Well, they have attacked you—I'm a witness to that. They've threatened you with bodily harm. There's that too. So, yes, I think you can shoot them and claim self-defense."

"You a Fed?" Damico said.

"Worse, he's a spook," Alex said.

She turned and saw a policeman standing at the corner of the church, facing the campo beyond. She heard the amplified voice of a woman who sounded like Marika.

"I've got a better idea. Maybe he can help. I hope you have your passports with you."

She and Javier started walking toward the officer.

CHAPTER 37

As Alex and Javier walked toward the Palazzo Grassi, she heard Turner yell something. When she turned around, they were gone.

"I don't know what to do with those guys," she said.

"We'll deal with them later," Javier answered. "Now that Ralph is either dead or on the lam, they've got nothing, and they know it."

"Desperate people do desperate things."

The sound of Marika's voice echoed through the calle between the church and the palazzo. When Alex reached the campo, she looked out across the pavement. A blue carpet, decorated with EU stars, ran diagonally across the stones from the edge of the canal to the palazzo's entry. To the left, in front of the palazzo, a heavy wooden lectern had been placed so that arriving officials could, if they desired, address the press and answer questions. Marika now stood at this lectern and looked out at the twenty journalists gathered to hear what she had to say. Alex caught her eye as Marika waited to continue; a surprised look appeared on her face. From the canal, a succession of motor launches briefly docked and delivered EU representatives and their staffs to the conference. These bureaucrats hurriedly walked the carpet, past the reporters, through the campo, and into the palazzo. None slowed or stopped. One looked at the microphone like it were an instrument of torture.

"Thank you for coming," Marika said. The crowd turned toward her. "Today is both a day of triumph and sadness. As you all know,

I have supported this herculean effort on the part of my country to become a fully vested member of the European Union, and this means integrating the euro into our monetary system. This will not happen in the next year or even the next two, but it will happen, I know in my heart it will."

Alex scanned the crowd. She assumed that Marika—knowing the United States had punted on her request—had promised these reporters more than a supportive remark on the euro. They wanted brimstone and red meat. "But during the last twenty years of peace, since the Dayton Accords and the imposition of a treaty among the various nations of Croatia, Serbia, and Bosnia and Herzegovina, a bloody stain remains— the stain of prejudice and injustice. How can we Croats move forward without bringing to justice those that murdered helpless Bosnians in our names? One of those murderers is now seeking the highest office in our country, and he has promised that he will return us to those days of genocide and ethnic cleansing."

Across the campo, in the far corner, a figure dressed in black stepped out of the passage and hid behind a large sign for the conference. Alex nudged Javier.

"Was that Ehsan?"

"Where?"

"Behind that sign with the blue EU logo."

"I don't see him, can't make out who it is."

A horn from an approaching boat turned their attention toward the Grand Canal and a mahogany launch easing itself against the quay. A young man in a striped T-shirt jumped from the boat and swung a line around one of the mooring posts. When the line was secured, a hefty man in uniform jumped to the quay. He then reached over the gunnel of the boat and helped a woman off. Behind the woman, an older, pudgy man in an ill-fitting suit climbed out. Another man, also in a military uniform, followed.

"And the most evil of these vile murderers is General Attila Kozak," Marika said, pointing to the launch. "That is the killer. That's him."

Alex recognized the man Marika pointed to. He was the man behind the slaps, the thick face, the man on the floor who received Marika's kick to the ribs.

Kozak waved to the gathering. One of Kozak's bodyguards turned toward the loudspeakers at the podium. Behind them, a vaporetto, full of tourists and Venetians, slowed and began to drift toward the San Samuele barge.

"That man, General Kozak, is personally responsible for the executions of hundreds of men, women, and children," Marika continued. "He was one of the leaders of the militias that bombed and murdered the citizens of Zenica and other villages in Bosnia. Look at that evil man—the man that wants the presidency of Croatia. He should be spending the rest of his life in prison."

Kozak, obviously hearing what Marika said, glared and started to move toward her. Colonel Vuković and one bodyguard grabbed Kozak's arm to steer him away. Kozak pushed them aside and continued toward her.

"Murderer!" Marika shrieked. "Killer, butcher, executioner!" She again pointed her finger at Kozak and braced herself for his charge. Shocked by what was happening, Alex turned back to the reporters and saw Ehsan pushing his way through the crowd.

"Why is he here?" Alex said to Javier.

"That son of a bitch? Nothing good."

When Ehsan cleared the crowd of reporters, Alex saw the pistol in his hand. He turned to Alex and Javier and smiled, then continued directly to the motor launch.

"He's going for Kozak."

Kozak was still trying to wrench his arm free from Vuković and the bodyguard. As Alex pulled her Glock from her backpack she looked back at Ehsan and then at Kozak and shouted, "Bomb! *Bomba!*"

The crowd, for a moment stunned at the words, began screaming and running toward the passageways.

A few paces from Kozak and his entourage, Ehsan raised the pistol and shot once at the bodyguard; the man twisted away and fell to the pavement. Turning to Kozak, he fired three times into the man's chest.

Directly behind Ehsan, the thunderous blast of an explosion lifted the vaporetto dock high above the canal and rolled it onto its side. The pressure wave from the bomb slammed into the side of the arriving vaporetto, instantly rolling the boat over, throwing passengers into the canal. Water from under the barge exploded upward higher than the campanile and deluged the campo and everyone in it. Alex and Javier were knocked to the paving stones along with most of those in the campo. The massive downpour of canal water rained over the prone bodies. A tidal wave of water raced across the canal, tipping gondolas and other small watercraft.

Alex was first to her feet. Her eyes went directly to Ehsan. He was trying to stand, the pistol still in his hand. He stumbled among the bodies sprawled across the pavement.

Alex looked out into the canal at the overturned hull of the vaporetto, dozens of people grasping at its side and struggling desperately to keep their heads above the frigid waters. She looked back across the campo and the carnage caused by the explosion and then to Ehsan. He was standing over the body of Kozak. He raised the weapon and fired again into the man's body, and then turned and pointed the weapon at Kozak's second-in-command, Vuković. He fired once into the struggling man, hitting him in the upper chest.

"Everyone down!" Alex yelled from halfway across the campo. She raised her pistol and fired.

Hit, Ehsan grabbed his shoulder with his free hand; he still held the pistol in the other. His hand came away bloody.

Alex braced herself to take another shot. Ehsan swung his pistol toward her; she fired again. The bullet hit the mahogany of the boat, just missing the man. Ehsan smiled and aimed his weapon at Alex. He pulled the trigger and fired. The slide slid back—the weapon was empty. The bullet missed. She calmly raised the Glock and steadied herself to fire.

From the canal, staccato bursts from an automatic weapon sounded over the screams of the victims of the explosion and the gunfire in the campo. Alex looked to the canal. A man in the back of a boat heading for the landing was holding an AK-47 and firing wildly above the heads of the people in the campo. Bullets impacted the stucco walls of the Palazzo Grassi. Everyone still in the campo threw themselves back onto the wet paving. Ehsan sprinted past the overturned San Samuele dock and toward the approaching boat. As Alex continued to fire, he jumped and tumbled into its stern. It accelerated and disappeared up the canal and away from the chaos. The screams for help from the campo and the canal were lost to the roar of the boat's engine.

CHAPTER 38

Alex and Javier stood in the center of the chaotic campo, stunned by what they had just witnessed. All across the piazza, dazed people were screaming and trying to stand. The only ones not moving were three figures lying on the end of a blue carpet near the edge of the canal. The blast had lifted Kozak's mahogany water taxi out of the canal and thrown it against the façade of the Palazzo Malipiero. Its stern hung precariously over the edge of the quay, its propeller still spinning, its engine vibrating the hull against the paving stones. The boat's driver stood, found his balance, then leaned toward the console and shut off the motor. Water still dripped from building façades and the bare branches of the trees in the campo.

In the Grand Canal, the overturned vaporetto, its black hull exposed, drifted away from the campo, people clinging to its sides, yelling for help. Others ran to the edge of the campo to assist those in the water onto dry land. The San Samuele dock, still secured to the quayside by twisted cables, sat half in and half out of the canal. Two women, hanging on to one of the ladders, screamed and waved.

Police officers knocked down by the blast now rose and helped where they could. Other officers began to appear from every alley entering the campo, guns drawn. Klaxons and sirens filled the canal. Some of the reporters, soaked and confused, sat against the surrounding walls of the palazzi, administered to by colleagues. Others sat on park benches, their heads between their legs.

"If we had walked faster, we would have been in the middle of all this," Alex said to Javier.

"If it weren't for your DEA friends, we would have been standing next to Marika."

"They are *not* my friends."

The force of the explosion had thrown the lectern against the wall of the Palazzo Malipiero. Pinned underneath was a struggling Marika, trying to push the heavy piece of furniture off her body. It wouldn't move. Javier ran to her side, grabbed the end, and lifted the lectern. Alex pulled Marika out.

"It was Ehsan," Alex said to Javier as he kneeled down to see how badly injured Marika was. "He shot Kozak and then turned the gun on Vuković. It had to be Fazlić and Radić in the launch. God, what just happened?"

In the canal, debris drifted slowly from the source of the explosion. She looked for Turner and Damico, but they were gone.

"I know, I saw Ehsan, I think you hit him." He pointed to the Glock she still had in her hand. "Hide it, now."

She jammed it back in the backpack that still hung loosely on her left arm.

"The explosion, it had to come from under the vaporetto stop," Alex said. "Nothing could have flipped that thing but a bomb."

Marika was now sitting against the lectern. She was clearly in shock. A thin stream of blood dripped from the corner of her mouth.

"It looks like a concussion," Javier said. "We need to get her to a hospital, fast. The lectern may have also caused serious internal damage."

Two yellow-and-orange ambulance boats pulled up to the quay, and emergency personnel began to triage the injured. One of the EMTs took charge of Marika and immediately began to check her vital signs.

All was chaos in the Grand Canal. Boats rescued people thrown from the vaporetto and other overturned craft. More than a dozen police and emergency boats drifted in the canal, scanning for survivors. One of the police boats secured a line to the overturned vaporetto hull to keep it from drifting farther down the canal.

A police officer grabbed Javier. "You were here yesterday. I remember the two of you. What the hell happened?"

"A bomb," Alex said. "It exploded under the barge. My guess is it was a diversion for the real reason."

"What was that?"

"The assassination of that man on the ground, Attila Kozak."

The officer turned toward the bodies in the campo and reached for his handset radio. Additional police soon arrived, and within minutes they outnumbered all the journalists and tourists that had been in the campo when the bomb exploded.

Alex saw a woman seated on the steps and leaning against the dark wooden doors of the Palazzo Malipiero. She was soaked and beginning to shiver from both the cold and shock. Lying on the ground next to her was Kozak.

"Maja Stankić?" Alex asked. "Are you Maja Stankić?"

The woman looked up at Alex, no recognition in her eyes. *"Što?"*

"Are you Maja Stankić?" Alex demanded again, this time loudly.

This time, the woman nodded. "Yes, I'm Stankić," she said in halting English. "Did you see they killed Attila? Murdered him." She glared at Alex. "You are that woman, Marika Jurić. It was you that killed my Attila."

"No, I'm the other woman you kidnapped two days ago. I should throw you in the canal. But unlike you, I don't kill innocent people."

"I never killed anyone, not like that man who shot the colonel and Attila"—she ran her hand through the dead man's hair—"and caused all this."

"You would have killed me if we hadn't been rescued!" Alex yelled.

"You are that American agent? We know all about you." Maja waved a thin finger at Alex. "My Attila would have become president. He would have changed everything; all of Croatia would have been better off. But no, you Americans had to stick your noses into the middle of all this. Now he's dead, murdered by those Bosniaks. Go away. I want nothing to do with you."

As Alex walked back to Javier, a medical attendant kneeled next to Stankić and started to ask questions.

"You okay?" Javier asked Alex.

"Yes, I'm fine. We were a day early," Alex answered. "This could have been stopped."

"You were right: something was hinky about all this," Javier said. "I don't think Marika knew about any of it. Her son used her to get revenge for his family. He wouldn't have put her in the middle of this."

"But he did," Alex said. "She's collateral damage and lucky to still be alive. Just like those poor souls on the boats. Damn, what a cold trio of bastards they are."

As they raced across the lagoon, Ehsan winced from the pain. Radić took off his undershirt and ripped it in two. He placed it as a compress on Ehsan's shoulder. The wound was high on the right shoulder, just missing the bone.

"You were lucky," Radić said. "That woman could have killed you. It's not too bad, just a groove cut through the top of your shoulder."

"What happened?" Ehsan asked, his clothes soaked in water and blood. "The explosion was supposed to be just enough to startle people, not overturn boats. Dammit, others may have died because of us. We only wanted Kozak."

"We were tricked," Radić said over the roar of the motor. "The bomb was more powerful than they said it would be. We were used. This is not what we wanted."

"No one will believe us!" Fazlić yelled. "We are now what we hate the most—terrorists."

As they exited the Grand Canal, two police boats passed them heading toward the site of the explosion. In minutes, they crossed the lagoon and approached the mainland. Fazlić slowed the launch and eased it into a boat slip buried within the industrial harbor of the Venetian municipality of Marghera. Three other rental boats, identical to the one they tied off, rocked in slips next to them. A large sign, visible from the lagoon, said *"NOLEGGIO BARCHE."* Below it, in small letters in English, it read "Boat Rentals." Across the lagoon, the ancient skyline of Venice etched itself against the late-morning sun and cold blue sky.

Radić placed the two AK-47s in the blue duffel bag. When he asked for the pistol, Ehsan shook his head and reloaded a full magazine, then placed the pistol into the shoulder holster under his bloody jacket. Radić shrugged and slipped the gun bag over his shoulder. The three walked the length of the narrow pier to the parking lot where Fazlić had left the rented white Toyota Corolla. Radić put the bag on the floor of the back seat and climbed in, Fazlić took the driver's seat, and Ehsan slipped into the passenger seat. Fifteen minutes later, after driving through the industrial neighborhoods of Marghera, they were on the A57 heading to Trieste and, later, Slovenia.

CHAPTER 39

To Ernesto Giuli, the three men looked like neither tourists nor water-
men. They were dressed in dark clothes and had looked furtively around
the marina when they walked past his cruiser. He'd seen two of the
men earlier, when they left the boat rental office and walked down the
ramp to one of the company's rental launches. He hadn't given it much
thought then. To rent the boat for the day was expensive, five hundred
and fifty euros. It wasn't his concern or even his money. Now, just a
little less than two hours later, they had returned. Instead of two men,
there were now three, and the new man looked wet. All very strange,
especially to a man who had spent his entire career driving water taxis
and barges around the lagoon. He thought of himself as a fair judge of
people and these three made him curious, extremely curious.

His wife, a stout but attractive woman, set a cup of coffee on the
console.

"Something happened on Grand Canal," she said. "The radio said
a bomb exploded near the Palazzo Grassi. Many people are hurt."

Giuli looked at the rented motor launch and then the white car
pulling out of the parking lot. He picked up his cell phone.

◆　◆　◆

Three senior Venetian police officers, dressed in blue fatigues, blue ballistic vests, and dark-blue berets, stood in the corner of the Campo San Samuele, interviewing Alex and Javier. One of the officers had interviewed the two Americans the previous afternoon. It was not going well.

They spoke Italian very fast and very loud. Javier understood only every other word. He tried to explain what had happened, who the shooter was, who may have set off the bomb. The police were only interested in what America's and, more specifically, the CIA's roles were in this *casi di esplosione di bombe.* Who the men were on the paving, now covered with blue plastic tarps, was secondary. "They are not going anywhere," one of the officers said.

Just as Javier retrieved his cell phone to call Milan, one of the officers' handheld walkie-talkies squawked. The man listened and then said something to his team. They all ran to a police boat, maneuvered through the chaos, and sped up the canal at high speed.

"They have a lead on where Ehsan may have gone," Javier said to Alex. "There's a report that three men just landed in Marghera, across the lagoon."

"My God," Alex said. "All this just to kill Kozak?"

"Looks like it. Sometimes the answer to the most complex problem is a simple one."

Alex kneeled next to the stretcher holding Marika. She was conscious, and color had returned to her face.

"Did you know about this?" Alex asked.

Marika shook her head. "No. I saw him. I saw him shoot Kozak. Then the bomb. No, I had no idea. Why?"

The attendant said something in Italian. Javier answered, *"Un momento."*

"We need to find him. Do you know where he is?" Alex asked.

"No. But you must find him before they kill him."

"We will try," Javier said as he kneeled next to Alex.

Other than the dead, Marika was the most injured of anyone in the campo. Others still moved around shaken, confused, but relatively unhurt. Javier walked alongside the stretcher as they placed her in the water ambulance.

"You need to give me the pistol," he said after the boat sped away. "I will dispose of it."

"It was your idea," Alex answered.

"And you thought today would be a good day to carry it?"

"Yes, I guessed right for a change."

CHAPTER 40

In addition to Kozak, Vuković, and the bodyguard, three other people were confirmed dead, and one person was still missing. All four were tourists with a travel group from Australia on the vaporetto. The initial news reports said that a radical Islamic cell, located in Bulgaria, claimed responsibility for the explosion and the killing of the hated war criminal Attila Kozak and his second-in-command, Oskar Vuković. Within hours, three other groups claimed responsibility too. All of them said it was in retaliation for the crimes committed against the peace-loving people of Bosnia and Herzegovina. One group, located in Syria, announced it was also a message to those European crusaders that wanted to stop the refugees from fleeing the corrupt regimes in Syria and Iraq. This was a warning that more Croatian and Serbian war criminals would be found and executed.

After two hours of interviews with the police, Alex and Javier returned to the safe house.

"That is so much crap," Alex said as she, Javier, and Nox sat in the office, watching the CNN International broadcast. "Bullshit. Dammit, we were there—that's not what happened. We know that those people had nothing to do with it."

"There is too much propaganda to be made from this," Javier said as he sipped his bourbon. "Spin, it's all about the spin."

"How?" Alex said.

"Ms. Polonia, it is all about prestige and marketing, even among terrorists," Nox said. "Whoever gets the first word out, wins the PR battle. And these people have become good at that. Look at the radical Sunnis' international recruitment programs for Syria and elsewhere in the Middle East. Their use of the Internet, social sites, and the darknet is impressive."

"That does not change the fact it *was* a terrorist attack," Javier said. "And Ehsan is responsible—he and those friends of his."

"They had a lot of time to prepare for this. How about the house we saw them enter? The one with the Muslim woman."

Nox reread an e-mail he'd printed earlier. "When the police went to the house, they found it empty. Some materials that could be used for a bomb were recovered, but no explosives or residue. If that is where they picked it up, the bomb was made elsewhere. By it exploding underwater, it is hard, if not impossible, to find the parts that may help to identify the builders. C-4 or Semtex would be my guess. It is available everywhere, most notably in some of the old Eastern Bloc countries. They made it by the kiloton before the breakup of the Soviet Union."

"Pleasant thought," Alex said.

"I don't like being used," Javier added, placing a piece of paper on the table. "Ehsan set this up as a way to publicly get to Kozak. It was as much about the theater of the act as the act itself. The United States will have to respond; the president will have to say something in support of Venice and Italy. Marika will make an issue of the US not supporting her demands on Kozak. This may provide a one-up to the Islamic terrorists—cleaning up a mess our government wanted nothing to do with."

"He put his mother in jeopardy," Alex said. "She's lucky. She could have been killed. How could he do that to her?"

"His hate and desire for revenge trumped everything," Javier said.

"Are they going to let her return to her hotel?"

"I don't know, and I have no control over what the Italian authorities do," Javier said. "If I could, I'd walk away from all this. That e-mail is from Langley, and they want me to liaison with the locals. I guess I'm here for a few more days. Have you decided against returning to Cleveland?"

"No, I'm going back. I had a chance to call my hotel, and they're looking for airline alternatives and standby options. Leaving this last-minute makes it difficult and expensive. No matter what my captain says, I think Ralph is in the wind. If anyone knows how to use the system, it's him. He really stuck it to me."

Javier's phone buzzed. "I'll be right back."

"Another martini, Ms. Polonia?" Nox asked.

"Please call me Alex. After the last few days, Mr. Nox, I believe that you can call me by my given name."

"It's Albert."

"I know. So, we have a deal?"

Nox smiled. "A fresh one, Alex?"

"Yes. Thank you, Albert."

Javier returned. "This is the latest: There was a witness at a marina across the lagoon, shortly after the explosion. Three men returned a rented motor launch and hastily left in a white Toyota. The witness looked at the photos I gave the Italian authorities and identified all three. A camera at the marina office was able to capture the license number of the car; it's being checked. They are also looking at highway camera feeds to find the car. Maybe something will pop up."

"A little spooky, don't you think?" Alex said.

"Technology is a blessing and a curse. Here in Europe, I guess, they are ahead of us when it comes to license-plate scanning."

"Not sure if it's a good thing or a bad thing," Alex said as she took the martini from Nox.

"Just tools. If the three stay off the main roads, it will be more difficult."

"Didn't you say one of the men lives in Trieste?"

"Yes, Asmir Fazlić. He works for a logistics company. Requires him to travel throughout the Middle East. He has property in Bosnia as well. They are asking authorities there to help stake out his place. The other, Cvijetin Radić, has an apartment in Zurich, also being watched. Switzerland will be too difficult to get to—too far."

"No reason for them to go to any of those places. They have been working on this a long time—just like Ralph. They have looked at every contingency, every escape route. They are not crazy Islamists with suicide belts. I think these guys want to live as much as anyone. They will have a safe house, somewhere they can lie low for a while, then, my guess, try to get out of Europe. Would they try to get to Iran?"

"Iran is Shia," Nox said. "These fellows are Sunni and are more connected to Saudi Arabia. That's where they might go. The help they received was probably from a Saudi Wahhabi group, different yet just as radical as ISIS and al-Qaeda. The major differences are their loyalties. The Wahhabis tend to support the House of Saud, now running Saudi Arabia."

"They have to get to Bosnia or Turkey first, then on to Saudi Arabia," Javier said. "No trains, no planes, at least for the next few days. Everything will be covered."

"From my experience dealing with illegals and immigrants in Cleveland, the world is a lot more opaque these days. Governments claim transparency, yet if you are off the grid, you can hide in plain sight. If there is no electronic trail, you do not exist. It's easy to disappear in the crowd," Alex said. "Look at those trying to join ISIS from Europe. They don't seem to have trouble entering back into Syria and Afghanistan, and their victims are fleeing the region by the hundreds of thousands. If they get that far, they will disappear."

Javier's phone buzzed again, and he left the room for a minute. "Marika is okay," he said when he returned. "She's at the hospital. Bruises and a couple of cuts to her legs. X-rays and scans are negative.

The police are questioning her, and she wants me there. Care for a walk?"

"A walk would be welcome," Alex said. "What about Ehsan and his friends?"

"The Italians and Europol have just hours to find them. If not, they will be gone."

CHAPTER 41

The three friends said nothing as they drove eastward on the lesser-used Italian back roads. Their detailed planning estimated that they would have just two hours after leaving the marina before they became the focus of an all-out search across northern Italy. Two hours to reach the Italian port city of Monfalcone and the border to Slovenia. Three times during the past month, they had tested this back door, and there had been no problem. The radio blared news reports of the explosion and the assassinations. When the reports of the civilian deaths and injured began, Ehsan turned off the radio.

He looked out the window. Farm fields, barren and waiting for spring, rolled past. "Our so-called brothers used and screwed us."

"It was a good plan," Cvijetin said to Ehsan.

"All plans are good until they are not," Asmir said, watching the road ahead for any signs of police or military vehicles. "How is your shoulder?"

"It burns, but I can deal with it," Ehsan said. "The bleeding stopped."

"Try to keep it stable, we'll get a bandage on it later."

Ehsan glanced at his watch. "One hour, one hour before we reach the border."

Weeks earlier, while Ehsan worked with his mother to assemble the documents against Kozak, Asmir and Cvijetin had prepared their escape. The most difficult and dangerous leg was getting out of Italy.

Near the hillside Slovenian border town of Opatje Selo, they told him, they'd found an unguarded road that allowed them an escape route up and through the mountains. There, in that Slovenian village, they had stashed a dented and rusted blue Volkswagen Rabbit several days earlier. They had left it with an old woman they found tending a garden next to the last house on the Slovenian side. They had told her they were going hiking for a few days, and they had given her one hundred euros to watch the car.

"No problem, just leave it there," she'd said as she lit a cigarette. "It will be okay. The mountains are a favorite hiking area, but there's not much to see. Just old rubble and concrete from the war fought here a hundred years ago. But go, enjoy yourselves."

"You two go on to Slovenia," Ehsan now said. "I'm going back to Venice. I must get back to my mother."

"No, Ehsan," Asmir said. "We agreed to see this through together."

"I need to protect her. The police will try to connect her to all this. I have to go. You two will do better without me. You know the route, and besides, I never did like the heat of the desert."

Cvijetin sat quietly in the back seat, then said, "Where do you want to stop?"

"There's a station at San Giorgio di Nogaro. I'll take the train back. Drop me a few blocks away; they may be watching the station for the car."

Near a small city park in the center of the village, Asmir pulled to the side of the road.

"You can't be seen in that bloody jacket," Asmir said. "Take mine. I have another in the backpack."

Cvijetin looked at the wound. "You're okay, for now. But it does need dressing."

"And take this," Asmir said, handing his long wool scarf to Ehsan. "It will help to keep you warm and maybe even hide your face."

"Thank you, my dear friends," Ehsan said. "I'll do what I can in Venice. *As-salamu alaikum.*"

The three friends hugged and said goodbye. Ehsan adjusted the shoulder holster under the coat and secured his pistol. He watched as Asmir turned the Toyota around, crossed over the railroad tracks, and disappeared over a rise. To the west, a fast-moving front had darkened the horizon, and a sharp, cold wind swirled with snowflakes. He zipped his coat, wrapped the scarf around his neck, and slipped on a black ski cap. He looked again up the road, in the direction his friends went. He knew he would never see them again in this life.

CHAPTER 42

Marika sat in a wheelchair in the small room off the lobby of the Hospital SS Giovanni e Paolo. Her wrist was wrapped in a white bandage, but nothing was broken or severely damaged. Her shoulder had taken the brunt force of the lectern, leaving a deep bruise.

Two uniformed police officers flanked a gentleman in a wrinkled black suit. His tie, a narrow bureaucratic black, was held in place with a fashionable silver clip. He sat directly across from her. For five minutes he said nothing, just scribbled in a notebook, unnerving her.

"I'm Detective Lugano, with the state police," he began. "Ms. Jurić, you may be in a lot of trouble. It is my job to figure out how much."

"There must be a mistake. I had nothing to do with this."

Lugano made a note. "What do you know about the explosion?"

"What explosion?"

Lugano made another note in his little book. "Earlier today you were injured during an explosion at the Palazzo Grassi. You were lucky—many died."

She looked up at the guards and then to her bruised hands. "I know nothing about what happened. I don't remember anything. Look at me. I'm a victim too."

"Where is your son—your adopted son—one Ehsan Abdurrahman?" The detective looked up from his notebook.

"I have no idea."

"Do you know Asmir Fazlić and Cvijetin Radić?"

"Yes, they are friends of my son's. They are also from Bosnia. They went to school with him."

"What is your involvement with the CIA?"

"How do you know about that?"

"We have talked with Agent Javier Castillo. He was there. He told us about your relationship. He was in the campo—he saw it all."

"Was he with that woman?"

"Which woman is that?"

"Alex something or another. They say she looks like me. I don't think so, but . . ." Her thought trailed off.

"There was an American woman in the campo with the agent." Lugano lifted a page and studied the text underneath. "She may have been the one who wounded the assassin. It says here that she took a shot at the man."

"She shot my son? That bitch tried to kill my Ehsan?" Marika looked at the investigator and softly added, "She's an agent working for the CIA. She says she's a detective on vacation from someplace called Cleveland. I don't believe it."

Lugano made another note. "She said she shot him to stop him from killing anyone else."

"Why?"

"Your son shot and killed Attila Kozak just as the bomb exploded."

"Kozak is dead? Bomb? My son?"

"Kozak was shot as he stepped onto the campo from a water taxi," the detective said. "Witnesses tell us it was your son. He shot two other people as well."

"No, it cannot be," she said. "He is not a murderer. He would hurt no one. If I had known, I would have stopped him."

"We have photos, news film, CCTV, and the word of a CIA agent to prove that it was him."

"They would not do this. I would not let them do this," she protested. "You are wrong. That's not what happened."

"They were seen leaving the scene of the explosion in a motor launch. So, Ms. Jurić, where are they?"

She stopped and turned her head away from the detective, then put her hands together on her lap. "I have no idea."

"What do you know about an Arab terrorist group in Venice?" Lugano pressed.

"I don't know anything about terrorists in Venice. I'm here to show that Kozak is a war criminal, he is the terrorist. Ask Agent Castillo. He will tell you that."

"What I want to know is where your son is and where the terrorists are."

"I do not know," Marika protested weakly.

The questions continued for another hour. Twice, the nurses came in to check on Marika. She waved them off both times.

"Where is your son?" the officer asked for the umpteenth time.

"I don't know. Please stop. I have no idea. I don't remember anything that happened."

Through the glass window of the room, Marika saw Javier and Alex. "Ask him, he knows what happened." She raised her bandaged arm and pointed at Javier.

The detective left the room, closing the door behind him.

Alex watched Marika through the window. The woman glared at her.

"She has told us nothing new," Lugano said to Javier. Seeing Alex, he did a double take. "Who are you?"

"A tourist," Alex said.

"What's your relationship with that woman? Are you her sister?"

"No. And no relationship at all," Alex said. "It's just a coincidence that we look alike."

"Passport, please."

Alex removed the new document from her bag and gave it to the officer. He checked it.

"No customs stamp, no entry stamps. In fact, this passport looks new."

Javier explained the theft of Alex's purse and the loss of necessary documents but conveniently left out the Kozak kidnapping and the rescue. "The government of the United States tries to help its citizens the best it can," he added.

"Since when?" Lugano huffed. "This is all too strange."

"You're telling me," Alex answered.

"My inclination is to arrest Ms. Jurić and hold her until her side of the story can be verified and her son is caught. She says she is staying at the Ai Reali. Is that correct, Special Agent Castillo?"

"Yes. She has a suite. She needs to rest. I believe that she was caught up in this and that her son used her as a cover for Kozak's assassination. I will vouch for her and make sure she doesn't leave."

"I've already taken her passport; she can't leave the country. In fact, I would ask you to ensure that she does not leave Venice."

"I have been assigned by my government to help as best I can," Javier said. "Is Ms. Jurić free to go?"

"For now," Lugano said. "I will have more questions tomorrow." He continued to stare at Alex, a question forming on his lips.

"What?" Alex said, exasperated.

"Nothing, Ms. Polonia. Stay around. I may have more questions for you as well."

Javier signaled a water taxi in front of the hospital. In the dark of the evening, the taxi then circumnavigated the island and entered the Grand Canal and the side canal that fronted the Ai Reali. Alex, Javier, and Marika disembarked. Marika hadn't said a word since they left the hospital. Alex could see that she wanted to ask about Ehsan but was never able to get past his name.

In Marika's suite, a news video of the San Samuele dock exploding and the boat overturning played over and over on the flat-screen TV sitting above the honor bar. It was mesmerizing without the sound.

Alex watched as Marika lit a cigarette, inhaled, and turned to Javier. "What happened, Agent Castillo? All I can remember is seeing Kozak arrive, then waking up in the hospital. Was what that detective said true? Did Ehsan do those things?"

"Yes. After he shot the bodyguard, Kozak, and then Vuković, he turned toward Alex. It looked like he was going to shoot her too."

"Is that when you tried to kill my son?" Marika said, turning to Alex.

"Yes," Alex said. "I had to stop him. I could not let him leave. Or kill me."

"Yet, as I've found out"—she pointed to the television—"he did manage to escape."

"One of his friends began shooting an automatic weapon from the canal," Alex said. "There was nothing else we could do."

"There it is. I knew that the two of you are CIA agents. This whole ruse of you being a tourist, it did not fool Ehsan or me. He knew, and now I'm sure. Were you going to take my place after this and then have the United States take all the glory?"

"What? You are crazy," Alex said. "Maybe as crazy as your son."

Marika swirled the drink that Alex had made and stared out the window into the canal. Smoke from her cigarette swirled around her head. "How could I have been such a fool? He left clues every time we talked about the war, subtle things about revenge and justice. I thought he was talking about his work, making sure that the criminals were eventually caught and prosecuted. I never imagined . . ."

"Vengeance can be a powerful motivator, especially if it is your family," Alex said. "In my profession, I have seen it more times than I want to remember."

"For the first few years he was with me, he was a lost child," Marika said. "I did everything I could to make him happy. We traveled, he attended good schools, he made friends—children like him who had lost so much because of the war. When he was fifteen, we took a driving trip through Bosnia and Herzegovina. When we passed through the Lašva Valley and stopped in Ahmići, he just stared out the window—wouldn't leave the car. When I asked him why, he said it was the ghosts. He could see the ghosts, and they wanted him to stay. Later, as an adult, he told me he did go back."

"I'm sorry," Alex said.

"Why are you here?" Marika asked Alex. "Why you, why us? Ehsan believes you are a spy working with him." She pointed the cigarette at Javier. "Who is this woman?"

Alex looked at Javier, then back at Marika. A hundred thoughts bounced around in her head. None landed.

"A very confused cop on vacation in Venice," Alex said. "That is it. Really—that is all it is. My life is a disaster. I came here to escape, to put it all behind me, even if for a week. Even in Venice, as I've found out, that is impossible."

Marika smiled. "Yes, that might be true. Maybe you are telling the truth. Like I believed that the Americans would help me." She glared at Javier. "Now Kozak and his jackals are dead, and you tell me my son and his friends are murderers and wanted as terrorists. I fear that the authorities will not let them live long. My heart is shattered." She crushed out one cigarette and lit another. "This is all my fault, not theirs. I should have let the dead lie in whatever peace they could find. There will always be men like Kozak; we have no way of cutting them out of society, short of what my son did. They are worse than cancer—cancer kills the body, but these vermin poison and kill the soul. Yes, I understand why Ehsan had to do it. He did it because the civilized governments failed him; they failed the ghosts of his family."

Marika reached for her phone and punched in a number.

CHAPTER 43

After leaving Ehsan near the train station, Asmir and Cvijetin headed east. Their only hope was to disappear into the ragged hills along the border between Italy and Slovenia. The Toyota wound its way among the roads flanked with patchwork fields of cornstalk stubble and barren vineyards north of Sagrado. After crossing the Isonzo River, they climbed the narrow road toward the village of San Martino del Carso. Signs along the road pointed to dozens of World War I memorials erected to the insane battles in these mountains a hundred years earlier, between the Italian armies and the Austro-Hungarians, that left more than a half million dead.

The midafternoon sun was now disappearing into thick clouds drifting in from the sea; the bare tree branches overhanging the road obscured the light. A gray haze of snow and fog rapidly developed as the temperature dropped and they ascended into the hills. Three miles beyond the village of San Martino, they began to look for the dirt road that would lead them to the Slovenian border and Opatje Selo.

"It was along here," Asmir said. "The odometer said three point six kilometers from San Martino when we drove it last month. It's along here."

"Everything is different now," Cvijetin said, staring out into the thickening fog and the snow dusting the ground. "Everything."

Asmir looked into the gloom. "There, the sign to Gorizia and Trieste. Only a little farther."

He slowed to a stop at the next intersection. He looked right, then left, into the thick murkiness; he could barely see the road ahead. As Asmir began to accelerate, bright headlights came up suddenly from behind, and a blue light flashed on the roof of the car.

"Police, dammit," Cvijetin said. "Go, go!"

Hundreds of dark-green Italian cypress trees—like tall black sentries—flashed by in the gloom to their right, and a granite slope, covered with scree and boulders, climbed upward to the left and disappeared into the fog. The police car kept pace behind them; there was no siren. They flew past the turn they needed to take to reach Opatje Selo.

"We can't outrun the police radio. We have to find a way off this road. There will be a dozen cars here in minutes," Asmir said.

Cvijetin reached between the seats, dragged the blue nylon bag toward him, and retrieved one of the AK-47s. He pulled the magazine, checked it, then jammed it back in place. He then lowered the window. "When I say 'now,' slow down. I'll try to disable it."

"Damn!" Asmir yelled as the rear end of a truck suddenly appeared through the fog directly ahead. He slammed on the brakes. "Now."

Cvijetin pulled himself through the window, aimed the rifle, and fired a burst into the grillwork of the blue-and-white sedan. The bullets instantly sheared coolant hoses and cracked the block of the engine. Steam forced its way through the edges of the hood. Cvijetin fired again; the left tire began to deflate. The driver of the police cruiser jerked the car to the side of the road. Its blue light was instantly lost to the fog. Cvijetin returned to his seat.

Asmir accelerated and drew close to the truck. The large shipping container secured to the trailer all but blocked the view of the road ahead. The truck began to slow. A highway median split the road on the left; a steel guardrail hugged the right side.

"Maybe he's just going to turn," Asmir said as more blue flashing lights appeared in his rearview mirror. "Police."

The truck came to an abrupt stop.

"Could be a roadblock," Cvijetin said. "What now?"

Beyond the truck, blue lights intermittently flashed. The fog and snow flurries enshrouded them.

"I'm going to try the other side. Hold tight."

Asmir turned hard left and sped past the truck, bounced through the soft median, and felt the undercarriage scrape the gravel. He turned into oncoming traffic. More blue-and-white patrol cars appeared in the middle of the road. He aimed at a gap between two of the cars and pushed the accelerator. The opening, only as wide as the car, allowed him just enough room to accelerate through.

Instantly, holes began to appear in the windshield to his right, and the rear window crashed. More bullets passed through the car, just missing his shoulder and head and puncturing the windshield. Then the shooting stopped. Using the side mirror, he looked back; the snow had completely hidden the roadblock from view. He turned to Cvijetin. His boyhood friend stared at him, blood over his hands and arms. With each beat of his heart, a small spurt of blood from his neck showered the dashboard.

"My God!" Asmir screamed and pulled to the roadside. He ran to the passenger's side and carefully helped his friend to the ground. Pushing against the wound was no use—the bullet had ripped away a quarter of Cvijetin's throat. His friend looked imploringly at Asmir, fear on his face. He grabbed Asmir's hand and squeezed it hard, then lay still. Asmir continued to push against the wound, screaming, "No!" Blood covered his arms.

Asmir released the pressure on his dead friend's neck. The wailing of sirens pierced the thick, snow-filled air. He reached into the vehicle, pulled the rifle from the floor well, and took a position behind the car.

He braced his arms in the *V* between the open door and the car's frame, and waited.

The police suddenly pushed through the fog like angry white wraiths flying and screaming from hell. Asmir intentionally fired into the roadway ahead of the vehicles. Bullets exploded off the pavement, leaving sparks as they ricocheted into the oncoming cars. The police cars pulled to the left and right and slid to a stop on the roadside. Officers dismounted and took defensive positions behind their cars. He continued to fire, every bullet aimed twenty feet over the heads of the police.

Asmir heard the return fire hit the rental car, heard the side windows explode. He raised the rifle and fired once more. When he pulled the trigger again, nothing happened; the magazine was empty. He kneeled to the side of his friend, kissed his bloody fingers, and placed them on Cvijetin's cheek.

"For our families," he said. He raised the weapon to his shoulder and began to walk into the falling snow and toward the police cars.

CHAPTER 44

From his seat, Ehsan watched the lagoon pass on both sides of the train. To the right, paralleling the railroad tracks, was the Via della Libertà, the vehicular causeway that led to Venice. As the train slowed and approached Venice's Santa Lucia terminal, three black SUVs roared by on the roadway, their blue police lights flashing through the front windshields. The falling snow swirled in great billows behind them. There was no other vehicular traffic entering Venice. He took a deep breath and wrapped his wool scarf around his face, hoping that his luck would hold and they would be looking at those trying to leave, not enter, Venice.

He swiftly walked through the station. Hundreds of passengers, stranded by the order to stop all outgoing trains, milled about. Some talked with police in military uniforms, distracting them as he walked past. More than once he saw people imploring the police to allow them to move toward the idling trains, trains that were not going to leave the island that day.

Ehsan found a small, half-filled coffee shop on the far side of the canal that fronted the train station. He ordered an espresso and took a seat in the corner farthest from the door. A muted TV hung above the back bar. On the screen, a microphone in his face, a policeman was talking to a reporter. Two dozen people stood at the espresso bar, cell phones to their ears, their individual voices lost in the babel of excuses and explanations. Occasionally, they would look up at the ongoing report of the bombing on the canal. The crawler at the bottom of the screen read "Six Dead." He slipped the scarf low enough to take a sip, his eyes never leaving the door. After turning on his cell phone, he saw ten messages—all from his mother.

His mother—she was alive. The last thing he remembered from the campo was her lying on the stone pavement, the wooden lectern on top of her. He shuddered to think how cruel he'd been to leave her—such an arrogant and stupid fool. The shock on Kozak's dying face did seem to make it all worthwhile; yes, vengeance was sweet, yet with a caustic, bitter aftertaste. Kozak and Vuković were now ghosts, the latest victims of a war a quarter-century dead. Yet, remembering how he'd left his mother—the woman who had saved his life and raised him as her own—cut sharply into his heart.

Then the paranoia returned. *Maybe it isn't her; maybe someone else is using her phone to trap me.* Perhaps that woman who looked like his mother—Alexandra something. Why was she here? And that fool CIA agent. Ehsan knew they could find him using his phone when it was on. Were they tracking him now? Were they just outside, waiting for him?

Then his face appeared on the TV, his passport photo along with photos of Asmir and Cvijetin. Next he saw the image of a white car silhouetted in bright camera lights, where a reporter stood facing the camera. The white car's windows were shattered, and the door was riddled with bullet holes. Flashing blue police lights reflected off the wet surface of the car; snow lay on the ground. A blue tarp covered something on the ground next to the car; a portion of one leg and shoe was left uncovered. The camera zoomed in on the ghoulish sight of the shoe. Ehsan recognized the black-and-white running shoe; it was the kind that Cvijetin loved to jog in. Crawling across the bottom of the screen was a message that read *"Due bombe esplose, sospetti mortar durante la separatory con la polizia."*

Ehsan's eyes drifted from the TV and the announcement that his friends were dead to the door of the café. Just outside, snow was thickly falling in the narrow passageway. Snow was unusual in Venice, but not unheard of. A mother wrapped in a coat dusted with snow hurried by, a child holding tight to her hand. A happy childhood memory materialized, of walking with Marika through the snow in Zagreb. They were on their way to get cocoa. The shops were all bright with Christmas, toys and great stacks of pastries filling the windows. He could still smell the chocolate. The phone vibrated in his hand—it was like he'd been shocked with a million volts. The screen read "Mother."

"Mother? . . . Yes, it is me . . . Are you okay? I thought you were . . . They were trying to get to Bosnia . . . Nearby—I want to give myself up . . . It wasn't supposed to happen this way . . . We were tricked . . . I need to see you." Ehsan looked out into the passageway; the people inside were reflected on the café's windows. More flickering images of the bullet-ridden Toyota filled the television. "I'm still here . . . Yes, give myself up . . . Is Agent Castillo with you? . . . To you and him only, no one else . . ." He looked at his watch. "One hour, near the Basilica di San Marco. There's a plaza to one side, with two carved red lions . . . Yes, that's the place. One hour . . . I love you too."

CHAPTER 45

"How did he sound?" Javier asked.

"Tired," Marika answered as she set the cell phone on the table near her chair. "Thank God. My son is still alive!"

"You are too injured to walk to Piazza San Marco," Alex said. "You barely made it this far. You should have stayed in the hospital."

"I knew he was alive. I knew it." Marika looked out the window at the falling snow. "I must go to him." She looked at her watch. "One hour, I must go." She stood and tried to take a step but fell to the carpet.

"Now, how are you going to walk halfway across Venice?" Alex said, walking over to Marika. "You can't even stand. Javier, for God's sake, talk some sense into this woman."

"I've tried. The one I should have been talking to was Ehsan."

"Don't let them kill him," Marika implored as she took Alex's hand. "They will if they catch him. You must stop them." She settled into the chair.

"You have to tell the Italians," Alex said. "You have no choice."

"Please don't tell them yet. Let me see him, and then you can arrest him. He said he wanted to give himself up, but only to Agent Castillo."

"So you said," Javier said.

"He did say it—he wants to give himself up. You have to trust him. You have to trust me."

"After what happened today," Javier said, "I can't trust him. I won't trust him."

"Please, Agent, for my love for my son, can you bring him here? Then take him to the police. Let me see him first, then . . ."

"Javier, where the hell can he go?" Alex said. "I'll go with you. I can help convince him to come with us and return here to Marika. Then we turn him over to the Italians afterward."

"The Italians, after what happened, will throw us all in jail," Javier said, turning to Marika. "Especially now that you've talked with him. It is all too dangerous. Suppose all this is a charade and he has another bomb. Then what? Hell, maybe he'll be wearing a suicide vest. Sorry, Alex, I couldn't live with myself if that happens. Too many died today, and it was all Ehsan's fault. Marika, this is the way it will play out. I'm going to talk with the Italians. When he reaches the piazza, he will be arrested. You can see him when you are better."

"I will never let anyone hurt him," Marika said. "No one. He is my son. I cannot bear to think of him in prison."

"Give me your phone, Marika," Javier said.

"You think I'll call him?"

"I don't want to find out. Phone." He held his hand out.

Marika gave the cell phone to Javier. He placed it in his pocket. "Alex, stay with her while I make some calls."

Marika watched as Javier left the small sitting room and disappeared into the bedroom, closing the door behind him but leaving it open an inch.

"Ms. Polonia, you have to convince him to let me see my son, to touch his face, to hold him in my arms. You are a woman; you know these things. I know he has to pay for what he's done, but he doesn't need to die."

"That will be his choice," Alex said. "Many people are dead because of him. There're a dozen innocents in the hospital."

"All those dead are on Kozak. If it weren't for him, none of this would have happened. He's the murderer—not my son." She reached for the cigarette pack on the table and shook it; it was empty. "I need a cigarette. Would you hand me my handbag?" She pointed to a leather bag on the floor near the end of the couch.

Alex grabbed the strap of the bag and passed it to Marika, who opened the flap and removed a package of Ronhills. She extracted one and lit it.

"You shouldn't smoke," Alex said. "It's not good for you."

"Really? Tell me something I don't know. But I assure you this is a lot more dangerous." Marika slipped her hand back into the bag and pulled out the Beretta, cocked the hammer, and aimed it directly at Alex. "Now sit. I will use this if I have to." Marika paused for a moment and watched Alex deliberately take a seat on the couch. "Agent Castillo, can you come in here?"

Javier walked back into the living room, slipping his cell phone in his pocket. When he saw Marika's pistol, he froze.

"Sit there with Ms. Polonia." She motioned Javier to the couch with her pistol. He sat. "This is what is going to happen. I am going to meet my son and then we are going to leave Italy."

"You will never leave," Alex said. "How can you even think of leaving this island? It's impossible."

"Nothing is impossible with a mother's love. Ms. Polonia, Agent Castillo will give you the knife from the top drawer of the cabinet. Then you will cut the cords from the blinds and tie his hands behind him, and then his feet. And I mean very tight—I will be able to tell. Also, remove my phone from his pocket and set it on the table."

Marika watched Alex do as she was told. "Now your turn. Please hand me the remaining cords."

"You come and get them," Alex said as she stood defiantly.

Marika stood, walked over to Alex, and placed the pistol's muzzle on the other woman's forehead. "On your knees, now."

"I thought—"

"A simple ruse; we all believe what we want to believe. Now, on your knees."

Alex lowered herself to the carpet. Marika then swung the barrel against Alex's head, knocking her out. She collapsed to the floor. One minute later, Alex was tied up as tightly as Javier.

"You won't get away," Javier said, looking at Alex. "They will find you."

"We will see. I know you have more than a professional interest in this woman. I knew it from the first time I saw you both together. She's okay. But for right now, I have to find my son." Marika took cloth napkins from the bar and gagged both of them. She put her coat on, wrapped a scarf around her face, and left the suite.

After the door slammed shut, Alex instantly rolled over onto her back and rubbed her face against the side of the couch, dislodging the gag. "Thought she'd never leave," she said. "You okay?"

Javier nodded, just a little shocked.

"Good, hold on one second." Alex rolled over to Javier's side and with her teeth pulled on the end of the rope that extended out from the slipknot she'd tied. It opened, and Javier shed the rest of the cords.

With his hands free, he removed his gag. "That was quite a whack to the head, you okay?"

"I have two brothers. My mother always said I had the hardest head of the three of us."

"Maybe I should leave you all trussed up—it's the best way I know to keep you out of trouble."

"How do you know I'm not Houdini and can get out of these in a second? Then I'll beat your butt. And besides, we don't have time, so please, cut me free."

"Smart-ass. And you look so harmless all tied up."

Outside, the snow had stopped, and a fairyland frosting of snow clung to the windowsills and rooftops. Footprints—small and feminine—had been left in the carpet of snow. They turned left.

"Better than bread crumbs," Javier said.

Chapter 46

Marika hurried down the dark and empty alley. The snow shower had passed, and aimless white flakes drifted about in the still air. She pulled her coat tight and rewrapped the cashmere scarf once around her neck.

She passed the Aqua Palace Hotel, crossed the canal, and turned left onto the narrow Calle Specchieri. Her son was just a few blocks away; all that mattered now was Ehsan. At the intersection with Calle Larga San Marco, a tall man appeared and stood solidly in her path, blocking any direction except where she'd come.

"This way," Ehsan said as he took his mother by the arm. "The police are converging on the piazza. I have a boat waiting."

Marika looked up at her son, and a thousand questions raced through her mind. "Why?"

"It needed to be done" was his only answer.

As they turned to retrace Marika's steps, two men blocked their way.

"Goddamn, you are hard to find," Duane Turner said, a pistol in his hand. "I made some calls. They say your husband is dead. So, where's the money? I'll shoot him if you don't tell me." He pointed the pistol at Ehsan.

"Who the hell are you?" Ehsan asked, his hand reaching under his jacket.

"Stay the hell out of this, and don't move. This woman and I have business to conduct. If you don't want to be hurt, tell us where the money is."

"Mother, who are these men?"

"These are some of Ms. Polonia's friends. We met the other day. I have no idea what they are talking about." She reached for her son, exposing her forearm.

"Mother?" Damico said. "Listen, bitch, who is this guy?"

"We need to go," Ehsan said, taking his mother's elbow. "The police will be here any moment."

"Police, what the hell?" Turner said to Damico. "Dammit, she's the broad from the other day."

A pistol shot snapped in the still air. Turner fell to the stones, grabbing his thigh; blood splattered the snow. Damico pulled his weapon and, turning toward Marika, raised his pistol. Before he could fire, Ehsan swung his pistol and clubbed the man across his face, opening a long gash on the man's cheek, and knocking him onto his partner. Turner yelled in pain.

"Mother, now," Ehsan said and pulled Marika away from the men. "Mother?"

"Why did you shoot them?" she demanded.

"We need to go now. The police are coming." He beckoned with his hand, reaching toward her. "Mother—now."

Whistles and sirens echoed through the Venetian canyons. Marika looked down at the men struggling to get up, then turned and followed her son. They began to run. From the next alley, Marika was shocked to see Alex and Javier burst into their path. Alex slipped on the thin snow, stumbled, and slammed into Marika, knocking her down. Javier slid to a stop on the slippery pavement. He pulled his weapon. Marika saw that her son already had his pistol aimed at Alex.

"If either of you moves, I will kill her," Ehsan said, his heavy breathing visible in the cold air. "Agent Castillo, is that how you want this to end?"

"What are you doing?" Marika said. "We need to go."

"Ehsan, it is over," Javier said. "The police are coming. There is no way you can escape. I know your mother had nothing to do with what happened, but you will have to pay. If you continue with this, I will see that she is charged with aiding you. Do you want her to spend the rest of her life in prison as a terrorist?"

"I have nothing, nothing—you hear me?" Ehsan said. "Since the day Kozak murdered my family, I was left with nothing—no past, no future, nothing."

Marika looked at Alex. "This woman raised you," Alex said, helping Marika stand. "She gave you your life and a future. How can you turn your back on her?"

Marika fumbled with her handbag as she reached her feet. She looked at her son. "Why are you doing this?"

"Mother, I'm sorry, but this had to be done. It was the only way my family could rest."

"Ehsan, your family would not have wanted this," Marika said, dropping the handbag and holding the Beretta tight to her side. "Asmir and Cvijetin are now dead. Is that what they wanted? Is this how you imagined all this ending?"

"We are soldiers. We knew this might happen."

"Soldiers?" Marika shouted. "You are children. Children do not kill innocent people."

From the far end of the plaza, beyond the red lions, Marika saw a dozen men in dark uniforms appear. Flashlight beams jerked about the ancient façades. The men stopped at the two DEA agents, and then half the group cautiously began to advance.

Ehsan looked forlornly at his mother, fear in his eyes. "Mother, we need to go."

"Ehsan, my son, I love you more than life itself." Marika reached out with both arms, pulled him to her breast, and kissed him on the cheek. As she tightly hugged him, she shot her son in the chest.

He stood wrapped in her embrace for a moment, his wide eyes looking into his mother's, then collapsed at her feet, pulling her down with him.

Kneeling at her dying son's side, she kissed her fingertips and touched his damp cheek. Slowly standing, she looked at Alex. "A mother's love. You must understand." She turned the weapon against her breast, fired one muffled shot, and collapsed onto her dead son.

FRIDAY

CHAPTER 47

Alex nursed a vodka on the rocks in the cramped office of the safe house. She listened to Javier as he walked the outside hall and talked first with Washington, then Milan, then Washington again. Morning daylight cut a thin shaft through a high window in the room and left a long, narrow strip of sunlight on the wall above Albert Nox's head. He sipped coffee.

"Is he in a lot of trouble?" Alex asked.

"He'll be fine," Nox said. "Once all this is sorted out."

"How the hell was he supposed to know this would all turn into a Venetian morality play? He was just a courier. There was no way he could know what went on more than twenty years ago."

"We are all condemned by our pasts," Nox said.

"Very Shakespearean, Albert," Alex said, lifting her glass. "And bullshit."

"With what is going on in Cleveland, old Bill Shakespeare could write a play about you, Alex," Nox offered. "Are you going home today?"

"I haven't heard from the hotel, or the police for that matter. They are trying to get me on a wait list for a flight somewhere that will connect to Cleveland. My captain wants me to be in his office as soon as I land. Not sure whether I'm being canned, arrested, or shot. None of the choices are all that appealing."

"I'd give you a commendation. None of this is your making."

"Yes, but that's what I get for showing up at the dance. A couple of weeks' vacation was all I was looking for, a few quiet days to myself. I am so screwed."

"Your ex-husband?"

"I'm sure he's gone. My partner says they are trying to break through the frozen block of ice that is the basement of the exploded house, but I am positive that he set the whole thing up. And it's still snowing at the site of the explosion."

"Winter in the Midwest, nothing more depressing."

"After the last few days here, Venice may rank with the Midwest. My romance with this enchanting city of La Serenissima is over."

"Your language skills are improving," Nox said. "Don't let the last few days turn you against her. She is beguiling and yes, at times frustrating, but still the queen she always has been."

Javier came back in. He shoved his cell phone into his pocket while Nox handed him a bourbon. "Well, it's not as bad as it could have been. It seems that our little pursuit Wednesday afternoon of Fazlić and Radić, to the Islamic safe house, led to three people, Saudis, who lived in Austria. Fingerprints found on the inside of a tin of coffee in the house identified a Saudi woman living ten miles outside Vienna. The Austrian police staked out the house. When she returned to the residence with two men, they tried to escape. None survived. The car they were in exploded. Government officials are not sure if it was suicide or gunfire from the police that set it off."

"And Fazlić and Radić?" asked Alex.

"They have been confirmed as the men killed at the roadblock. The report says that Fazlić tried to shoot his way out but was killed when he attacked the police head-on. Radić died from his wounds. The police were lucky to spot them. Seems that they passed by a truck weigh station and their license plate was scanned. It matched the one that appeared on the CCTV at the marina. A local police car saw the vehicle as it passed through a small town in the hills near the Slovenian border. They could not outrun the police radio."

"Ehsan?"

"CCTV at a train station sixty miles from here, toward Trieste, caught him heading back to Venice," Javier continued. "They saw someone dressed like him walk through the Santa Lucia concourse. His face was wrapped in a scarf. The timeline works. I just don't get Marika. Why?"

"I can only come up with love," Alex said. "She shot her son to prevent him from spending the rest of his life in prison or worse. She just could not live with that. It's all so tragic. It started back in a war that no one understands and ends here in a city none called home."

"One more sorrow in centuries of Venetian sorrows and deaths," Nox added. "It was Byron who said, 'I stood in Venice, on the Bridge of Sighs, A palace and a prison on each hand.'"

"I'm needed in my own prison," Javier said. "They want me in Milan tomorrow and Washington next week. The blowback from the Kozak assassination still needs to be dealt with. The right wing in Croatia and that PR woman friend of Kozak's are trying to make it look like the United States is behind the assassination. Something about an imposter sent here to Venice to impersonate Jurić and that we are behind Marika's death."

"Great, just great," Alex said. "Have you heard about Turner and Damico?"

"Turner is in the hospital with a leg wound, lucky to be alive," Nox said. "Damico's face is bandaged from a bad laceration that did not improve his looks, I'm told. They did not arrive as official federal agents—as you suspected, they were after the money for themselves. I would say they are going to lose their government salaries. And they had guns, and the Italians do not appreciate visitors with guns, even 'gun-happy' Americans, as the sergeant called us. The last report I heard was that they will be thrown out of Italy as soon as they can walk. When their hotel room was searched, they found a small address book. One of the numbers was for a cell phone, area code Cleveland. It belonged to a detective in the Cleveland police department; the number was also on Turner's cell phone. Do you know a Robert Simmons?"

"Not Bob? He was my partner until all this crap with my husband blew up. Bob couldn't be the leak."

"No, it was his new partner, the one that replaced you. Wasn't hard to trace Turner through him. The idiot left Turner's number on his own phone. Your captain is following this up. I have to wonder about your Cleveland detectives."

"They are like every police force: there are bad apples, and then there are peaches like me," Alex said. "And sometimes they are just plain stupid."

"Our agency cleaners have also finished with Kozak's suite at the hotel," Nox added. "There is nothing left to connect Cleveland or the United States with anything to do with Croatia. There are suggestions, in some of the correspondence and e-mails that were found on Ms. Stankić's computer, that the Russians might be involved. It is being pursued. And they found your purse, Alex."

"I've had dealings with the Russians in Cleveland," Alex said. "Not a nice bunch. I really would like the things in my wallet, particularly my ID and shield. There are some pictures, my old passport—not that it had any places of interest stamped in it—and about three hundred euros. I could really use that right now."

"I will see what I can do," Javier said. "If not, it will be sent to you in Cleveland. We have your home address."

Alex looked at Javier. "Of course you do. Gee, golly, thanks. But right now, outside of the euros that you lent me, I'm still broke."

"I'll lend you a few hundred more," Javier said.

"My hero. That's the least you can do."

"They did find a suitcase. Are you missing a fine German aluminum suitcase?" Nox asked. "Alex, think very carefully about your answer."

"No, it's not mine."

"I'll ask one more time, an aluminum . . ."

"No, it's not mine," Alex insisted.

"More's the pity then. They estimate that there are a million euros stuffed in the thing. All nice and crinkly—and unmarked. Too bad it's on its way to Milan with Javier. If the Italians find out, they would want it."

"I used to like you, Albert. That was not nice."

"I'll walk you back to your hotel," Javier said.

"I would like that," Alex said.

The snow had melted off the paving stones but still clung to streetlamps and restaurant tabletops. The wind had died to nothing; at that hour of the morning, the streets were quiet, still, almost tranquil.

"Hard to believe all that happened in just the last four days," Alex said, holding Javier's hand.

"I'm sorry that you got all mixed up in this. Then again . . ." He stopped, turned her face to his, and kissed her, deeply, longingly, knowingly. "I would never have met you."

She melted into his arms, his warmth almost more than she could hold.

"Do you mind if I cry?" she asked, a tear coursing down her cheek. "I need a good cry."

He squeezed her tighter. Her sobs, soft and gentle, dampened his ear. They held each other, each not wanting to be the first to let go.

They walked the rest of the way to her hotel. He didn't ask; she didn't offer. Alex only said, "I don't think I can be alone, Javier. Please don't leave me alone. Dammit all, I don't want to be alone."

Later that afternoon, the front desk called and said they had managed to reserve a seat on a flight out of Venice that night; she would be routed through Heathrow to a nonstop flight to Boston, then on to Cleveland. Giuseppe's business card sat near the phone on the small desk. Alex called the young man who had first carried her into Venice.

The bow of the mahogany water taxi cut through the light chop of the lagoon, spreading a *V*-shaped wake outward from the stern. Her hands on the stern's chrome railing, Alex stood and watched as Venice, framed in the double wake, receded. The wind rustled her blonde hair. Behind the iconic skyline, the setting sun, a bright-yellow button, tried vainly to warm her face. Javier held her tightly around her waist.

Has it just been four days, less than a week?

She raised her face and kissed him, for the thousandth time that day. Her one black carry-on bag rested on the deck near the cabin's door. They walked back into the cabin.

"Warm enough?" Javier asked as she sat next to him, slipping a blanket over their legs.

"Yes." She snuggled close to the Texan. "You?"

"Warmer than I've felt in a long time."

"Sometimes you can be so sweet."

"And the other times?"

"I'm saving that."

Giuseppe's wondrous mahogany motor taxi continued on across the lagoon, toward the airport. The two lovers, holding each other's hands, watched La Serenissima dissolve wistfully into the setting sun.

ACKNOWLEDGMENTS

For research on the Bosnian War, I used movies and two books. The books provided background and detail necessary to tell the brutal story that was the Bosnian War. David Rieff was there during the fighting; and within months of the declared peace, he published *Slaughterhouse: Bosnia and the Failure of the West*. Also contemporary and published soon after the war's end was Mark Almond's *Europe's Backyard War: The War in the Balkans*. I recommend them both. This was, as with all wars, a horrific struggle between cultures and religions.

I want to thank the editors and marketing staff of Thomas & Mercer for backing this story. I express a specific thank-you to Matthew Patin, developmental editor; his efforts made this a stronger narrative. And most significantly, thank you to Jessica Tribble, my editor, for believing in Alexandra Polonia and to Sarah Shaw for handling the marketing. When it comes to author relations, they are a special team in the Thomas & Mercer world.

I am honored and pleased to call Kimberley Cameron both agent and friend. It was her idea that pushed me into telling this story. I am thrilled to be a part of her agency, Kimberley Cameron & Associates. I join a tribe of amazing writers whose careers are what they are because of this incredible person.

And of exceptional note, thanks to my wife, Bonnie, who's been the love of my life for forty-seven years and is involved in every book I write. Her keen insight, ideas, critiques, edits, and especially friendship and patience make these miracles happen. To be honest, they are as much her work as mine.

ABOUT THE AUTHOR

Photo © 2010 Penelope Lippincort

Gregory C. Randall was born in Michigan, raised in Chicago, and currently lives in the San Francisco Bay Area with his wife. He is the author of the five-book series The Sharon O'Mara Chronicles and the Detective Tony Alfano noir thrillers, *Chicago Swing* and *Chicago Jazz*, set in 1933 Chicago. His young adult novel, *Elk River*, won critical acclaim and awards from the Independent Book Publishers Association and the Northern California Book Publishers Association. Gregory and his wife also operate an independent book publishing company, Windsor Hill Publishing.